ABOUT THE AUTHOR

Tarah DeWitt is an author, wife, and mama. When she felt like she had devoured every rom-com available in 2020, she indulged herself in writing bits and pieces of her own. Eventually, those ramblings from the Notes app turned into her debut novel. Tarah loves stories centered around perfectly imperfect characters. Especially the ones who may have just enough trauma to keep them funny, without being forcefully cavalier. She believes laughter is an essential part of romance, friendship, parenting, and life. She is the author of *Rootbound*, *The Co-op*, and *Funny Feelings*.

Also by Tarah DeWitt

The Co-op
Funny Feelings

Rootbound

TARAH DEWITT

PIATKUS

PIATKUS

First published in this edition in Great Britain in 2024 by Piatkus

1 3 5 7 9 10 8 6 4 2

A CIP catalogue record for this book is available from the British Library.

ISBN 978-0-349-43895-5

Typeset in 10/14.5pt ITC Mendoza Roman Std
by Jouve (UK), Milton Keynes

Printed and bound in Great Britain by Clays Ltd, Elcograf S.p.A.

Papers used by Piatkus are from well-managed forests
and other responsible sources.

Piatkus
An imprint of
Little, Brown Book Group
Carmelite House
50 Victoria Embankment
London EC4Y 0DZ

An Hachette UK Company
www.hachette.co.uk

www.littlebrown.co.uk

PROLOGUE

TAIT

As I sit at the café on the most beautiful day of the year thus far, with a crystal clear view of the snowcapped Sierras, sipping on a perfectly foamy cappuccino, I can't help but think of . . . wounds.

The festering, infected, gaping kind that are notoriously hard to heal—to be precise.

When I was in nursing school we learned about wound debridement: the act of removing the dead or damaged tissues in order to improve the healing potential of the remaining tissue. I can't help but find it darkly ironic that, broken down, that word is de-bride-ment—exactly what the process of divorce is: un-becoming the bride. The wound happens, that initial break, the injury that calls for the divorce. Could be a sudden, forceful injury. Could be something small and almost indiscernible—something that turns putrid. Whichever it is, the wound is there, and needs to be addressed.

Then, the painful debridement continues each time you need to take apart a piece of that marriage—property division, monetary division, closing and changing every damn account you ever had. It's a necessary process, because as petty as it might be, I refuse to share a Netflix account with my ex-husband and his new fiancée—lest my wounded self be infected further by knowing what shows they're enjoying together, on the sectional we painstakingly picked out after three months of sitting on every option within a fifty-mile radius.

Then there's the restaurants you most enjoyed, the hobbies, the photos . . . that one dress he loved with the tiny hole in the seam . . . the one you haven't yet mended since it reminds you of the time you both dressed up and cooked a three-course meal at home, got wine-drunk together and ended up having sex in the dining room. That rip happened when, even after eight years together, he got worked up enough to almost tear that dress off of you.

Some of the more painful, more necrotic "tissues" to remove are the subsequent relationships: our entire friend group, the in-laws that were my family. After all of that, when the wound is this big, it's no wonder a complete amputation is what many recommend.

"Let that shit go," my sister Ava says. "Cut them all off completely, because you know that keeping them around will inevitably lead to them dumping info on you about him that you don't want or need. I know it's painful now, Tait, and I know how much you loved them, too, but you have to get protective of yourself here. You already decided the same thing with the house—that it's not worth the memories. I think you need to decide that with everything else, too."

Ava is ferocious, free-spirited, and despite being just under four years younger than me, has suddenly become the big sister in our dynamic since the divorce began. I hate that.

I hate that I haven't been able to hold my head high and

push through like so many other problems in life—with copious amounts of sarcasm, distractions, overeating and then over-exercising, perhaps even some girls' nights mixed in. My "girls" are nonexistent now. Sure, some still called and made an effort for a bit, but I knew it was out of guilt. After all, no one really wants to take the adulterer's side, so of course they wanted to *seem* like they chose me, instead.

But I'm not the witty, fun friend they once knew anymore, anyway. I was half of a whole and now I'm just . . . half. I can't even recall the last time one of them called or texted, and don't know what I would say at this point if they did . . . I barely know how to attach my thoughts to my feelings these days, anyway.

But as much as my family life may have lacked, I thank the universe that I was given a sister, and that she has the family she has. I think we both had the same idea when we found the people we wanted to be with forever; that our family had been broken, and that the most cathartic thing for us was to relish in establishing our own. The only problem is that mine is . . . no longer, and she has been forced to absorb me into hers. So, of course, she worries excessively, and feels responsible for me now.

She is actually responsible for my favorite person on the planet, my nephew Jack. Jack was born the day after Cole had told me he was leaving me. I'd been getting out of the shower (had not even wrapped myself in a towel yet) when he told me. I remember every word of that conversation vividly. I remember how it felt like my head was going to explode because of the blood rushing to it; I remember not absorbing his words entirely because I was blindingly fucking pissed that he couldn't wait until I was at least not naked to shatter my world. How when the words did sink in, I bawled and yelled like a wounded animal. How he knew me and my pride well enough to just leave.

The next day, my brother-in-law, Casey, called and told me that Jack was on his way—two weeks early. Because that's the singular constant in life, isn't it? That one minute you are completely obliterated by it, and then in the next moment, it carries you toward something else, regardless of whether or not you're still emotionally reeling.

So, I took off the towel (that I had managed to wrap myself in), got off the top of bed that I had cried myself to sleep on, dressed and went on my way. I arrived at the hospital, and as I walked into Ava's room, Jack made his screeching debut. He was a sturdy, eight-pound boy in spite of his earliness, with dark brown hair, his father's nose, and his mother's ears. He stole the remaining shard of my heart instantly. He is now just over one, and I'm absolutely certain he's the smartest and greatest one-year-old to ever live.

I let out a dark chuckle to myself, thinking about my whole debridement thing, when Cole shows up.

"Care to let me in on the joke?" he says with complete sincerity. And while his tone is casual, he wears a desperate look on his face.

I pause for a second, trying to get past the knee-jerk reactions that still happen. We were together from the time that I was sixteen up until twenty-six, so I suppose it will take more time for them all to fade . . . There's the dip in my stomach when I see his classically handsome face, his broad shoulders and size, just over six feet and strong as ever, I'm sure, despite the fact that he's thinned out a bit. He looks more like he did when we met at sixteen this way, still clean-shaven since he can't grow a great beard, black hair, kind brown eyes, a strong nose, and a wide mouth that always looks like it's on the verge of a smile. He's in his station uniform, which I've always loved. Every time I see it, I can't help but be proud of him: the youngest battalion chief in the history of our county's fire department. Like riding a bike, I want to grab his hand as I would have before, yank him down, and plant a kiss on his lips, pulling out that dimpled smile. Taking a beat to return to reality, I manage a closed-lip smile and say, "Hi. Did you want to wait for your drink?"

"That's okay, I'm not going to order anything," he says, and sits.

"Okay, did you bring everything that you need me to sign?" I ask, trying for an easy, unhurried tone. He immediately looks uncomfortable, and I have to stop myself from saying something to ease it.

"Tait, I—yes, I did. I don't want to use up your time. But, yeah, I did."

"I have a pen this time," I volunteer. Won't ever make the mistake of *not* having one again. There's a time limit on how long one can keep it together during these things, and, like developing a substance tolerance, over time that ability increases. But, in the beginning, not having a pen and having to frantically search for one, all to end up having to ask strangers around you, while swallowing back tears . . . well, it leads to a pretty pathetic scene.

He hands me the documents and I immediately proceed with the signatures. He's had the decency to mark everywhere with those little signature tabs to make it "easy."

I suppose it is the least he can do since I'm giving him what was once our home. He wanted to buy me out for a small amount, but I simply don't need the money, and since he didn't want any of mine, this seemed like the easiest way to just cut ties and for us all to move on. Neither he, nor his new fiancée, Alex, seems to mind that they'll be sharing the home *I* helped design, on the land *I* helped to purchase with the inheritance given to me by my grandparents. It *is* a great house, if I do say so myself—so I imagine that's why.

We don't have any children together. Ostensibly, this is a blessing . . . or so I've been told.

I'm on the second to last page when the bastard has the nerve . . .

"I miss you, Tait. I—I know I shouldn't say that and don't deserve to, but I miss you being my best friend. Allie does, too. I am so sorry," he says, for about the billionth time, and with enough earnestness to make me furious. My ears heat, the anger catching in my throat.

I have worked so, *so* hard to hide the anger and the bitterness. To just proceed with cleaning this wound, to do everything that I can to improve the healing potential of what's left of me. But the pain of it just keeps coming, and it blooms all over again at his words. I simply can't yell anymore, so I choke out a whisper: "And how do you think I feel, Cole? Don't you think I wish that I could just be happy for you? You gave me no indication that you were even remotely unhappy, that anything was even wrong. You just up and ripped my heart out of my chest and threw away over ten years of being half of my soul—let alone my best fucking friend. I didn't know you were even slightly less than happy, Cole. I didn't know."

Tears are falling freely from his eyes, as they normally do. I don't want to be angry anymore. I have moments of it, but I find that it's a useless emotion in this scenario. I'm just incredibly sad now. Sad beyond tears. The kind that goes bone deep, numbs you and makes you aware of when you need to remember to breathe.

"I wasn't. I just . . . we fell in love, and it was beyond our control. I don't want to hurt you more. I just can't stand the thought of you thinking you should've done anything differently. I *know* you, Tait, I know you probably think you missed something, but you just have to understand that you didn't. Please understand that. You're fucking perfect, and always have been. After my dad died, and then your mom right after, I realized that we only get this life, and I realized I was more scared to not let myself feel than to face the consequences. I owe my life to you—I wouldn't be who I am without you. I will always regret that I hurt you, and that I lost us, for us."

I huff out a sigh. "I don't know what you want me to say. Stop concerning yourself with what I might be thinking, or who I'm blaming and just please, please let this be the last of it all, Cole." I hate how my voice shakes at the end of it. I want this to stop. I send up a silent prayer to be woken up, if this is all just a nightmare.

A tear wells over and falls from my eye, and I hate that, too. I quickly scribble the last signature.

He must sense my desperation for the emotional purge to stop, so he moves on.

"This was the last of everything for the house, so it should definitely be all of it, now. Allie's brother is a notary and said he'll verify everything for us. He'll reach out for anything he needs . . ." He pauses, flicking his glance up to me and back down. "I don't expect you to right away, but my mom has made it abundantly clear that she loves you more than she loves me right now. I hope you'll eventually have a relationship with her again. I know she misses you, too."

I can't muster up the emotional energy to address my relationship with Clara. I don't want to dwell on how she has been more of a mother to me than mine was, how desperately I wish I had a mother to help pull me through this time, to eventually pester me about *getting out there* again. I can't marinate on how much I miss cooking with Clara, or how I miss her still wanting to take pictures of us all the time, even as adults.

I *miss* feeling cared for, feeling precious to someone, and the self-loathing that this actualization brings me is a daily dose of acid, burning and sour.

I can't get further into that now, weary as I am. So I haul my body out of my seat, turn away from the view, and say, "Bye, Cole. Be well."

It occurs to me that for some sick reason I *do* want him to be well. To grab his happiness and love with both hands and just go with it, because, despite my best judgment, despite the fact that I love myself enough to know that I deserve better . . . I still love that idiot, too. That boy who became a man, who held me through my mother's death and the complicated grieving that accompanied it, who supported me pursuing a career (and then supported me flipping the switch and changing it, despite years of school and money going to the former). We grew up with each other. We used to joke about how lucky we were to have found great sex at sixteen—at least great chemistry that grew into great sex. To have grown up and still grown *with* each other. He and his family, our friends—it was all so . . . great. I never took it for granted. And now I know what it's like to have no hopes for that kind of love again.

I believe him, that it was out of his hands to fall in love with her. I have to. Because believing that our life—and even more than that, our friendship—was all a lie, or just simply not enough . . . well, it would empty me out entirely.

SOMEONE PASS THE BONE SAW . . .

ONE

TAIT

2 YEARS LATER

"If you don't shut that thing off I swear to God, Tait, I will grab the next bottle of champagne that floats by and use it to smash it to pieces."

Ava is concealed in giant shades, her waist length, beautiful, raven-black hair—hair that I still get jealous of as an adult—pulled into a messy bun, wearing no makeup, and suffering what appears to be an impressive hangover.

"Well, well, aren't we chipper today?!" I laugh as I put my phone on silent. "It's just my boss, couldn't possibly be important or anything, but since you were *quite* insistent that you wanted to continue last night's fun, here we are!"

She groans. "I was a completely different person then. I clearly don't get out enough and let the evening get away from me. Also, you were keeping up with me. How are *you* so perky?"

"I haven't gone to bed yet. I might still be a little drunk," I explain.

To be fair, I'm rocking the same general look that she is:

workout leggings, an oversized Fleetwood Mac tee, the same crazy-ass, wobbly bun on my head, sans makeup . . . but my bun is vaguely blonde, and I guess I'm just not radiating pain the same way she is.

"Ha. Nice. More like you didn't have a three-year-old riding the high of his ring bearer power to wrangle into bed. He was on another level."

"Not that I'd share this with the bride, but he did steal the show, didn't he? Kid has some moves." I pay tribute and mime his little robot routine.

She laughs. "His enthusiasm for the Ying-Yang Twins should probably make me reevaluate a few things."

The waitress comes to the table, then, and offers a quick intro—Penelope or something, I think. Despite not being in quite as bad shape, I'm not exactly thriving at the moment, either. Still, I can't help but poke the bear sometimes.

"Hair of the dog?" I say to Ava. "I know it's hard to get past the idea, but one more is usually the cure."

She laughs darkly. "You did *not* just quote our mother to me." Then, turning a little green around the gills, "Fine, you order it though, I'm afraid to speak it."

I smile up at the waitress—a cute platinum blonde with bright red lips and pretty doe eyes. She's practically bouncing on her toes and is probably much too bubbly and bright to get stuck with the Logan sisters on this particular morning.

"Okay, we'll do a round of mimosas, and we may as well start off with a good starch. Hit us with the cheese tots."

"GRRRRRREAT choice! I'll be right back with the mimosas and just let me know when you're ready to order those meals, gals!" Penelope exclaims.

"Okay!" I wince and give her an awkward thumbs up in an effort to match her enthusiasm.

Yup, definitely too bubbly for us today.

I look back to Ava, already anticipating what's about to come out of her mouth.

"Gals? What are we, eighty-five?" She snorts.

"She's sweet and it's Sunday brunch. She's probably just excited for her tips. By the way, where are Jack and Casey today? They were more than welcome to join us."

"I know, but they were happy in the hotel room and nursing their own kind of hangovers, I think. They were both propped up in bed watching *Paw Patrol* when I left."

I smirk at the mental image. Jack is a mini Casey these days. And, despite his jokes and various sarcastic comments about missing sports, I know Casey loves just about every kid show out there. Except, apparently, something called *Caillou*—who is akin to the devil's spawn, according to him.

"Kayla was so grateful for how you came through last night. Thanks again. I've never gotten the warmest vibes from her and now she's already texted me twice today to make sure I passed along her thanks."

Kayla is Casey's cousin and the bride of the wedding we're recovering from. Her photographer's flight was rescheduled so that she could attend her niece's birth, and then delayed last minute. She wasn't going to make the ceremony. There would still have been a videographer, and the photographer was there in time for the reception, but I get that it would have been pretty devastating for those memories of the rest of the day to go un-captured.

"It's no problem, I'm glad it worked out. And I hope she's not still pissed. I know I wouldn't have missed Jack's debut for anything either," I say.

"The photographer offered her a *full* refund and still came for the reception, plus you're basically the best photographer upgrade ever, and took her wedding photos for free—which I still don't agree with, by the way. If she's still pissed, she's an idiot."

I dust my shoulder off sarcastically. "True." I smile.

The mimosas arrive, and since I know it'll end up doing us some good, I pour each of us a glass before second thoughts take hold. She likes a 50/50 ratio of juice and champagne in hers, whereas I prefer mine to taste like it drove by an orange grove and picked up an orange essence, so I make them accordingly.

"Ugh. I mean what's even the point of the juice when you do it like that?!" she says with more venom than I think she intends. I respond with an unladylike gulp.

"Hey, last time I just wafted the orange juice towards the champagne. I did this for your benefit."

She shrugs me off before changing course.

"No, but really Tait, thank you. I know you haven't taken wedding photos in a while, so I hope that was okay? You're okay, right?"

Irritation flares, whipping through me with surprising force, and I have to take another sip before answering. I staple the nonchalant smile onto my face.

"Ave, we were dancing and having a blast all night. I took full advantage of getting to party during the reception. I could have just jetted home after the ceremony. You were with me. Did I look broken or even upset to you?"

She smiles at that. "No, no you didn't. In fact, I did catch you flirting with that groomsman at the bar—who asked Casey for your number, by the way. You were doing great for a minute there—" She sighs and her tone flattens. "—and then spent the whole night dancing with the three-year-old instead."

She's right, I haven't done wedding photography for quite some time. But it's less nuanced than what I photograph now, and it was actually refreshing to have some specific parameters to follow: simply capture the happy people on their happy day.

"Hey, that was not on me. I even asked what's-his-face—"

"Ryan. He was literally the best man and was introduced numerous times throughout the night, Tait."

"—*what's-his-face*, to dance. He wasn't into the *fun* dancing and did not even participate in the conga line. You *know* how I feel about that. He just wanted to chat, and I could tell he was working up to ask for a slow dance, which is the lamest."

"Oh my god. Someone not dancing at a wedding is not an in-depth view into their psyche, Tait. He was smoking hot, is single, has no baggage, and is a *doctor* for fuck's sake. I had high hopes. I know you avoid the rugged ones these days, but we both know that's your type, and he is very outdoors-y. He seemed extremely nice, too. Did you actually *ask* him to dance?"

Our tots arrive then, and we both shovel some onto our plates a little too quickly to be dignified. Desperately wanting to change the subject, and not having any great comebacks in my addled arsenal at the moment—I am disturbed that she has caught on to the fact that I avoid a "type"—I reply lamely, "My, my, Ava Jean Pruitt. Such language! From a mother no less."

She tosses some food back and doesn't reward my dumb remark with a response. I don't blame her. The attempt was as subtle as a gun, and about as sharp as a marble.

Since I can't help but hate when she's disappointed, and wish she'd stop letting her worry over me take away from her own happiness, I give in.

"Okay, I *may* have just said that I was going to go hit the dance floor. But the invitation in that is implied. And it is a legit theory. If he can't fun-dance at a wedding, where everyone of all ages is fun-dancing and there's zero excuse to be self-conscious, then he's probably just not that much . . . fun. And you know that slow dancing doesn't count either—the combo of the wedding atmosphere, booze, music—that's just a dude trying to make a girl feel twitterpated enough to hop into bed."

She rolls her eyes, the expression exaggerated as she attempts to chew an overlarge bite. "I'm choosing to ignore the *Bambi* reference, but we will need to circle back to the fact that you need to start spending more time with grown-ups and probably less with Jack. Why is fun always your first and *only* priority, though? What about a genuine connection with another human? We both know that the moment they actually do have anything else going for them, you lose interest. I'm not saying it had to be hot doctor Ryan, but Jesus, Tait, there's always something. You need to break the dry spell. It's time."

I sigh, and decide to give one more shot at lightening the mood. "Remind me to avoid hungover you next time. Booze takes you deep whereas it leaves me floating happily in the shallows." I continue before she can protest, "BUT, I do get it and I love you. I wanted to just have a good time. I'm glad it happened to be right by home and everything, too. And, most importantly, I don't need a *person* to be happy, or to have a good time. I'd hoped you would have known that by now." She rolls her eyes some more at that and I sense more of a lecture coming, so I press on. "You *know* that I am now the proud owner of an air fryer. I am on a first name basis with all three of my Amazon delivery drivers, Ave. My life is full of joy."

"Tait. Be serious. You know their names, their wives' and girlfriends' names, shit, probably even their dogs' names, but do they know *anything* about you?"

Le sigh. I was not prepared for this version of Ava this morning. I *like* shining a light on others. I *like* how I make other people feel: important. I *like* keeping things light and without permanence right now. I chase these good and simple feelings.

And, okay sure, she might be right, I do avoid what I once *may* have considered my type. However, there's a real purpose behind that, too. I most likely only find that to be my type because I was with the same person for over ten years— most of which were my very formative years as far as all that is concerned. How do I know that's what I'm even really into?

My ex-husband was my first and only love, but it went deeper than that. He, his family, our journey together—it created roots in me that I hadn't otherwise had. Roots that were effectively ripped up. I am growing anew here . . . I am *happy*.

So yes, I avoid the rugged, blue-collar men—the ones who come home dirty and have calluses. I find them to be too direct; they try to cut too quickly through the getting-to-know-you part, and elicit too strong a response for the comfort zone I've established. I also have a theory that they're generally just more self-aware than is good for me. I still need simple, uncomplicated distractions for a bit. Besides that, I have a sister, brother-in-law, and a nephew that I adore. I have a dream career. And I have had occasional sex in the last few years! *I have!* It's not as if I have closed myself off to that entirely . . . Nothing to write home about in that department, which is why I'm not dying to hop back in the saddle. I just have no interest in a relationship in general, and I don't feel the need to give more of myself away again—not when I know exactly how it feels for it to disappear in an instant.

No thanks.

Hard pass . . . Actually, it's a bit sad how *easy* the idea is to pass on.

I've worked hard enough to become whole again and happy, alone. I had the love story and the drama that came with it, and now I will happily choose to be the fun aunt who travels the world and has her own grand adventures. Life is whole enough. I'm no longer scared of loneliness. I've faced it and learned to enjoy my own company.

"Ave, I've got you guys."

Still not feeling it, she won't look at me. But she eventually relents and says, "I'm just really nursing this thing. It's been a couple years since I had a good hangover, and I just have been thinking about some shit lately." She pauses, darting her eyes to her plate as she pushes around a tot. "I got another letter from Dad which always brings out the worst, and I just want you to be happy because you deserve all the things—*you* deserve love and everything with it. More than anyone else."

Something about that last part doesn't sit right with me. "Wait, what's that supposed to mean?"

She gives me a quizzical look from behind her sunglasses. "Huh? Just what I said—that you deserve to be happy."

"Yeah, but what do you mean, 'more than anyone else'? More than who, exactly?"

She blows out a sigh. "I didn't—I didn't even mean anything by that. I didn't want to bring this up at all. I wasn't going to." She puts her face in her hands. "Fuck my stupid, pickled brain."

I raise an eyebrow at her and wait.

She takes a deep breath. "I did some social media stalking again . . ."

"Goddamn it, Ava. I told you to stop. I don't even have any accounts besides my work page, which is work only, so I clearly don't want to know. *You* told me to cut everything off. Why is it *you* who wants to know more?"

"I don't know T, I'm sorry. I guess I think—well, maybe I hope to find out that he's gotten fat or something."

I know that's not all of it. Not even close. But I understand to an extent. Cole was like a brother to her. We did grow up together through all those years. When our relationship ended abruptly, it effectively ended theirs as well, and just as much out of the blue.

That being said, the last time she did this it ended in complete disaster . . .

She came across his wedding photos. It'd been a wine-soaked night at my place, and against my better judgment, I ended up scrolling with her. That was all that it had taken for me to learn *my* lesson . . . I would have hoped it did the same for her.

Cole and Alex (known by her friends as Allie) had their wedding in our—*their*—backyard, with all of our shared friends making up the bridal party. It was a small wedding by the looks of it. Perfect, really . . . The love radiated, almost cloyingly so, from the photos. Ava continues before I get the chance to tell her to stop, that I don't want to know any more.

"Alex is pregnant."

I manage not to pause this time.

"Of course she is, Ava. They're married and happy and in epic fucking love. Not some high school sweetheart kind of bullshit. They're both fucking heroes. That's the natural

order of things, to have a baby next. So of course they are. I'm
not shocked, and I am fine."

The mimosa starts to turn on me and I reach for my ice
water with a shaky hand.

Bubbles returns at that moment. "Ladies, are we ready
to order? I *highly* recommend the lobster Benedict. Orrrrr
the churro waffles! Orrrrr do we need another round before
food?"

I want to bite out that *we* don't need anything since *she* is
not actually sitting with *us,* but I maintain composure and
don't dissolve into complete petulance.

"I actually will take the donut holes, the California
omelette with the breakfast potatoes, and a side biscuit with
gravy, please."

"Great, two plates for that to share?"

"Nope, sure not." I offer her a saccharine smile.

Ava throws me an anxious look, orders the breakfast
sandwich and her own side of gravy, and Bubbles floats away.

"You know, it's rude that you stay as fit as you do," Ava
says, as if all it will take is a thinly-veiled compliment . . .

"I'm hungry and going on no sleep. Leave me be. And
you're one to talk."

I work out to keep the demons at bay which usually means
I work out five days a week, sometimes twice a day. I'm an
active hobby addict because digging into a dark place and
sweating my ass off means I'm out of my thoughts, frankly.
The subsequent endorphins don't hurt, either. Still, I am
equally passionate about good food so I'm certainly not thin.
Ava is five foot ten with long, willowy, graceful limbs, while
still not lacking in the curves department. I'm five foot five
with a similar shape plus a healthy amount of muscle, just
shoved onto a shorter frame. I'm not complaining—I am

admittedly self-conscious about my legs at times, and would happily take a few inches from Ave, but I've got a trim waist and physical strength, and I do what I need in order to be happy in my own skin. I'll never deprive myself of a good meal. This world hands out enough shit sandwiches, so I'll enjoy a tasty one whenever I can get it.

"So, the letter from Dad, huh? Who actually sends letters still? The man can clearly afford a cell phone, or send a damn email," I say.

"Yeah, it was a little different this time, but mostly the same as always. He thanked me for my response again, even though my responses are, *again*, mostly just short answers and telling him not to feel obligated to continue to write. He asked me to send my best to you. He still sent us all plane tickets, one for Jack to have his own seat and everything. He apparently set up an account for Jack, and gave me all the info for that which caught me off guard . . . I haven't looked at it yet or anything. The only thing different was that he actually asked if he could come here, if we would see him if he did, rather than just asking if we might consider visiting them. He stopped asking for your address a few letters ago. It was still *him,* but sounded a little . . . desperate, rather than mostly aloof like normal. He even signed it 'Dad' this time."

"Wow. Reeks of desperation," I reply.

She flaps a hand. "Yeah, I don't know. Just small differences I suppose. Casey being Casey and the eternal sap that he is wants us to go out there. He tries to convince me that regardless of the awkwardness 'it would still end up being a cool vacation.'" She includes the air quotes, which come off a bit forced, and I can't help but get the sense that she might actually *want* to go . . .

I don't really have a response for that. I can't sort through my feelings about Ava and her family getting reacquainted with our estranged father, and I suppose it's not my place to even have feelings about what she decides with that, anyway. I know my feelings and my experience, and that's all I need to know.

My mother was never the happiest person, and she didn't always make the best choices. The consequences of those choices sometimes fell on us, to be sure. But, she had been left, too. She had been abandoned, and never recovered. The only difference between her then and me now is that I don't have two daughters to drag down into my despair with me. She moved us to California, putting a few states of separation between her and my father, and to be closer to our grandparents. I haven't seen Charlie Logan since. I was seven, and Ava was three. He started writing to Ava and I when she was fourteen, and I was eighteen. At that time, I had no desire to write back. I didn't need to. Up until that point I had craved a family environment; one with a mom who wanted to be involved, who was warm, or just a bit more interested. Mom was damaged, somehow, but did her best . . . I wouldn't be who I am if she hadn't been who she was. And she was there, which is more than I can say for Charlie.

But by eighteen, I'd fallen in love and was busy making memories with a new family. I felt complete and excited about the rest of my life—plus, I was still being a teenager. So, I never wrote back. I was finally enjoying feeling like I had something good and *whole* in my life, and had zero desire to dwell in my broken home's past. Charlie occasionally called, but I never had anything to say, and he was stoic at best. I never wrote back to his letters like Ave did.

Ava has always seemed to care more about her origins

than I, though. She recently got into the idea of us doing those DNA kits, and pitched it to me with feigned nonchalance. It was under the guise of knowing our ethnicities "for Jack," but it occurs to me now that maybe she just has always *cared* more. I suspected that she was interested in it segueing into a connection with Dad's family. Like, maybe, an online thread would lead to a real-life one, or something. And, maybe, doing it together gave us collective permission to do so.

I don't understand why I *should* care about my ties to Charlie, or any of the Logans, for that matter. The last real effort he ever put forth was sending me my first camera as a graduation gift—so, ten years ago now. Hell, we didn't even invite Charlie to our weddings since that would have meant that he (and by extension, the rest of his family) would have needed to be involved in the rest of our lives. Plus, it would not have been fair to my mother, who was already in the beginning stages of illness by then.

Our meals arrive and the rest of the conversation is light and pleasant. That, combined with the striking blue of Lake Tahoe in the background, warm-yet-fresh air, and a contented, full belly, make me ready to catch up on that shut-eye by the end of the meal.

I squeeze Ava and send her on her way. Thankfully, they don't have a long journey home—only about an hour down the hill in the foothills, where there's no tourist seasons and it's an easier place to raise kids. Where I also used to live.

I head back to my little A-frame on the west shore, feeling more numb than I probably should given the news of the day. I try to tell myself it's a sort of peace I'm feeling and not that deep wave of depression getting ready to pull me under. It feels as if I've almost been waiting for this, though: the final confirmation that life—Cole—has moved on completely. That he's getting what I couldn't give him, and that however bad he may have felt for not being able to continue loving me, his happiness is too great to not sail on forward.

I get home and all but collapse on the bed, ignoring the constant vibrating of my phone, and sleep.

TWO

I wake with a start, drenched in sweat, to find that it's completely dark outside. "Great . . . ," I groan. The headache has arrived, and sleeping the day away will totally screw up my circadian schedule for days.

I, at least, have a flexible work schedule. Well, no *real* schedule to abide by, anyway, and plenty of time off. I've admittedly slowed down on work the last few years and am beginning to run low on funds—a fact that's officially burrowing an anxious hole in my brain.

I currently work for a publishing company doing research assistance and photography for various journalists, authors, and their subsequent story developments. I got my "big break" on a photo that I took, which included a small piece of poetry I wrote on my (then) blog, about five years ago.

I have no idea how the blog came onto Gemma Nola's radar, but my photo of a canyon that had been half devastated—almost perfectly split down the middle, in fact—by wildfire, with the accompanying short poem, somehow inspired a novel. Because she felt set on using the photo and poem, she offered me credit in the foreword, as well as a stake in the profits. That angsty (but highly entertaining), epic family drama novel turned into a group of three, each of which she had me privately commissioned for. People's reviews of the books almost always stated how they loved having photography to coincide with the settings. Adult novels with pictures, who knew? We went on to collaborate on a coffee table book that focused entirely on the photography: the inspirations behind the variety of settings featured.

I've since developed a suspicion that Gemma is agoraphobic, hence why she doesn't go seek out these inspirations for herself, and I've never even been able to get the woman to meet in person, *but,* it has also worked to my extreme favor. The publishing company was so happy with the success of those books that they referred me for other jobs, which led to a healthy portfolio that resulted in more work—for the magazines it publishes, more books, digital artists and publications, etc.

It may have been too good to be true. Kept me busy for a while, but after my divorce, I have simply lacked motivation.

I am beginning to get the sense that Deacon Publishing regrets their investment in me. I've done a few spreads for magazines over the last two years, but haven't exactly jumped at each opportunity they've thrown my way. Just enough to keep my job.

I PAD OFF TO THE kitchen, scraping up the remnants of my bun that are stuck to my neck, when I hear my phone shudder.

"Shit." I forgot to turn the sound back on. I scoop the device out of my purse, and my stomach drops. Twenty-three missed calls, thirty-seven texts, and five voicemails. *What the?*

I verify that none are from Ava, meaning an emergency is

unlikely, but see that they're split pretty evenly between Gemma and Fletcher, my agent from Deacon. Rather than trying to go through every text or voicemail, I go with the quicker option available and push call for Gemma.

She picks up after two rings.

"Taitum."

"Gemma, I am so sorry I missed your calls. I—I was out with my sister today and left my phone at home." I decide the lie is easier than explaining that I chose to dedicate my attention elsewhere.

"All's forgiven—that is, assuming you accept the assignment?"

"Oh, ummm. I'm not exactly decided yet. I'm sure it will work out, but I just need to iron out the details."

I'm met with utter silence. Deeply regretting not going through those voicemails or texts, I decide to gamble . . . After all, I very much owe my comfortable life to Gemma Nola. I've been sent to all of my favorite places at her behest: Scotland, Spain, New Zealand, Switzerland . . . I've seen places that look as if they couldn't be real, like they should only exist as screensavers. She could have kept her moment of inspiration to herself all those years ago and not chosen to even acknowledge my photograph, or my blog. The poem aside, she had her story inspiration and could've ran with it. The books would have been equally successful, I'm sure. I could still be doing all freelance work, or not traveling at all and simply doing family photography.

And, as sad as it is, my job is all that I have at this point. It's allowed me travel to places beyond my imagination, where I have met fascinating people, and I've experienced an inordinate amount of fun. These experiences are everything I have—they're what has built me back up to my whole self.

Or this version of myself, at least. Having a career that I'm passionate about is the only piece of me that I tended and grew on my *own*.

Aside from that, this kind of assignment and entity of my job is my favorite—research with a focus on imagery. I'm suddenly gripped with the need to get away, to throw myself into work so that I don't lose this, too.

Peter the Prime guy and his Pontiac rebuild progress be damned! He, and the other two (Jose and Ted), might miss me, but they'll still be here when I get back!

At that very real thought—and the cold-water reality that washes over me with it—I suddenly know what choice I need to make. Unlike almost all the other assignments over the last two years, I *know* I need to do this whatever this is. I owe it to Gemma, and more importantly, to myself.

"You know what, I've got everything covered. I would love to dig into it for you."

She laughs loudly, a bit harsh and phony, but the one I know as her normal laugh.

"Oh Taitum, I have *such* a juicy story brewing and it's absolutely PARAMOUNT that it revolves around this place. This—this family legacy of a ranch that continues to fight for its own existence. And I know you must think every angle has been seen with that show's infamy—*Lord,* that hot extra and all. Anyway, I know you and your keen vision will capture so much more than what has already been exposed to the masses. I need that inside view."

I FEEL THE BLOOD BEGINNING to rush to my head again, that all-too-familiar sensation that makes it sound like words are coming from a distance. I instinctively know the place she's referring to, but decide to hold out hope that I'm wrong . . .

"Uh . . . remind me the name of the place again, Gemma?"

"Logan Range, that marvelous ranch right outside of Sun Valley where they film that show, *Dollar Mountain*."

FUCK.

MY FATHER'S RANCH.

THREE

I manage half-hearted responses and wrap up the call as quickly as I can, missing every other itinerary detail I'm sure she was attempting to share, but desperately needing to get my bearings.

So. Maybe my confirmation on this particular job was just a *tad* premature.

Shaking myself out of my stupor, I quickly decide to act.

Gratitude aside, the anxiety over the would-be awkwardness of exploring my stranger-for-a-dad's ranch is far more potent than my pride. After quickly brainstorming my approach, I decide that I better just go directly to Fletcher to explain why I'll need to withdraw, and flat-out admit the blunder. I'm sure I could share it with Gemma, but it seems like the more efficient option to come clean to the people who write the checks, first.

Gemma couldn't have known about my ties to the ranch since she only knows me by my pen name—Tait Leigh. Frankly, Taitum isn't even my name, I just don't correct her. Besides, even if she'd known my last name, Logan is common enough.

Starting off in the blog world, being young(er), jaded, and

self-important enough to think that my name needed to be catchy to be recognized, I decided a pen name was for me.

Also, my last name at the time was Van Rijckevorsel. So—yeah, there's that.

Obviously, I will owe them an explanation on my flip-flopping, and the further I let this go, the more details I'll have to give. I decide to call Fletcher when it occurs to me that it is, in fact, 12:30 A.M. and no one will be in their office until nine. I don't think it wise to blow up his cell phone at this hour, either.

PANIC CONTINUES TO PERCOLATE, THOUGH, and I eventually give up any hope of falling back asleep. Instead, I attempt to pick up a book, do some yoga, look online at dog shelters for a dog that my laptop and I both know I won't end up committing to, and even complete an eleven-step skincare routine that consists of rubbing every sample I have amassed onto my face, before I finally concede to do some reconnaissance. . . .

Dollar Mountain is the newest hit show to take over the nation. It would've been impossible to avoid it being on the fringes of my awareness with the various billboards, memes, and quotable one-liners constantly being shared or talked about—even without having a regularly active social media account. It is *the* highest rated television show out there after two seasons. Ava confirmed that it was Logan Range after the first commercial for the pilot featured the same stone barn from our childhood. The barn looks like something that belongs on an old English estate rather than a working cattle ranch, but, slightly behind and perpendicular to that is a sprawling white ranch house with a wraparound porch—all Americana.

I decide that it seems sensible to watch a bit of the show so that I know exactly what I'm turning down. Plus, I hope I can glean some focus points to share with them for whoever they replace me with, possibly earning me a few forgiveness points. After all, it's not as if I'll actually be watching Charlie, or his new family. Just about all the memories I have of the Range itself are pleasant ones.

It doesn't need to be personal.

I'm not invested.

I prop myself up on a mountain of pillows and start episode one . . .

TWO EPISODES INTO THE SEASON, around 4:30 A.M., I watch the scene that sparked the "hot extra" phenomenon. A six-and-a-half-foot scruffy Viking in a cowboy hat. He only sticks out like a sore thumb because he's standing as stiff as a statue in the background of a scene where Joseph Dollar—the patriarch of the family—is beating the shit out of one of his unruly sons. The entire aesthetic of the scene is thrown off by his looming and awkward presence in the background. I snort. You can't get a clear picture of his face, all you can discern is his size and that he's got dark auburn-blonde hair that brushes the top of his collar, and a closely cropped beard. When the camera pans over him he even passes a quick, uncomfortable glance into the lens. The eyes are probably what all the fuss is about. They're a light gold, framed by the kind of lines that weather a man's face, but (annoyingly) make him more handsome. It couldn't be more obvious that this guy is not an actor of any kind. I imagine the television crew pulling him out of some diner booth out there, thinking that using him would add to the realistic atmosphere. It has the opposite effect. If anything, he eclipses the too-pretty actors and actresses of the show; the ones with artfully distressed clothing and bodies manufactured in gyms, versus digging posts and pulling barbed wire fencing.

The show is . . . well, it's wonderful.

A modern-day Western that pays homage to family and all the drama that entails, with entertaining and dramatic storylines that are rooted by breathtaking landscapes. There's artful symbolism, satisfying romance that doesn't feel earnest or phony, and enough dysfunction to be endearing.

Still, from what I recall of Charlie Logan, I remain as confused as when I first heard the news that he allowed them to film on Logan Range, *his* family's legacy.

The Range is the real mistress that he loved so much; the one he left my mother and us for. There was another woman, yes, but long before she came into the picture, my mom had made it abundantly clear to my dad that she never intended to be a ranching wife or a ranching family. She wanted us to grow up with friends and extracurriculars and choices, not to be duty bound to our forefathers' legacy. When my grandfather died, any one of my two uncles, or my aunt, could have taken over Logan Range. But Dad decided it was his to continue. My mom always told us that we were the family he could've chosen, but didn't.

Mom held her ground, and we eventually moved to be nearer to her parents. I don't even recall the exact time the divorce became official, just that he never followed. After that, he seemed to easily fade from our lives. Charlie became too wrapped up with running Logan Range to maintain his relationship with his daughters. He remarried and started a new family instead. He remarried and had a baby within two years or so.

I wonder if perhaps, just as in the show, the ranch itself was struggling financially? Hence the reason for allowing the show access . . .

But, since I'm not invested and since I hold no claim of connection to the place, it's none of my business. I decide to be thorough, though, and do a quick Google search. I'm further flabbergasted to read that the place is not even a working ranch anymore: it's been converted to a guest ranch. They run guided hunts out of it during the season, and host guests and tours. It states that the guest ranch is completely booked for the next two years given the show's production seasons.

So, Charlie left us to run the ranch, and it's not even an *actual* ranch. He supposedly worshipped his family's legacy so much that he abandoned us for some idea that he never actually upheld. Right on. Wonderful.

I EVENTUALLY MANAGE A FEW hours of restless sleep, and call Fletcher's cell at 8:00 A.M.

"Tait—was just calling you. First off, good morning. Secondly—thank you for being you and for being available to drop everything and take off."

I try not to read into that and the implication that I've got no personal commitments holding me back. Joke's on him after all, I've got my air fryer. *Cue sad trombone.*

"Oh, um, that's what I'm calling about . . . Fletcher, I am so sorry, I completely messed up. I can't go."

He laughs, clearly assuming I'm joking . . .

"No, Fletcher, really. Listen, I feel there's a conflict of interest here—somewhere. And I really hope that this information can remain confidential, but"—I blow out a breath that gusts static through the phone—"that ranch is owned by my father. I have spoken to him *maybe* three times in the last twenty years, Fletcher. This would not be a good situation. It always goes better when people are excited to have me and are welcoming. *They* would not be welcoming or excited to have me there, and the whole assignment would just be . . . full of distractions. I'd be wasting your time and Deacon's money, and this seems like a story Gemma is very excited to develop." Big inhale. "There's definitely a lot of great photography there, though, so I know anyone else would jump at this. There's the landscape, wildlife, multiple houses on the property. There's a house that one of my uncles lived in with its own dock on a small lake—well, it's a pond really—but I haven't seen it in any of the episodes yet . . ." I ramble until he has to raise his voice over me.

"Logan—Logan. *Tait!* Listen, Tait . . . you clearly already have memories and an idea of the place and its surroundings. From what I hear, the owner is rarely even around any of the TV crew. We have an extremely small window of time that this is available to us for access, before shooting for the winter episodes begins. *You* were specifically requested by one of our highest grossing clients. I already arranged for an entire coinciding article and spread to be done for our travel magazine, and our entertainment magazine for the show, too. I had my assistant book your flight this morning—you're supposed to leave *tomorrow.* Why did you agree to this if you couldn't do it?"

I fess up to how I mishandled the situation.

"Alright . . ." He sighs, and I can almost hear him gearing up to pitch. "While I understand that this is a—difficult situation, why not try to look at this as an opportunity? Oftentimes when art is emotional, we do our best work—or so I've heard, right? It's a miracle that we were so easily granted access to this place. They've had to lock it down like Fort Knox. Also, hey, some of the actors are going to be there while you're there! You'll get a chance to meet them! From what I hear, some even stay in the bunkhouse and everything!"

"Fletcher, I just—I really don't think I can."

"Tait. You can. And, I'm asking you, please . . . *please* don't make me regret how hard I pushed for you here." And then, more gently, he adds, "You can have the sales rights on all of the photography for other projects if you'd like, too. Given the journalism aspect along with Gemma's book, this could be very lucrative for you."

I swallow around the lump in my throat, thinking about the dwindling, dismal state of my bank account. I'm swept by some unnamed force (one that's *actually* named "impending poverty"). "Okay . . . *okay,*" I practically shout. "How long will I be there?"

"That's my girl! We've arranged for you to stay there for six weeks."

"SIX WEEKS?! Wha—Fletcher, the longest assignment I've ever been on has been two!"

"Yes, well, I had to give you ample time for the book and make arrangements for both magazines as well. If you do your best work quickly, we could always arrange to bring you home sooner, but it's going to be four weeks, minimum."

"O-okay."

"Great. Isabel is sending you your flight details shortly, and Gemma will be in contact with you about any specific focus she needs, etc. Also, Tait, please squeeze in some fun for the rest of us." He huffs a satisfied sigh. "Oh! Lastly, if I have something couriered over to you, could you take it

with you to get Sadie Dollar to sign it for me?! That girl is
a pistol!"

"Umm, sure. Yeah." Why the hell not.

"Wonderful. Contract and details coming your way."

AGAINST MY BETTER JUDGMENT, I am now invested . . .

FOUR

Explaining to Ava that I was jetting off to Idaho for a couple of months at dear old Dad's went both better—and worse—than I anticipated. I expected her to be on my side at least a bit—to be pissed and frustrated, or even nervous for me. I would have expected her to feel a little betrayed, perhaps, that I was breaking the unspoken agreement to still not allow him back into our lives after Mom's death . . . but, after breaking it down to her, she laughs.

"You're lucky school already started, otherwise I would be taking off with you. I would pay good money to watch this."

"What? Why?" My sister is a brilliant calculus teacher, has a notoriously good memory, and is what I imagine folks consider a traditional genius. However, her deep love for both trashy reality TV *and* Lifetime/horror movies makes me inherently suspicious of anything she would "pay money to watch."

"I just—would. Dad is, well, I'm not entirely sure he actually wants a relationship with us," she says. "I think he tries, but maybe just out of guilt? He and I have found our little comfort zone, but that's because we have Jack to use as our buffer. And that's all through letters. He will not know how to even start with you. And you . . . you have always managed to make every new surrounding look like it feels like home, and people always love how much you *want* to capture the whole essence of a place. Part of your charm, and what makes people welcome you, is how complimentary you are. I cannot imagine you going to our once family home and acting like it's nothing to you, yet still needing to poke around the place. You're going to have to be polite despite yourself so that they don't suspect you of wanting any claim to it, you know . . . It's the one place and group of people you won't bring yourself to charm to death, but you'll have to toe the line and not be a complete bitch, either . . ."

I scoff, but she tramples on with a laugh.

"They'll latch right on to any angry vibe and close you off, fast. I can just see your whole 'I don't even watch the show and I don't even want to be here' act now. And Dad's reaction when he sees that it's you—oh my god, I bet he has no idea what you even look like! I've sent him pictures of us, but mostly Jack—never you."

"Well, your sense of humor skews a little fucked, per usual. And trust me, I'm just as aware of how easily they close people off."

She sighs impatiently, letting me know I'm in for a lecture.

"Tait, listen. I've been wanting to have this conversation with you for a while. And I don't mean to come at you hard like this, again, but . . . you are constipated."

"Excuse me? I'm quite regular, thank you."

"No, you are dealing with some major *emotional* constipation. It's like you've clenched too long and turned it off or something. And, trust me, I love that you come and stay with

Jack as often as you do, and I love you as a friend and a sister, but I worry that you're really out of touch, or that you're just not all the way processed or something." *Because I don't have a life of my own.* I hear the implication in the unsaid words.

"Ave—" God, I don't want to do this right now . . .

She continues before I can cut her off, though. "Remember when Jack went through that phase where he got scared of having to sit on toilets to poop? After falling in at the really loud movie theater one? He'd barely touched it, but the shock of the water plus the loud flush traumatized him . . . and he absolutely hated having to sit on the toilet after that. He held it so long that he developed encopresis, Tait! He has been fully potty trained for over a year now, and he still has full-blown little boy shit-splosions. The doctor said that the nerve damage done means he could continue having accidents for a few *years*. All that potty training work, and this genius, sweet little boy is still having sharts that are painfully embarrassing for him. If you don't *feel* again, and actually take care of your emotional business, it won't just go away. The same thing is going to happen to you. You're going to shit your pants . . . emotionally."

THIRTY SECONDS PASS BEFORE I can respond to that, and even then all I muster is, "Wow."

"Shit doesn't just go away, sister. It must pass!"

"Wow."

"Alright, Owen Wilson, my analogies aren't the most eloquent, but this is what motherhood has done to me."

THEN, THE THOUGHT OCCURS TO me. "Oh my god, Ave, you're *right,* he has no idea what I look like!"

"Huh? Oh, Charlie, you mean? Tait, he's still going to know that it's you."

"How? *How* would he know, though? Really? The amount of people that go there now to do, like, set photography for the show alone—just the sheer amount of outsiders that roll through there now has to be huge. They have an actual guest ranch that people rent out to stay at. I bet none of the family themselves even pay attention to names that come across their list. They're probably just vaguely aware that someone from Deacon publishing is coming!"

"That's a lot of 'probablys' and, Tait, I didn't mean any of that. I think this would be *good* for you. Mom is not alive. You are not being disloyal to her. You don't owe anyone anything—Jesus, we didn't owe it to her when she was alive, either! I really think it is ok to reestablish this connection."

"No Ave, I think you just made things way less complicated for me. I'm going to just give myself another name and he'll never even realize it's me." I decide to brush past that last part about connections. I have all that I need in her, Casey, and Jack. I'll—I'll get a dog, for real this time, when I get back, or something, too. Maybe I'll agree to a blind date to really appease her.

"Tait, oh my god, come on—"

"Gotta pack . . . I love you. Kiss Jack extra for me ok? Tell him he's not allowed to learn anything new until I get home."

"T . . . crap. Okay. I love you, too."

Something pops into my head, then, because there were no pictures on the website and no specific info about their family. Vague details that I've avoided but know Ava's looked into before, so I grab my phone again and fire off a text to her.

Me: Hey, I know you told me before, but what is our brother's name?

Ava: I want to give myself credit and remind you that I really tried to remain the sullen, uninterested teenager in solidarity with you . . . until Jack came around and softened up this hardened heart of mine. But, his name is Grady.

Ava: I'm actually a little jealous. I know you were being sarcastic with calling him 'brother' . . . but I hope you will at least try, for me. It'll be good for you.

Me: Love you

Ava: Don't think I don't see your non-responses here. Also, Charlie is going to know it is you, loser. Love you, too

I quickly fire off a text to Fletcher.

Me: I went ahead and checked into the flight. Just curious, I didn't see on the itinerary who will be grabbing me from the airport? Not sure Uber will take me that far.

Fletcher: The Range has offered transportation. Look for someone holding a 'Deacon Publishing' sign.

Me: Perfect. Thanks!

I do a mental fist pump. They don't have my name yet, otherwise I'm sure I'd be looking for a "Tait Logan" sign. All I need to do is pick a different name to go by. Simple enough.

I latch on to this hope.

FIVE

TAIT

One air fryer kissed goodbye, an Uber ride, three flights, and two layovers later, I'm in Idaho. Last minute flights are never the most ideal, so my flight path was wonky to say the least. I'd planned on brainstorming the name plan during the time, but the anxiety has my thoughts in disarray. A tangled mess of avoidance.

I can't go with Taitum. That's too suspicious and might stoke an ember of a memory that'd have them looking too closely and spotting a resemblance. Responding to LeighAnn might be doable, but that presents its own issues. Picking a fake last name is making me want to scream.

Mentally setting it aside, I chose a less productive path and indulged in some in-flight cocktails in an attempt to calm my nerves. But as I'm riding the escalator down to the baggage claim area, I'm wishing I'd had about three more. The edge I had attempted to take off has been firmly put back on, and I'm no more settled on details.

I wipe my sweaty palms on my jeans and scan the drivers with signs.

It takes about a millisecond to find mine. Viking-cowboy-Thor is a head taller than the rest, even without the cowboy hat. He's wearing a baleful look on his face, haphazardly tapping the Deacon Publishing sign against his thigh, other hand firmly planted in his pocket. He looks about as excited as I feel at the moment. I'm not shocked that he works for the ranch, since, even from his brief debut, it was blatantly obviously that he wasn't meant to be working in television. I *am* shocked, however, that he's been sent on this particular errand rather than being put to work back on the Range—surely they have other staff for this kind of thing now?

Like calls to like as they say, and his eyes lock with mine. I feel my features arrange themselves into my typical resting bitch face, hardening, shielding over. I refuse to be the first to break eye contact, and manage to make my steps determined. His gaze turns from bored to stern, which only makes mine sharpen.

Right as I'm approaching the proximity that I've mentally prepared to greet him in, a ponytail whips me in the face.

"*Oh my god.* I totally recognize you. You were in *Dollar Mountain* weren't you?" Ponytail exclaims.

He nods and smiles tightly. Of course, the Neanderthal is mute. I decide to leave them to it and beeline for the luggage when I see one of my four bags dropping down the chute onto the conveyor belt. I grab the first bag and wait. Try to breathe through my nose and gain control of these anxious butterflies. Instead, to my shame, tears prick the backs of my eyes. I see the bag with my more precious camera equipment and step closer so that I can get it as quickly as possible.

Part of this anxiety is from the typical worry that everything made it safely, I decide. Feebly.

A hand shoots in front of mine to grab it, but before the

expletive escapes me, the owner of the hand says, in a gravelly voice, "Deacon Publishing?"

Ah, I see he managed to escape his fangirl. I sniff. "Oh—yeah, thank you. Nice to meet you." I think I forget to smile, and turn for the other bag.

"Nice to meet you too . . . Tait?"

My head whips around so fast I feel something pop in my neck. "Ouch—what? How did you know my name?"

He gives me a bored look and replies, "The luggage tag."

Fuck.

Christ on a fucking cracker. At least they are very old tags that still say Van Rijckevorsel, I think? He doesn't ask about the last name, so I don't mention it.

"I'm Henry. I'll be driving you out to the ranch. I'll take these two bags out to the truck and then come back for you, alright?"

I manage a nod.

As soon as he turns to leave, the panic surges. My heart hammers in my throat and the tears threaten to spill over. I'm not going to get to avoid *any* of this like I'd hoped. I feel like a marionette with my strings being pulled. I'm being played in something that I am not remotely prepared for . . . Why didn't I prepare better?

I'm tired and the combination of the cocktails and residual flight anxiety is just getting to me, I decide. After all, *I* have done nothing wrong here. That family—the one who didn't care enough to even remain in touch—should be the ones afraid of *me*. And Charlie . . . *his* actions are the foundation for all of this. I am not the one at fault. I am not after anything from them. I've made a successful, amazing life for myself in spite of the people who left me. A life I will uphold and cling to with every fiber of strength in me. I've got this.

I toss back my head to knock the tears out of my eyes and decide, in that very moment, that I'm here to do my *job*—one that will result in awe-inspiring photos, and one hell of a story, and there's no reason for anyone or anything to get in the way of that.

SIX

HENRY

I get the bags packed in the back seat of the truck and make sure they're wedged in securely. I assume little miss sunshine back there won't want her precious camera equipment to get thrown in the bed, and since I know that Mrs. Logan will have my balls if I make the ranch look bad in any way, I decide that's the better course of action. I need to muster up the energy to be more . . . personable . . . but fuck, I have plenty of real work back at the ranch to be doing, and this girl flew into the wrong airport. Not to mention, I can already tell that the woman I just met is going to be about as warm as a glacier.

Something nags at the back of my mind, though—her name, Tait, and something about the way that stare cut right through me. Eyes that at first look almost brown, but up close are actually a dark mossy green. She's tan, but I guess she's from California after all, so it's likely fake. Her blonde hair is a wavy mane down her back and around her shoulders, wild. Almost like she'd been yanking at the roots the whole way here. She's definitely not what I would have expected, though. I guess I'm small town enough to think that a Californian photographer would show up looking completely underfed, in head-to-toe black, rocking oversized glasses, or something. This girl showed up looking comfortable, in what Grace and Grady like to refer to as "athleisure," and a jean jacket.

I could also tell through her gray workout leggings that, objectively, she's got shapely legs (the term "thighs that could crush a watermelon" comes to mind) and couldn't help but notice a sizable rack. *Objectively.* Again, California, so probably all fake (for all that I'd be able to tell). I should reel in the judgmental tone to those thoughts, but I feel immediately agitated by the woman, with no idea why.

I turn to head back only to find her charging headfirst at me like a buck ready to lock horns, rolling a bag with each arm behind her.

"Let's roll!" she exclaims with a jerk of her blonde head at the truck.

The change in demeanor is jarring, a little manic. I silently take and load the other bags while she gingerly hops in—as if trucks are her regular mode of transportation, or something. I laugh under my breath, thinking about the last date I went on. She'd worn a skin-tight skirt and ended up needing me to give her a lift to get in and out every time. She probably thought it was cute and funny—maybe an excuse for me to touch her . . . I found it annoying.

I'm not jaded enough to think that it's *them* and not *me* who's causing my love life to be a veritable wasteland.

"So, Henry. How far is the Range from the airport?" Tait asks, cutting into my philosophical thoughts.

"Well, since you flew into Boise instead of Hailey, we are looking at about a three-hour ride."

I catch one eyebrow shoot up and a little head shake.

"I didn't book my flight, Deacon did. I hope this isn't too much trouble."

The slow and precise way she says it, combined with the curl of her eyebrow, makes it clear that she couldn't care less about the amount of trouble it is. Something about the determined set of her jaw, the way she juts out her chin with the small cleft in it, her pouty bottom lip—it gets under my skin and I want to needle her more.

"Nah, what's an extra six hours of my day when it could have been a total of one? The work will still be there, waiting for me, tomorrow. Along with tomorrow's work."

I see a muscle in her jaw flutter out of the corner of my eye.

"Would you mind if I play music? That seems like a pleasant enough way to pass the time," she asks.

"Sure," I reply. I don't offer to help her figure out radio stations. She whips out her phone and manages to sync it to my Bluetooth immediately. I flinch and prepare for the worst . . .

. . . And am pleasantly surprised when the first song is by Chris Stapleton. Not my favorite of his, but tolerable at least.

The next song throws me off, though. Hootie & the Blowfish?

Song number three is, straight up, an oldie: "The Chain" by Fleetwood Mac.

After that, the chaos continues.

I'm subjected to Justin Bieber, followed by George Strait, the Eagles, Katy Perry, Tom Petty, Post Malone, Shania Twain, Queen, then a few in a row that have the most filthy and/or violent lyrics I've ever heard (uncensored, and the girl doesn't even bat an eye) . . . She mouths "spank me, slap me, choke me, bite me" without so much as a hesitant glance in my direction. It takes more than a song to scandalize me, but the unflinching, relentless randomness of this has heat creeping up my neck.

Oh, sure, now we're back to some country.

I can't take it anymore, and frankly, I'm starting to get a little afraid.

"What. Is. This." I try (and fail) to keep my tone neutral.

She is momentarily shocked that I burst our long-standing bubble of silence.

"What? It's Tyler Childers."

"I know who *this* is. I mean what is this whole goddamn playlist? There is absolutely *no* rhyme or reason to any of it."

"What do you mean? They're all good songs—that's what it is!" she says, not trying to disguise her offense.

"No," I manage to respond with an annoyed sigh.

"Ummm excuse me, what do you mean *no?*!" she sneers.

"I mean no, I can't follow along with this. It's distracting my driving. You need to group a playlist together by at least *similar* genres or something. This is different decades, different tempos, different genres, and different everything. This is psychotic."

"Oh, sorry *Deliverance,* I left all my dueling banjo tunes back home. Are you for real? It's fucking music!"

"Sure as hell is not *fucking* music, not sure what kind of fucking you're into, but this mash-up would not be good to fuck to."

Woah—what was that? What made me go there? But I press on.

"Also, really? '*Deliverance*'? You know you're in Idaho, right? Not exactly known for being backwoods or toothless. I know I got a purdy mouth." I bare my teeth at her in the biggest smile I can manage.

Her mouth hangs open at that and it takes everything in me not to piss her off more and poke my finger in it. I know I'm being a dick, but I'm (mostly) serious, and seeing her temper flare is the closest I've been to hilarity in a while.

She doesn't grace me with a response, but disconnects the phone and puts in her headphones. Relieved, albeit a little let down she didn't attempt a comeback (not sure what that is about either), I go back to driving.

The girl is attractive, there's no doubt about it. But I've been attracted to plenty of women before. Tait Von Frankenstein, or something to that effect, practically wears a "fuck off" sticker on her forehead. She's either attached, or not interested. Her face completely shifted when we locked eyes earlier. She came down the escalator looking a bit wide-eyed, and immediately shuttered that expression. I'm not sure if I should feel suspicious of this yet, or what it means . . . Something about her continues to pester my brain, though, and I'm determined to find out why. Maybe she reminds me of someone?

I can't help but feel protective of the Logans. They took me in fifteen years ago when I was just sixteen, gave me a summer job and raised me up from there. I had a dad who loved me in the way he knew—which was to ignore me as much as humanly possible, and tend to his own vices. While doing the latter, he got into a bar fight over who knows what, ended up accidentally killing a man, and going to prison. After that, I was sent to live with my aunt, Grace, and by extension, Charlie. The Logans put me to work, caught me up on school, and changed my life. I sometimes could do without Charlie's brothers—namely the one that pimped me out to the TV producers as an extra. That shit has followed me since. They had a great laugh at that—still do.

For the most part, though, the Logan family is all the family I need. Helping maintain the ranch, working outdoors, guiding hunts, driving cattle for the ranchers who still lease out the land—it's what brings me contentedness. It's all I know how to do, and all I could ever want to do, and I never would've had the opportunity to know it if not for them. They've made me a part of their family, and as a guy that never knew what that was before, they'll have my loyalty for life.

But like me—like us all—they have their own skeletons and demons. I know Charlie has two daughters out there that he hasn't seen in decades. Only after a long whiskey night will he mention them . . .

I SLAM ON THE BREAKS, forcing Tait to nearly smack her head on the dash.

"Alright, dude *what the fuck*." She whips in her seat to face me.

"Tait . . . that's—that's a fairly unique name," I say.

It's the eyes. I see the resignation on her face when she accepts that I know.

"Yeah, it is."

"What's your last name again?" I ask.

"Logan. My name is Tait Logan. And yeah, I'm Charlie's daughter."

SEVEN

TAIT

"And the reason you neglected to mention that? Along with why you're here? The book research seems like a pretty far-fetched excuse to operate under," Henry says accusingly. His tone is much less venomous than it was when it came to my playlist, but he's clearly suspicious.

"There's a very simple explanation for this. But can we pull over or something? I'd prefer not to get wiped off the road," I say.

He seems to just take notice that we are stopped in the middle of a two line highway and pulls the car over accordingly. As soon as he flips it in park, he returns his hawkish gaze back on me and lifts his eyebrows, prompting me to continue.

"Okay, I *am* the photographer for the publishing company. That's entirely true. It's purely coincidental that the author who commissioned me wants her story to revolve around the Range. I tried to convince them that they'd be better off using someone else for the project, but with the scheduling crunch and short notice, they pushed me to. Honestly, when I told them it only motivated them more."

I hope that keeping it simple will get him off my back. I'm not exactly someone who shies away from confrontation, but something about this guy's stern, cold stare and booming voice make me feel like I have something to feel guilty about—a feeling that I find extremely unwelcome given the circumstances.

"So, you expect me to believe that some writer—someone who, it sounds like, has already seen the show—chose *you* to do her ground work for her? That *you* didn't use the fact that it's your family ranch to get yourself the job out here? Now, of all times?" He pauses, and then, as if that needed further clarification, adds, "When it's suddenly a famous ranch tied to a famous show?"

Fuck. Well, when you put it that way . . . I start to see how it must look: as if I took no interest in the Logan family until things suddenly appeared to be going quite well for them, as if I want a piece of that, or something. I only ever considered how I did *not*. How I did not need to trudge through yet another emotional journey in life. I can't help but let out an overloud guffaw, and he rears back at my weird laugh.

"Sorry, but no. I want nothing from the Logan family. I need *nothing* from the Logan family. I have never once asked for anything from them. I am here to do my job, you can believe me or not, I really couldn't care less. Also, I'm doing the photography for two different magazine articles, too, not just the book. Lastly, is it actually any of your fucking business?"

"It *actually* is. When I'm not busy chauffeuring I have a real job. Security being breached makes that job much harder. You wouldn't be the first person who came sniffing around either hoping to claim something, or someone—or to feel like they're a part of it."

I bare my teeth. "Well, if you can get the chauffeuring done without me leaping from this truck and into oncoming traffic, then I am sure you will find in no time that I am after none of those things. I want to do my job. That means taking pictures of the pretty things, and being on my way. That's it."

He doesn't need to know that my job is so much more than that. I always describe each photo, the smell of the air, the weathered feel of the stone, the worn hands of the people . . . I do my best to give clear inspiration and see the history of something, the craftsmanship and love that went into an old building, the wildness, the colors and contrasts of an untouched landscape. He doesn't need to understand that my work is the only thing that hasn't gone numb for me, that I feel every bit of it.

"What was with the last name?" he asks.

"Huh?"

"On the luggage tags. Did you make that up, hoping you could come here unrecognized? Seems a little nefarious to me." His brows lift in a facial shrug, and I struggle not to scoff.

"Clearly you're not into crime drama, Sherlock. Why would I use my real first name?"

"Answer the question."

"It is my married name!"

"Then where's the ring?!"

I only realize that our voices have continued to raise when I feel the little balloon of tension begin to deflate, then. I imagine I can hear the flatulent noise being expelled out of it, and my indignation with it.

"I changed it back after I got divorced," I reply once I'm in control of my senses.

"Did you change it back after the show aired?" he asks, clearly not one to give up.

"Oh my GOD. Will you please let up? I couldn't care less about the precious show. I only just watched part of it to figure out what my boss's thought process might be. I promise you, I will be in and out and on my way."

Then, hoping that some honesty might gain me an ounce of mercy here, I add, "This is going to be hard enough for me. I'll be honest, I *had* hoped that they wouldn't recognize me. I figured that might make it easier to do my job. If *you* are any indication of how I'll be treated, then I can see that this is going to be a long six weeks, just as expected."

That seems to land how I'd hoped. His expression softens and he blinks a few times, making me wonder if he hadn't through our entire exchange. I also can't help but notice that he's got nice eyelashes for a man. Because of course he does.

"Sorry . . . Charlie is, well—" He winces with a frown before finishing, "He's like a father to me. The ranch is my home. He hasn't had the easiest time with his . . . family life, lately, with all this going on. And since the show began our whole MO has been bombarded. I feel a little overprotective, I guess."

I'm not sure why this statement immediately fills me with rage. He's being genuine enough and the man clearly has no social filter to begin with. I tamp it down as best I can, heat rising and burning my temples before I manage a reply. "Well, it's all safe from me. Charlie hasn't been a father to me for the vast majority of my life, and the ranch will never be my home. I'm not interested in digging up the past."

He studies me for a moment longer, then, and I have to stifle the urge to throttle him. I hold his stare until he comes to some sort of internal decision, his expression smoothing before he says, "Okay, then. Would you mind if I called ahead? I don't want to just show up with . . . this"—he nods my way—"without warning." I roll my eyes at being referred to as *this*.

"Go for it. You'll save me the trouble of explaining all over again."

HE STEPS OUT OF THE truck and walks some yardage away. The man is big, probably six and a half feet tall, I note—purely for the sake of being able to describe him to the police—and handsome, to be sure. Hemsworth-esque. But, as with many of his kind, he ruins it with speaking. I also decide that Wranglers are highly underrated on men. As are men's legs. There's something to be said about strong, thick legs on a man. The arms and shoulders and chests—they're all great, but . . . good legs usually lead up to an equally good manbutt. *Yep,* can confirm.

I am vaguely aware of the fact that my brain is choosing to deflect and assess (ha, ass-ess) him at the moment, rather than wonder who exactly he is dialing and what he might be saying.

Having him do the explaining may not have been the best choice given his obvious bias, but I'm not controlling enough to care. I'm almost relieved, knowing that the family will now be doing their best to avoid me rather than trying to welcome and show me around, telling me the history of the place, inviting me to family dinners, etc. I don't know if they would have anyway, though. Maybe things are run by Henry now? Maybe they have managerial people who handle all the outsiders while on the property?

I once spent two weeks living in a castle in Scotland, with

(surprisingly) what I would imagine is the truest picture of an ideal family, aside from Cole's. They weren't without their drama and fights—especially among the older generation. But they had game nights and movie marathons, Sunday dinners with extended family, chores around the farm. They were some of the most warm and loving people. People who never pried deeply into my personal life, but simply included me in all of theirs. I was party to all of their traditions and idiosyncrasies, all while they continually shared the anecdotes and history about their castle home. I still keep in touch with them over email, though correspondence has slowed . . . Admittedly, my replies are fairly surface level. I share details about my sister and her family often, but I don't have a friend group, let alone my own family to speak of anymore, and I fill my days with whatever makes me feel good, which seems boring to write about . . .

HENRY BEGINS HIS MARCH BACK to the truck, brows furrowed under a lock of floppy hair that's curled over his face. He's somehow managed not to have one of those hat tans with the pale forehead that most farmers and cowboys end up with, which makes me wonder if he's got a streak of vanity and takes care to avoid it?

Again with the deflecting, Tait.

He hops in and puts the truck back in gear without making an attempt to look my way. I want to maintain the illusion of my detachedness enough that I refuse to inquire about the call. It's hours that go by, each minute pushing me farther up this hill I'm determined to die on.

Eventually he relents, huffing an agitated sigh through

his nose. "I spoke with Grace, Charlie's wife. Relayed everything you told me," he says.

In for a penny, I still refuse to give anything else by asking for details. "Thanks," I reply.

He chuckles and shakes his head. I refuse to ask about that, too.

WE TURN ONTO A GRAVEL road, the nervous fluttering in my belly too strong to worry about music or making conversation. I've let about eighty-seven different scenarios mentally play out—carefully developing what my responses will be to each should they occur—when suddenly, the stone barn is in sight.

I lose my grip at the same time Henry seems to speed up. "Wait . . . please wait," I say, voice embarrassingly tight.

I grab the wrist of the arm on the steering wheel, and he visibly flinches, but doesn't pull away. I feel the coarse hair under my hand and wonder if I hurt him? I look at my hand—my fingers don't *nearly* meet all the way around the big wrist and I'm not even squeezing him.

"Your hand . . . is extremely, extremely sweaty," he says flatly.

I jerk it back and wipe both on my pants, letting a nervous laugh barrel out of me.

"Sorry."

He looks at me, brows dipping before his expression softens into what I determine must be his pitying look. And then he offers me an encouraging nod.

For some reason, the gesture bolsters me. I take a deep breath, face the house and say, "Okay. I'm ready."

EIGHT

Tension rolls off of Tait in waves as we pull up past the barn and stop in front of the house.

I wonder what exactly she expects to find here? Whatever she thinks she recalls or seems to know of them doesn't align with the family I know, at least. If she's here to do her job, they won't stand in her way.

I feel validated in that thought when I see Grace already waiting on the porch with their son, Grady. Grady reminds me of one of the pack llamas on the ranch with how his head is weaving to and fro, looking for his first glimpse of her.

To her credit, Tait manages to get out of the truck smoothly despite her obvious discomfort. Shoulders back and head held high, I can't help admiring her.

Personally, I avoid painfully awkward and uncomfortable exchanges whenever I can. I'm definitely *not* one of those people who has to slow down past a car wreck because of some morbid curiosity. Shit, I'm tempted to fast forward through the awkward and embarrassing scenes in my favorite movies, even after seeing them numerous times. I don't enjoy secondhand embarrassment or discomfort, or other people's business in general. So after she gets out, I immediately proceed with driving her luggage the three miles out to the cabin Grace told me she'd open up for her. It feels a little like abandonment, but not enough for me to stick around. I don't miss the filthy look thrown at me in my rearview mirror, though.

Replaying my phone call with Grace, I linger on the lack of shock I sensed from her. I suppose at this point, everyone really has wanted a piece of the place since it became famous, so perhaps she's been expecting Charlie's estranged family to come around. Still, it's September, the time when the unused buildings are shut up for winter before the work of winterizing the occupied ones begins. This particular cabin has never been used aside from a very short period of time . . . before.

It's the newest construction, twin to mine from the exterior, with more modern finishes on the interior. The bunkhouse is plenty empty right now though, too, and much farther away than the one that I share the pond with. It feels a little like betrayal to so easily move this stranger into this specific cabin . . .

I mentally give myself a shake and a reminder that none of it is actually *mine*, anyway.

I've grown used to the dull pain that comes whenever I see the new cabin down the road from mine, but passing this time to unload Tait's things brings it a little closer to the surface. I sort through my keys to find the one I know I still have.

Inside, Grace has already had everything taken care of and prepped. It's fully cleaned, minimally furnished. There are freshly folded towels laid on the dining table. It still smells new even though it was built over three years ago now. I quickly set down the first two bags and go unload the other two. I don't know for certain if there's an extra key that

Grace already had made or anything, but I'd rather not risk needing to be asked for it later, so I toss the spare key on the counter. It's something I'm completely unprepared to do, but I quickly jet out before the emotion—whatever it is I *should* feel—has a chance to take hold.

Directly across the pond is what I know of as *my* cabin. Charlie's younger brother, James, used to reside in it until he built his home on the farthest eastern ridge of the property. He manages the outfitting entity of the Range now, which means that we rarely see him. He's one of three guides, the others being Charlie and myself. I usually only co-guide, since people-ing is not my strong suit. They spend a great portion of the year scouting and doing predator management, and will spend much of October and November doing guided elk hunts. It's fairly obvious that they're two grown-up kids living out their dream of riding around quads, shooting, and sleeping under the stars—though no one will accuse them of not taking their jobs seriously.

My beauty, Belle, greets me with a bark and her usual mouth-grab on my forearm when I get home. She's been cooped up much longer than normal today. I typically bring her everywhere, so I let her outside and throw her ball for a bit. She eventually takes off after some grouse and I head inside, somehow more worn out than if I'd been on a days-long hike, when my phone dings.

Grady: This is the most excitement we've had around here in YEARS. And Charlie isn't even home yet!!!

Leave it to Grady to find entertainment in anyone else's pain. Where I avoid the awkward, Grady would be the kid to prep the popcorn. He's only twenty-one, though, and still

thinks humor has the power to cancel out any other emotion. I should remind him that we have an Emmy-nominated
show that is filmed here for six months out of the year off
and on, and all the excitement *that* has unleashed.

Me: Go easy on the girl.

Grady: Mom wants you both to come up for dinner tonight.
I didn't get Tait's number before she zoomed out of here
like a bat outta hell, so will you go knock on her door, be
the neighborly boy next door I know you are, and pass
along the invite?

It's then that I hear the telltale crunch of gravel and look
up to see a Logan Range fleet truck fly past my window. The
brat is blowing up enough dust to suffocate anything nearby.
"Shit!"
Belle.
I jog out just in time to see her fly out of the meadow and
after the cloud of dust. She's bred to herd and gets even more
ornery about folks that drive too fast. She's also a mean bitch
to anyone but the immediate family. I sprint a few steps
before reason sets in, and turn around to quickly grab my
keys and go after them in the truck. The last thing this
woman needs is a dog bite to start off her trip here—also the
last thing I want to be responsible for.

Sure enough, I hear Belle barking from a distance when I
get in the truck. I jam over as quickly as I can, but can't see
what's going on through the billowing dirt in the air. The
barking stops, my dread rising. I bolt out of the truck and
send up a silent prayer that she doesn't already have her by
the ankle.

The dust puffs up around me and I squint and flap at it stupidly with my arms, frantically searching until it settles and reveals—

Belle sprawled out on her back, getting her belly rubbed.

TAIT'S SMILING, TOO—THE FIRST SMILE I think I've actually seen from her. She's got perfectly straight, bright white teeth. The smile completely transforms her face, somehow.

It immediately makes me think of the time that LeighAnn prepared a five-course, gourmet meal to celebrate Grace's fiftieth birthday. LeighAnn claimed she "wanted to bring some culture" to our "hick asses." Instead of a traditional cake, we were each served a personal crème brûlée—something I'd never tried before then. Grace commented on how they were so pretty, she didn't want to break them, to which LeighAnn exclaimed that cracking it with the back of our spoon was the most satisfying part . . .

Tait's smile reminds me of that.

It's a bit like cracking the top of a crème brûlée—the top is great, but that's good shit underneath. Cracking it really was strangely satisfying, too.

Almost more stunning than that is my typically badass dog—the one I've seen go toe to toe with a wolf before—upside down with her tongue lolling happily out of her mouth.

"Is she yours?" Tait asks, smile clinging.

"I'm honestly not sure anymore," I mumble suspiciously. "She doesn't normally take to strangers."

"Oh, well. I love dogs. Maybe she knew how sad I'd be if she didn't take to me. What's her name?" She makes a silly face and puts it up to Belle's snout and I flinch, about to call out, but Belle gives her a happy lick.

I make a noncommittal noise and call her to me before she can cause more chaos. She sprints over and sits by my feet, staring up at me with her happy-dog grin.

"Belle."

Tait pouts a little, and I'm disturbed at how that disappoints me.

"Wait. Belle? *Ha*—Beauty"—she points to Belle, then points up at me—"Beast."

I ignore it.

"Grady sent me a message to ask if I'd invite you to dinner at their place tonight. I guess you took off before they had a chance to get your number," I say.

"Oh—uhhh. Okay. I really just want to get settled tonight, I think. Pass along my thanks, though?"

"Or, why don't I just give you their numbers so that you can?"

She sighs, but pulls her phone out of her back pocket and looks at me expectantly. I give her the details and tell Belle to load up, when Grady's comment about being neighborly comes to mind.

"Listen, Tait. I don't know your history. I do know the— well, *these* Logans, though. I know if you give them a chance, they'll be more than accommodating with your work. And it's probably not my place to say, but they're not normally this welcoming to outsiders, aside from the obvious people who come for filming or to stay as guests, of course," I clarify, oddly defensive. "But for them to immediately invite you to dinner . . ." I don't need to explain that they could've set her up in one of the guest cabins or even the bunkhouse, as well. "They've gotten much more protective of their privacy in recent years. I'm just saying you might consider it."

"I'm sure they're just suspicious and want to vet me before

I wander around the place. But you're right, I need to make it clear to them what I'm here for, and that's my work . . . Which, I will do, but tonight I just want to get settled," she replies firmly.

I nod and turn to leave, when another thought occurs to me.

"Oh, uhh, I may as well get your number, too, and you mine. We've had a few security issues here since the show began and if you see anything suspicious, or need any help, I'm nearby. Out of all five thousand acres, there's surprisingly only a few pockets that don't get some kind of cell service."

We exchange details, and I head back to my side of the pond.

NINE

TAIT

Once I get inside the cabin, I immediately set to unpacking. When I turned thirteen, my mother gifted me with *The 7 Habits of Highly Effective Teens*. I know, I know, very moving stuff—just what every thirteen-year-old dreams of. I only ever skimmed over it, but I memorized the main ideas in case she ever prompted me. "Do First Things, First" has been my go-to life hack since.

Which is why I immediately set to settling and getting familiar with my surroundings. Having spatial awareness, first, is what grounds me. Once I unpack my equipment, clothes, and toiletries, I decide to rearrange the living room area a bit to better highlight the giant steel and glass doors that look back out over the pond. The way the furniture currently sits, it leaves a gaping area in the middle of the room.

Space is great, but not empty or unusable space . . .

Deflecting again.

It's a habit I've accrued, fitting myself into a space and immediately making it my own. I try to find the best in it, highlight the good and the beautiful. It's something I absolutely cannot do here, though. I cannot ignore the hurt that this family has caused by their apathy, simply because it feels nice and looks better that way right now. After all, you can hide all the wires in some cute aesthetic way, throw them in some well-fitting basket, but if you unplug them altogether, things are no longer functional.

A wave of reality balloons its way through me and I have to sit down. I feel like I've been watching my life over the last twenty-four hours from underwater—clear enough to make out the shape of what's going on, but not exactly cognizant, either.

As soon as I exited the truck, I thought my legs were going to buckle beneath me. Luckily, that feeling was immediately replaced by annoyance when Henry abandoned me to face everyone alone. I'd expected his looming presence to help give me a reason to hurry off to wherever my place was and get set up. I had no idea they'd lend me my own vehicle. Plus, he'd been privy to my sweaty hands and anxiety, so I'd hoped he'd stay and be my buffer.

The exchange replays in my mind . . .

A gangly boy—probably as tall as Henry but half his body weight—gives me an emphatic, whole-body wave, taking the porch steps in two strides before he envelopes me in a bear hug . . . or, more like what I would imagine a giraffe hug would feel like. Grace meets me with, well, grace . . . har har.

I don't blame her for my mother and father's split, just like I don't blame "the other woman" entirely for mine. It always takes two, and we're all adults who don't require anything of one another at this point, other than mutual respect. But, she offers a warm and kind smile, eyes glossy.

"It's so great to finally meet you," the boy says. "You have no idea how long we have wanted this. As soon as I found out I had sisters out there. Tell me everything about California. Do you

know how to surf? I'm kidding, I'm sorry. The production crew is normally here regaling me with tales of the Golden State, but it's off-season and I'm bored of all these same faces. You are beautiful, by the way. OH! I'm Grady!" Grady says without a breath.

"Th-thank you. It's really nice to meet you, too. I'm Tait. I'm really looking forward to photographing this place."

"We are really grateful that you're here," Grace says softly.

Grateful? That catches me off guard. I should've said I'm grateful for the opportunity to work here. I didn't do anything for any one of them by coming here, so why grateful?

"Grady, let's get Tait a truck and let her go get settled," Grace says, eyes staying on me.

Grady leaps back up the steps in about one-and-a-half strides this time and heads inside. Grace keeps me under her gaze, assessing. She's very pretty, kindness exuding from her and Grady both. The smile lines all around her eyes and bracketing her mouth are deep, her chestnut hair corkscrew-curly. The furthest thing from the dark, icy beauty that my mother possessed.

"Charlie's up on the ridge today. He didn't know you were coming, otherwise I can promise you, he would be here himself. He's going to be so happy to see you, and so happy you decided to surprise him."

I feel my face smile awkwardly, so I look down at my feet. She's being perfectly polite, not pushy, and clearly wants to welcome me . . . I manage to say "Thank you," stiffly.

Just then, Grady emerges with the keys. I hold up my hand, desperate for him to understand, and—oh thank God he gets it—he tosses them promptly.

"The fleet trucks are in the stone building over there. If you stay on this road, you'll come to a pond with two cabins; yours is the second," he shouts to my retreating form.

It's then that I notice that a secondary stone barn structure has been built out behind the main house. The driveway has been continued on over to it. It matches the original barn almost exactly, but since I know the original one to be the stables, I figure that the other must be the garage.

I march in the direction of the barn, clicking the button to find out which truck is mine, get in, and do my best not to peel out.

It's not until later that I realize that I didn't manage a goodbye, or even a brief chat about my outline for the photography. I only knew that I needed to catch my breath and get back into my own space.

So now, here I am. Sitting on the leather couch, looking out the giant steel sliding doors at the pond, attempting to catch that breath still, when . . .

"*I'M . . . COMING . . . OUT! I'M COMIIING OUT!!!*"

"*I'M . . . COMING . . . OUT! I'M COMIIIING OUT!!!*"

. . . plays from somewhere around me. I briefly wonder if this is the beginning of the psychotic break/aka shit-splosion Ava promised I was headed for before I hear a *knock, knock,* and a female voice shouts, "Sorry!!! I forgot about the door-bell! I know it can be jarring."

Still in shock, I rise rigidly and open the door . . . only to stare into a face that looks almost identical to mine, but in, like, fifteen years.

Same dark blonde hair, same olive skin tone . . . the eyes are different, though. Hers are a striking denim blue, the same shade as Ava's.

"Hi!" she says brightly. "It's about time we got you out here, girl. Do you remember me?"

Her smile is infectious as she bounces in place. I feel my face smile back, but I'm still suffering from the shock of my mental breakdown à la Diana Ross, and she continues before I get a chance.

"It's okay, honey. I forgot what I went to the grocery store for this morning, so I wouldn't remember either. I'm your aunt LeighAnn. Can I give you a hug?" And she does.

It's been so long since I've *been* hugged that I naturally fall into it. Don't get me wrong, I have hugged, but maybe it's only an older sibling thing—we are the ones who do the hugging.

The last hug that someone held *me* in was when I ran into my ex-mother-in-law at the grocery store in my former town. I, of course, looked like trash (because one never runs into anyone one knows when they are put together, only when they are mid three-day-eating/sci-fi-series-binge, still wearing a stain of the previous night's wine and still picking Oreo gunk out of one's teeth). I was only going out to replenish the necessary supplies. I was also clearly reflecting how I felt internally, and she held me tight enough for me to burst into tears in the middle of the chip aisle.

I moved shortly after that. And discovered grocery delivery.

LeighAnn is holding me that same way now, and it elicits the same response. I feel my throat thicken, and I break the hug before I let myself fall apart.

"LeighAnn, of course I remember you. You taught me how to French braid in the same day you taught me how to shoot a compound bow," I say, and the smile that surfaces is almost genuine. LeighAnn is seven years younger than Charlie, and was always my favorite.

Her grin warms, and I invite her in to sit down.

"No, no, I can't sit still for long anyways. Once Grady texted and told me you were here, I had to see you and catch up. And I thought I could show you around and get you reacquainted with the place. A lot has changed, but then again, a lot hasn't. Fancy a walk?"

Noting that she didn't say anything about making me join for dinner, I decide that this is my safest bet to appease everyone. My instincts aren't picking up any bad vibes from her, but I guess that she's trying to feel me out as much as she wants to get me reacquainted. Knowing what I know of this family, I suspect that I'll need to quickly squash anyone's suspicions about my motives and goals from the jump. LeighAnn seems like a good enough place to start.

"Sure, let me change my shoes."

"Sneakers might be comfy but you'll want some decent shit-kickers for around here."

I smile and quickly lace on my hiking boots. Shit-kickers they are not, but they'll do.

We head out in a silence that's anything but comfortable . . . LeighAnn keeps switching up her pace, but I don't know where to start with the conversation, so I am determined to sit back and let her take the lead. After about five awkward minutes, she begins.

"So—our Tater-Tot is all grown up, huh? What are you, twenty-eight now?"

"Yes, ma'am." The nickname was always the worst, and still is, but I refrain from telling her as much. She'd often watched Ava and I, and was always around from what I can remember, so I'm sure she's just trying to remind me of that and get us on comfortable ground.

"Don't you have a birthday coming up?"

"Yep. Twenty-nine in a little under a month."

"That's right. You share a birthday with my daughter, actually. She'll be twenty-one in October. Lucy. She's at Boise State."

"Wow, congrats—what's she studying?"

"She's doing the pre-vet program. She was a lot like you

growing up—could spend all day with the horses. Have you gone to the stables yet?"

"No. I, uh, just got here and wanted to get set up."

"Of course. Well, we have a herd of wild horses that's been spotted over by the eastern ridge and valley lately—they'd be awesome to photograph."

Oh good, she knows what I am here to do, there's my pivot point. "That'd be amazing. Thank you for the tip."

"No problem. I already know you don't need my advice, though. Your work is beautiful. I found Ava on Facebook a few years back and have seen some of what she's shared. And her family. That husband of hers is adorable—the baby even more so."

"You and Ava are Facebook friends?" I struggle to keep the incredulity out of my voice.

"Uhhh, yeah. She never mentioned it? I think she and Grady are, too? They've done some messaging back and forth . . ."

"Oh, yeah, that's right," I manage to say quickly, hoping I glazed over my confusion. The hurt that I feel is quickly over-shadowed by the fact that it's obvious that Ava wanted this—this reunion—way more than she let on. She must've lied out of thinking that I'd chastise her or judge her? I don't exactly know, but leaving me here with egg on my face is still pretty un-sisterly. Especially when she knew I was coming here. Did she know about our cousin, too? Actually, what the fuck?

"Tait?"

My head jerks up and I realize that I've stopped walking. "Sorry—I spaced."

"It's okay, sweetie. It's probably overwhelming being back here, too. I'm just glad that you finally are," she says sympathetically.

Maybe it's the exhaustion, the overwhelm, but the familiarity and earnestness has my nerves flaring again. The fact that everyone is being warm to me is utterly confounding.

"I'm sorry, but I need something to be clear, here: I came here to do a job. I have an author looking for inspiration for one of her stories—I'm not looking to add a chapter in mine. I'm *good* on all of that. I really appreciate the kindness, but we haven't been family for over twenty years, LeighAnn, and I'm not looking to be now that it's suddenly convenient for all of you." I turn on a heel and start heading back to the cabin.

"Tait—wait. Will you wait, please?"

I stop and look at her.

"Tait, I understand what you must think—of all of us, I do. But Charlie made it explicitly clear that we needed to give you guys space. And with everything that happened, we just thought we were being respectful of the . . . situation." Her hands flail while she speaks, a habit of mine, too. "I won't say more than that, other than I don't approve of his methods and have made that abundantly clear over the years. But the idiot had good intentions. He didn't know how to navigate his way through by the time things got too far away from him, but it's always been obvious to the rest of us that he's never stopped thinking about you girls."

And then I snap. "How? How has that been made obvious? What has he done? He writes the occasional letter—to Ava. We've had about three phone conversations since I was seven, and he came to see us zero times." I make a zero shape on one hand for emphasis.

"Tait, your mother wouldn't allow it."

"My mother has been dead for over four years, LeighAnn. What about then? Couldn't afford a plane ticket? What stopped him? Seems to me that he got so busy building a new, beautiful life for himself here that reconnecting with anything that reminded him that he tarnished the great Logan legacy just became too inconvenient for him."

I can see her fighting to say more, but she doesn't argue with me further. My chest is falling and rising with anger, swiftly followed by bitterness *at* this anger. I don't want it, damnit. I jerk my shoulders in a shrug, like I can shake off the heaviness.

LeighAnn lands on her words. "I'm sorry you feel that way. Just know that we all have suffered, even when we've triumphed. You're young, but life, love . . . none of it is ever black or white, all good or evil. There's always more to the picture," she says.

This is nothing that I don't already know. I had to realize that parents are people, too, at a much younger age than most. My mother wasn't *only* my mother—that wasn't the entirety of her identity. And her struggles made that part of her life more difficult. She was an addict, she was angry, she was funny, she was sad, she was vain, she struggled with her insecurities. She just . . . struggled. And she never fully recovered from her heartbreak. I learned before the age of twelve that I would need to be responsible for my own life's direction, and that I could love her without letting myself be dragged down, or blaming her for some missing components in my life.

Ava struggles more with her anger toward our mom. She's always resented that Mom's bitterness took precedence in our lives. I, on the other hand, hold tight to the knowledge that she was *there,* where Charlie was not. I find the good in our memories, adjust my mental exposure to them to enhance their colors where I can. My grandparents (her parents) weren't around long after we came back, but I was able to make memories with them, too. We didn't have some epic family dynamic in any aspect, good or bad. Sometimes, sure, Mom didn't come home until morning, and once in a while she would be passed out on the couch—likely more from the exhaustion of being a single parent over anything substance-related. But she never hit us or screamed at us, she never subjected us to weird boyfriends. She also didn't take much interest in what we were doing, but I think that's part of what has made Ava and I self-reliant. I always thought that when we grew up, had babies . . . that then, maybe being a grandma would connect us in a new way, that we would get a chance to bond better. But, she died, and I never got the chance.

Charlie, on the other hand, never even tried.

"I just hope we'll have the opportunity to get to know each other a bit," she continues, softly. "And here's the thing. You're here anyway, right? I know it's probably a bit brazen for me to say . . . but whatever comes of it, you're not going to be able to compartmentalize this entire trip, so you may as well dig in. Lord knows that Charlie will be a lot less pushy than me, so I just hope you'll give him a chance," she says, and turns to leave.

"LeighAnn . . ."

"Yes?"

"Does—does Charlie know that I'm here yet?" I ask.

"I'm not sure, sweetheart."

"How old is Grady?" I decide to get as many of the bare-bones facts as I can, hoping not to be caught off guard again.

"He's twenty-one, also," she says. But I don't miss the subtle change in her body language. She doesn't care for being the one answering questions. Interesting.

"And they don't have any other kids, then? Any other *cousins* I should know about?"

At that, she folds her arms and closes off completely. After considering her reply, she says, "They don't, no."

Ah, so when I start to interrogate it *is* unwelcome, I see. Well, I'll be damned if I'm going to be the one under the spotlight, here, the only one that has to answer for my choices.

"Okay. Please tell Grace and Grady thank you for the invite, but I'm exhausted and just want to catch up on sleep. I'll head to the house after breakfast tomorrow to talk about the timeline and where to get started with work."

"Sure thing. I'll be back to do a real tour though, soon." She offers me a sad smile before she heads to her car and on her way.

I HEAD BACK INTO THE house, collapse on the bed without even taking off my shoes, and fall asleep.

TEN

Growing up in Wyoming, before my dad's drinking got away from him, we spent a great deal of time outdoors. He used to say to me, "Stay close to nature, and nature will stay close to you," before promptly dropping me off somewhere in the woods and challenging me to find my way back on my own. His intentions were good, even if the execution was lacking in fatherly warmth.

He meant that spending time in nature kept your instincts on. We get so clouded by our reliance on our devices and convenience now, that as a species we've lost some of our wilder intuition. I suppose since I continue to spend as much time as I can in nature, that's why I'm able to still hear some of mine.

Which is also why, when I wake up a little after midnight with my hackles raised, I know something is wrong. We've had a slew of paps break into the ranch, crazed fans who are mostly harmless, and three different stalkers who were most definitely not. And since most of the actors have their own personal security when they're staying here on location, the real risk is that any one of these idiots could end up hurting themselves and try to hold Logan Range liable. They're all from cities, of course, and don't take the perils of nature seriously. One girl, a determined nineteen-year-old from San Diego, said that she knew that if she "could just meet Duke Wade, he'd see how great we could be together." This particular girl hiked for two days during winter. We found her nearly frozen only about two miles away from the main ranch, just over a ridge. She later admitted that she'd walked along that ridge for hours before collapsing. If she had just gone up top, she'd have seen our valley. That's Idaho country for you, though. The steepest and most dramatic ridge lines that break even the most seasoned hikers and hunters. I think she ended up losing a toe or two . . .

Belle is already on point at the door. She's a Queensland Heeler, so not exactly a pointing breed, but her body language is obvious. I throw my boots on over my sweats and a jacket, and grab my pistol. September might still be warm during the days, but the temperatures usually make a dramatic drop at night.

It's just shy of a full moon, and I know the surrounding landscape like the back of my hand, so I don't need a flashlight. I follow Belle through the meadow a ways and down toward the bottom of the same ridge that the lovesick teenager got stuck behind . . .

I think I see movement in the tree line, but can't be too certain. I make a sound to get Belle over to my side and we make our way through some of the outlying brush. I don't want whatever it is to see me coming and hide—if it's another one of these crazy fuckers we will absolutely press charges.

We make our way around and catch up enough that I can make the shape out of the thing . . .

It's moving on two legs—I think? But, there's a huge hump where it's back should be and I can't make out the legs. It's obviously a human of some kind. It's huddled around something, taking short steps here and there. What the fuck? What the hell is it? A wendigo?

Christ, Henry. You're a thirty-one-year-old man, don't go getting yourself worked up thinking it's some made-up creature.

The moon is shining in the clearing to our left, but through the trees it's too hard to discern the thing. I take the pistol out of my jacket pocket and lay it down on the ground, deciding that there's only one way to find out. I've got thoughts of killers and stalkers in ghillie suits running through my mind, and I refuse to make myself liable to some sue-happy asshole.

Before I can change my mind, I launch out after it, Belle at my heels. She passes me as the thing turns and tries to lunge away. Belle knocks it halfway down and I hurl my body to tackle it the rest of the way, hearing the air whoosh out and a strangled noise escape. Definitely human.

I wrap my arms around it as its limbs flail. My hand closes around something and it slightly gives under my touch—squishy?

"What"—a strangled gasp—"the"—more of the noise—"*fuck?!!*" it says. "That's my BOOB!" the voice manages to push out while trying to swallow back air.

I run my hands down and sure as shit, I feel how the body tapers in at the middle, and back up and out where boobs would, in fact, be . . .

Fuck. Recognition surfaces . . .

"Tait?!!"

TAIT

Anyone who's had the wind knocked out of them knows those noises that you make. The angry noises coming out of me sound . . . hideous. They're weird, strangled moans—way more akin to a terrible bout of diarrhea than sexual. He's got his hands on either side of my waist, his legs wrapped and locked around mine, with my ass smashed against his lap. Being wrapped up in his big limbs has me flustered and pissed off enough to hiss and writhe, but my backpack separates my back from his chest and is making it even harder for me to breathe.

"Yes—you"—*gasp*—"dick!"

He comes to and lifts his hands and feet straight into the air like a fainted goat. I, in turn, struggle like a turtle caught on its shell and try to right myself. I'm seeing spots, and as I roll back and forth against him, my ass comes into contact, repeatedly, with him *there,* and he lets out a little grunt that flusters me even more. After what feels like the longest ten seconds of my life, he grabs under my armpits from behind, and rights us both to standing in one swift motion.

I whip around, ready to tear him to shreds, but my vision swims. I groan, and sit down.

"What are you doing out here?" he says accusingly.

I hold up a finger and he seems to remember that he tackled me like a defensive lineman.

"Shit, I'm sorry. Are you hurt?"

The finger remains up and I work to get my breath steady again.

He's shifting from foot to foot with his hands on his hips. The bastard *should* be nervous—as soon as I catch my breath it's over for him.

"What on earth are you wearing?" he asks.

The *nerve* of this guy.

"You better hope you didn't break any of my equipment!" I snarl as I take off my parka and open up my backpack with my camera equipment.

"*No.*" I groan when I remember that I had my actual camera in my hands right before I was hit by the truck that is Henry. I see it on the ground, very obviously broken.

"Shit. I'm sorry. I didn't know it was you." His tone is etched with irritation. He stalks back the direction he came, picking up something from the ground and tucking it away. He whips back around to me, all hints of apology lost. "What the fuck are you doing out here at night, unarmed and wearing this—this dress-coat thing?!"

"This dress-coat thing is my old swimming parka! It's warm and comfortable. I wasn't headed out in the night worried about fashion, you knob! And, armed? Why the fuck would I need to be armed?"

"It's . . . brown . . . and shiny." He's fixated on my coat, the corners of his lips pulled down in disgust.

"Our mascot was the banana slug! Also, YOU BROKE MY CAMERA!"

"And for that I am sorry, but what were you thinking?"

"I was thinking that it's a full moon, and I had light. LeighAnn told me about a herd of wild horses, and I don't know—I figured I could get some interesting pictures one way or another. I woke up and couldn't go back to sleep, anyway."

He nods, jaw clenched and nose flaring before he looks down. Belle licks my hand and paws my leg for attention, before I comply.

"For the record, the horses are nowhere near here, but I will replace your camera, and anything else that was broken. I'm sorry again. And for the—" He gestures to my chest, and then looks down again, *rightfully* embarrassed. Shifts on his feet anxiously.

I study the man. He seems contrite enough, maybe a bit panicked. So while I don't understand why he took it upon himself to act as a one-man army, my guess is that there have been reasons for it in the past.

"It's alright, most action I've had in a while." I cringe, not sure what possessed me to say that.

A laugh escapes him in a rush before he replies, "Me too, actually." He grins.

Yeah right. That smile is a complete panty-melter. The moon is shining just enough that I can fully see his face clearly, now. The smile lines around his eyes deepen, and the ones around his mouth dimple, almost meeting each other. His hair is mussed and sticking up in a corner, like he just woke up. We both deflate at the same time, and laugh at the sheer ridiculousness of what just happened.

"Why are you up?" I ask, tension broken.

He laughs at that, too. "Oh, you know. Some caveman instinct told me there was danger nearby. Clearly I'm out of touch." He shuffles his hair away from his face and scratches the back of his neck. The movement causes an impressive bicep to bunch, and my body responds with traitorous warmth. Why, all of a sudden *now* my sexual appetite decides to make herself known on my hierarchy of needs, is beyond me.

"Well, I guess we may as well head back now. Not going to get much material . . ." I pick up the remnants of my camera. Henry grabs my coat and backpack.

"I'll take tomorrow off and we can head into town to look for a replacement. Let me know what else?"

"Uh, this is a five thousand dollar camera just FYI, and it's insured for these kinds of reasons. Well, maybe not *exactly* this. But really, it's okay."

"It's fine. It's my fault. I'll cover it."

I already know I'm not going to let him buy me a new

camera, but, rather than argue it out tonight, give a noncommittal nod.

We start to make our way back, my sides and back aching. I take a weird step and hiss.

"Fuck, you're hurt, aren't you?" He reaches for me before jerking his hands back, obviously unsure whether or not he should touch me again, eyes rounding in concern.

"No, no. Just took a weird step. I'll be fine, seriously. It was a misunderstanding."

"No, let me at least take a look when we get back to the cabins. I'll just make sure nothing is broken or anything," he says.

At this point, I'm so keyed up and sleep deprived, and can't start my work tomorrow anyway. I'm also starving, so I cave.

"Okay, but on the condition that you let me raid your food, and your booze," I reply. I decided to go out and seek work when I woke up in the middle of the night and saw that my cabin was devoid of any kind of sustenance.

"Works for me." He smirks and walks closer to me the rest of the way back, keeping his hand out as if to brace me. I shiver and realize that I'm in the pajamas that I changed into before I gave up and headed out for the night—braless, and in a too-small fitted T-shirt that says "Taco Belle" on it, with my favorite hole-ridden black sweats. Last Halloween Ava and Casey dressed up as Beauty and the Beast, with Jack in a Lumière costume. I bought this so I could join in their family theme (as Ava demanded) but added my own twist. I carried around a twelve pack box of tacos all night for effect.

In the dark the getup is fine, but I know once we get inside my nipples will be on full display. I try to grab my coat from Henry as we step on his porch, but he doesn't let it go.

"I don't think this should be allowed in my house, sorry." His nose scrunches when he spares my coat a horrified look.

"I'm cold."

"Then go inside, where it's warmer," he offers. He looks down as I fold my arms across my chest and understanding lights his face. "Oh." And then he smiles again, and opens the door. He tosses my coat on the nearby rocking chair, solidifying his stance.

I roll my eyes and head in.

ELEVEN

I do realize that I'm in a strange man's house, in the middle of the night, after he has attacked me in the woods, felt me up, broken my camera, and playfully taken my (beloved) coat away . . . and I further realize that I hadn't considered *any* of it until this point. I mentally shake myself while simultaneously hearing my own subconsciousness's voice purr. *So what? He doesn't give off that threatening vibe, and what's the worst this could lead to?*

Mmhm.

Clearly, he has more consideration for my self-preservation than I do, because he offers my coat back to me, looking a little disappointed. "I was kidding," he says dully.

He probably assumes I'm into him, as I'm sure most other warm-blooded females are.

I attempt to wrap my coat around me and feel something pinch in my side again. Henry catches my wince.

"Go sit down and let me take a look at your side."

Just then, because I haven't been put through enough torture tonight, my stomach chooses to let out the most audible, long-winded, gurgling growl that has ever occurred, *ever,* and I'm reminded of what sent me out into the night to begin with.

Henry's eyes go wide and he holds his hands up in surrender, as if I'm in charge of my stomach's auditory tendencies. "Or, I can feed you first?" he says, eyes on my midsection.

I sigh. "Thank you. There's not a scrap of food in my place." And then I catch the complaint in my voice and try to cover it.

". . . Not that I *expect* to be fed or the groceries to be stocked for me. I was invited to dinner and everything, and could've gone into town for food if I hadn't fallen asleep. I just—I'm starving," I elaborate.

He chuckles, the sound skating through me. "It's alright, go ahead and sit. I'll make a drink first. Assume you don't feel concussed?"

"No, my head is completely fine, actually." Minus the fifteen-year-old boy that's taken up where my libido resides.

"Any preferences?"

"I'm not picky, thank you."

I head over to the sofa. Everything is surprisingly tidy and nicely appointed. No detritus piled up anywhere. It makes me suspicious of how often he's actually here.

He heads over to the kitchen as I'm mentally grappling with another wave of self-consciousness. I've been assuming he lives here on his own this entire time—maybe it's so tidy because his girlfriend (or wife?!) keeps it that way?

"Are you alone?" I blurt out before I can think better of it.

"What?" He looks at me quizzically, head rearing back at my shout.

"I mean, is your girlfriend or anyone going to be woken up by us?"

"Do you plan on being particularly *loud* for any reason?"

"What? No!!" Then, realizing how loud *that* was, "No, I mean—"

He laughs again. "Relax, I'm kidding. Yes, I live alone. Just Belle and I."

At the mention of the latter, I pat the seat next to me to get her on the couch before I blow out a breath. It's not lost on me that he didn't clarify being unattached. Unfortunately, being in the single world, even in the smallest degree that I have been, has taught me that some men choose not to be transparent about those things for a reason.

Scratching Belle's ears and petting her soft fur calms my frazzled nerves. I'm pleased to smell something delicious coming from the kitchen; my stomach mewls in agreement.

Henry emerges with a grilled cheese and what looks like a cocktail, and I can't help but steal a glance at his gray sweatpants *effect*. There's something a little too intimate about him serving me food in his bare feet. When did he shed his boots? I'm genuinely annoyed at my baser attraction to him. It's been so long since someone besides myself participated in my orgasm. I sigh, suddenly very *aware* of everything he's doing. I remove my shoes and feel my eyebrows come together on their own accord as he brings the goods in front of me. The food, too.

"What?" he snaps at my expression. "Sorry I don't have any fresh sushi on hand, Sunshine." Ahh, yes, there he goes ruining it with speaking, again.

"No—sorry that my face—made a face! It looks fine. Great. Really good. Thank you," I stammer. He plops the plate on my lap and the drink on the table in front of me before he sits on the end of the chaise.

I'll wonder in a minute why he's sitting so close to me, when I clearly exasperate him so, but for now the smell of melted cheese and buttery bread steals my focus. I'm shocked when I bite into it to find something sweet and tangy. I must wear that expression on my face, too, because before I can ask, he says, "Apples and cheddar. Mrs. Logan always made them that way."

"It's delicious, thank you."

I wash it back with the drink, a whiskey and ginger ale number that warms me up from the inside. I have a swig after every bite, losing myself to the meal. The end comes too quickly, though, and I'm forced to look back up at Henry's sour expression.

"Which side hurts and where?"

I roll my eyes and lean onto my side, exposing the one that's pinched. A burp escapes me in the motion, but I'm either too sated or too immune to being embarrassed tonight to care.

"Sexy," he says flatly. I lift my arm to pinpoint the area, then use my opposite hand to lift up my shirt to look at it.

An angry, reddish-purple bruise has already mottled the skin over the front of my ribs, but it's the back that hurts. I roll onto my stomach to grant access to the area in question.

The awareness hasn't dulled with the meal, so when he slides the hem of my shirt up a bit further, I feel the touch of his rough fingertips shoot right through me, my stomach somersaulting.

He gingerly prods at the area in question, eliciting an annoyed and muffled "Ow" from me.

"Nothing's broken, but you've got a nasty bruise, and . . ." He chuckles softly, chuffing out a breath of air that hits my side. ". . . It's in the shape of a perfect circle."

"What? Let me see!"

"Not sure how to do that, unless you're an owl and can turn your head all the way around," he replies dryly.

"Where's your bathroom?"

He gestures to the hallway, and I remember that our cabins are essentially the same layout. I'd only been here a handful of times as a kid, but it has definitely been updated since. He doesn't offer more help than that, so I go off on my own. As soon as I open the door to the would-be hall bathroom (at least from what I recall at my place), Henry is up and behind me, his very large hand over mine, awkwardly taking the door handle. "Not that one, next one on the left," he says gently.

His proximity throws me off again, close enough to see chest hair poking up from the neckline of his shirt, oddly obscene . . . and he's so tall and warm, smelling like grilled cheese and something else that's just . . . man and/or man soap and warm leather. *Actual* warm leather, like the best books always say, and why is it always *warm* leather? How is warmth encapsulated in a scent?

My musings are cut short when he turns around and heads back toward the living room. Mercurial might be an understatement with that one.

I get to the bathroom, flip on the light, and audibly gasp because *ohmygod* it is the bathroom dreams are made of. The slate floors are heated under my feet, the room itself larger than my kitchen back home. A vanity with a sink dons either side, with there being a second arched door past the vanity on the right, and a built-in stocked with fluffy towels just past the one on the left. Straight ahead to the back are what appear to be large double sliding glass shower doors that lead to a slight step up and into a shower *room,* with a massive freestanding tub inside the shower, toward the back. There are two large windows over the tub, no doubt looking out and over the pond. On the left wall there are multiple shower heads, one handheld and one rain head that looks like it's big enough to wash an SUV. On the right side is a built-in bench. I suppose you'd end up spending so much time in there that you'd like a place to sit down.

I'm not sure how long I gawk, running my hands over the marble slab walls in the shower room (yes, I let myself in), but it must've been awhile because Henry stomps in, irritation written all over his face. I opt for honesty again.

"I don't even remember what I came in here for, but I'm having an out-of-body experience in this bathroom," I tell him. His hands go on his hips and he spares me another one of his exasperated looks.

"Do you even appreciate all this?" flies out of me, incredulous.

"What?"

"I mean it—there's no body wash or anything in here. I assume you shower?"

"I use mine, in my room. I'm sorry if *your* facilities aren't up to your standards, though."

It takes me a minute to process what he says, but I snap a little more, then.

"You really assume I'm some kind of snob, don't you? You're taking a compliment and reading into it as some kind of complaint or comparison, when it's not."

"You're the one who asked me if I even appreciated it, Tait."

True. I did do that, so I hedge, "You just did it over a facial expression not fifteen minutes ago, though. You're the one who tackled me in the woods, in the dark, and told me to come here, yet you're continuing to act like *I'm* up to something."

He sighs, and I see thoughts processing on his face. He seems to struggle with something, grasps it, and then finally spits out, "I'm sorry."

Realizing that I've been talking to him from his shower, I mournfully step out. This puts me back at an even greater height disadvantage, so I'm forced to look up at him.

"It's fine, I don't exactly assume the best of people myself. Especially being here. *But*, I'm going to be stuck here for a month and a half, and honestly, Henry, I could use some kind of friend. One who's not related to me." I'm not sure what about him—given that he's especially cranky, menacing, and rude—elicits such transparency from me, but it feels almost good to be recklessly vulnerable this way. Knowing that there's an end date, and that he's not sharing any of my DNA, helps.

He seems a bit flustered at that too, but responds, holding out his hand. "Truce?"

I take it, shake it firmly. "Truce." I grin, not one to miss an opportunity. "Especially if you let me have this bathroom to myself sometime, for like, three hours."

I expect him to laugh at that, or even roll his eyes. He does neither, just intensifies his look, and his grip on my hand and says, "I think I can do that."

I inhale sharply when a vision comes, unbidden, of those rough hands on my bare hips, piloting me as I grind on his, him seated on the shower bench, steam billowing around us. His face and chest are covered in sweat or water or both, mouth open and brow furrowed in pleasure . . .

"You want another drink?" he says, and I'm jerked back to reality, where I am still holding on to his hand and awkwardly slow-shaking it. I whip away as if burned, but recover nicely with a two syllable "Ye-es."

I go to leave when he grabs my arm with his obscenely large hand, and I very briefly wonder if the tension was felt mutually, but he says, "Your bruise—did you get a look at it?"

"OH! NO!" Overly loud and frantic, I hop over in front of one of the mirrors and lift up my shirt, turning around as much as possible. He's right, it is an insanely perfect circle, already welted and purple with red dots.

"Oh, God." I groan. "It's from my lens . . . the one in my backpack." The hilarity of it all—the last 24 hours, the reality of where I am, the fact that I have yet to even see my estranged father—it all hits me then, harder than in the woods, and I bust out laughing uncontrollably. It's my ugliest laugh: cackling, bubbling, frothing at the mouth. Eventually Henry grabs me, gives me a little shake, but when I look up at him, I see him fighting a laugh too, and it begins anew—this time with him losing it alongside me. His laugh is pleasant though, deep and rumbling . . . Mine is a psych ward unto itself.

Spent, panting, and wiping tears from our eyes, we eventually make our way back to the living room, with the occasional aftershock chuckle between us. It's the same feeling of old—the one like having a friend over for a sleepover, and staying up too late, when you can't stop laughing even if it's at nothing.

I decide to sit at the island this time and watch him as he makes us each another drink.

"Your laugh. It's awful," he says, but he smirks appreciatively at me.

"Thanks, I know. How long have you been working here?" I ask, feeling like the ice likely broke alongside my camera.

"About fifteen years now. Grace is my aunt." He slides another drink on the counter in front of me. He grabs one of the stools next to me and swings it to his side so we are sitting across from one another.

"Ah, I see." And then I recall something he said earlier. "Wait, you call your aunt 'Mrs. Logan?'"

He lets out a disgruntled noise and shoves a hand through his hair. "No, uhhh, your grandma—Emmaline, Emma. She's who I call Mrs. Logan."

Oh, wonderful. Dear Grandma. I have blessedly blocked her from my mind until this point. I manage a nod and take a sip of my drink. There goes another attempt at small talk, barreling to the ground in a ball of fire.

God, I'm tired, but not tired enough. I know if I head to bed, my thoughts will keep spinning.

"You like cards?" Henry asks, looking at me beneath a raised, sympathetic brow, and I could kiss him for his deflection.

"Love them."

WE PLAY CARD GAMES FOR what feels like hours. Gin, 5 Card Draw, High Spade/High Hand. We even make an attempt at Cribbage until we both decide there's too much thinking and math involved, and switch back to Gin. He regales me with light, funny stories from some of the outfitting trips he's guided on. One in particular leaves me in stitches, about a man from Seattle who thought he was lost and actually blew a foghorn despite being twenty-five yards away from a gravel road, *and* from Henry. I'm not sure if it's the image itself, or the put-out face he makes while he repeatedly says, "He thought he was lost after maybe ten minutes. Ten minutes! Not to mention, it was still fucking daylight!" By the time he finishes, I'm wiping tears from the corners of my eyes.

The conversation stays light, both of us cleverly avoiding anything that could turn heavy; sticking to our work, places I've been to and seen. He's an active listener, asking for pertinent details here and there, seeming genuinely interested. I find that I enjoy sharing, actually. Having the chance to talk about some of the places I've seen reminds me of their beauty and wonder, again.

Eventually, I simply cannot hold my head up any longer, though, and put my face to the cool countertop. Henry gets me up at some point and shuffles me to a bed, where I pass out before my head hits the pillow, and fall into a dreamless sleep.

TWELVE

HENRY

Despite only getting a few hours of sleep, my eyes shoot open at their typical five A.M. It's as if I just laid her down, though, for how very much aware I am of Tait's presence in my house. I could've listened to her happily prattle on all night, talking about some of her favorite places and experiences. Whenever she got to a particularly funny story or anecdote, her volume would increase more and more as she was telling it until she was effectively shouting by the end, completely oblivious.

She'd apologize when she realized that she'd been yelling, and instinctively I know that someone's made her feel bad about it before—a fact that slides an angry, oily feeling through my skull.

Yet, she's got a quiet confidence about her, never coming across as boastful or phony, just excited to share the things that I was, surprisingly, excited to listen to. As she got sleepier, her eyelids got visibly heavier, and her tired voice took on a husky tone that shot straight to my groin. The girl can't lose a card game sportingly, though, no matter how unaffected she tries to act.

My mind drifts back to the conversations from the night

before, and shit, I smile when I remember how good we both were at keeping it light, only once turning cringe-worthy on my end.

". . . GRADY GOT ME TO MAKE *a Tinder profile once, but I didn't last a week," I said.*

"Oh, come on. You seem like the kind of guy who'd love getting to know new people. Veeerrryyyy approachable, you are." She laughed.

"Har-har, Yoda. What about you? Do you sign into a profile while trekking the globe and check out the market in that area?" I winced, because I was trying to keep it light, but I'm so out of practice that it came out harsh, judgmental.

Her face fell, but she covered it with a sad smile. "Nah. The idea of dating anyone ever again sounds . . . exhausting."

I laughed through my nose but looked down at my cards, understanding her meaning but also feeling . . . sad about it. She continued on before I could come up with a subject change.

"My sister Ava is married to her best friend, and he's incredible. Jesus, he loves her so much. But they've been together for a billion years now, and Ava always tries to tell me 'God, Tait, I miss the newness. You get to have that exciting feeling again when you're infatuated with someone and want to see them all the time, when they want to see you all the time and skip things just to be together. That's the best part.' She tells me she misses that part, but I know better. I KNOW what comes with that. The idea of all that useless shit in the beginning just exhausts me. Always needing to look your best, smell your best, show your best angles, be hairless—oh but still be fun, can't seem high-maintenance or anything. Heaven forbid the guy knows I have a functioning butthole. And all those mindless, meaningless questions . . ." She made

a disgusted face and groaned. " 'What's your favorite color?' Barf. Give me a fucking break. That's not the best part. The best part is when you get past all that and get to feel that peace, when you know the other person feels for you what you feel for them, and they've already seen you at your worst, smelliest self, or love the effort you've put into being high-maintenance and can actually appreciate it. When someone's gotten to know all of that and still wants to get to know you more as you change and grow—to figure out the changing you, and you them. That's the most intense and best feeling."

Holy shit . . . our eyes locked, and I hoped she could see that I knew what she was saying. It was on the tip of my tongue to ask how you get to that point without the other shit, though, and what the fuck you do when you get there and find out it's all a lie, when she laughed, and made a swiping motion with her hand.

"Did I lose you when I said 'functioning butthole'?" she said with another forced laugh and pleading eyes, and that was my cue for that subject change.

"So . . . uhh . . . what's your favorite color?"

THE NIGHT STAYED PRETTY SURFACE-LEVEL from there, but every time she laughed, it was all I could do to not immediately try to elicit another. I swear each one is different, full of unbridled, cackling joy.

And while I'm glad to be on friendly terms, I'm in touch with myself enough to be annoyed at how much I look forward to seeing her again and spending time with the woman while she is here. Obviously, I need to get out and do some socializing. Maybe I'll make plans with Duke . . . Maybe she'd want to join?

"Fuck, idiot, give her some space. You *would* pick the most unavailable woman to start showing interest in. She needs a friend, not some moron drooling over her," I say to my own reflection.

She is, in the most literal sense, a woman of the world. She's traveled far and wide, and she's obviously tenacious when it comes to her goals and aspirations. I'm confident in myself in plenty areas of life, but I'm way too simple for her.

I decide I would rather not test our newfound friendship over awkward coffee, so I move to head out as quietly as I can to take on some of the earlier chores before I have to head into town with her. I'm confident that she can let herself out.

As soon as I take care of my human needs and get my jeans on, I hear a banging on the door. I try to skirt down the stairs as quick as possible, but as soon as I get to the bottom, I look across the great room to see Tait already there, opening the door.

To Charlie Logan.

He sucks in a breath and looks at her, then over to me, with my belt unbuckled and shirtless. I swear his eyes go back and forth at least ten times. Tait glances over at me, and then must realize what Charlie is seeing because she does a double take, and then looks back at him and crosses her arms. *Is she . . . ?* Yep, she's going to go ahead and let him come to his own conclusion here, something that immediately has me flustered.

"Nn-Nnnnn." (Shit, I haven't stuttered in years.) "Charlie, hey. This is not what it looks like." The look he spares me is humorless, though, so I give Tait a look that I hope conveys *"pleasefortheloveofGodhelpmewoman."* She rolls her eyes and looks back to Charlie.

He visibly flinches under *her* glare and says, "I wasn't expecting you here."

Oof.

"Ahhh, yes. Funnily enough, I wasn't expecting you here either. I didn't know if I should expect you anywhere, at all, actually since you didn't deign to come by yesterday when I got here, despite not seeing me in—oh, what has it been—twenty-plus years?"

She's not being *completely* unfair, I guess.

He takes off his hat and shuffles awkwardly on his feet. To his credit, he meets her eyes again before he replies, "You look so much like your mother."

Fuuuuuckkkk.

I've never been (nor do I suspect that I'll ever be) the guy that knows the right things to say to women, at the right time. But, even *I* know that this was the wrong thing to say. The rage on her face and the color change of it has me turning around to head back upstairs.

"Don't you dare leave. I am," she says quietly without turning my way. Shit, how do women do that? In one swift movement she scoops up her coat and backpack, and is out the door and on the march.

I expect Charlie to head out after her, but he doesn't. Just eventually blows out a long breath and steps inside.

"Well, that went about as good as I thought it would," he declares.

I take that moment to finish getting dressed, not sure if I should admonish him for not going by her cabin, surprised that I feel a bit defensive over Tait, nasty retort or not . . .

I come back out to find him wearing that same humorless look on his face from before, though.

"What *was* she doing here, though? Grace told me you got her from the airport, but that should have been pretty early still?"

I fumble for the right approach to the story until I settle for the blunt overview. "I attacked her in the woods because I thought she was a trespasser, then invited her back here to check her for . . . injuries. She crashed and I didn't want to wake her to make her go back to her place."

An eyebrow raise is my only indication that he heard me, so I offer up a few more details. Eventually, I can see he's become lost in his own train of thought, so I go make coffee and a quick breakfast.

I bring him a cup and offer some scrambled eggs and sausage, which he declines. He's normally such a jovial guy—opinionated to be sure, but one who normally can crack a joke and move on from tension pretty quickly. He's good at picking up on something even when it is not exactly put down, always carrying on, making him a natural leader. So, seeing him lost to his own mood and thoughts is . . . new.

"Charlie . . . what exactly is the story there?"

That seems to get him back to earth. "It's complicated, and then again, not," he replies.

"Well, she's an adult now. I'm sure she understands that. Maybe part of her took this job in the hopes of finding out?" I offer.

"That's the thing," he says with a sigh, "I don't know if learning my side would make her want anything more to do with me anyway. Not after all this time."

THIRTEEN

Once inside the privacy of my cabin, I waste no time before taking a shower hot enough to match my temper. The shower might not be in its own spa-like room, but it's clear that the place has been done up with high end finishes. It took me a solid ten minutes to figure out the various side jets and the handheld option. Something turned on a radio, another thing turned on some lights. Long after I was done, I stood under the scalding water—hot enough to hurt a bit—until it *almost* succeeded in melting the thoughts away.

Look like my mother? If only. The man had to have been blind not to see how I much I look exactly like him. Me thinking I could ever play him for a fool and have him not recognize me—it would have been futile. To be so aloof, and then to not even attempt to remedy the situation.

I'd be lying if I said I didn't enjoy the confused, almost accusatory look on his face when he was drawing conclusions about me being at Henry's, though. As if Charlie Logan deserves any say in my life, let alone my sex life.

I get out and catch my reflection in the mirror, looking like the Heat Miser with my reddened skin and steam curling off of me. I'm starving again, so I'm determined to get into town to buy groceries as quickly as possible before I have to start the rigmarole of getting a new camera. I check the weather app on my phone, and in the process see multiple missed texts and calls from Ava, and one missed call from Gemma.

Ava is going to have to wait until I am open to hearing her reasons for keeping me out of the loop, because for the time being, I'm oscillating between angry, confused, and hurt. I already know that I'm not in the place for hearing her side. The one thing that is unforgivable (that she is well aware of) is making me be the last to know. While she didn't necessarily lie outright, she never once shared her true feelings—which clearly leaned more open to rekindling with the Logans, since she's already established some form of connection. Not communicating this to me, though, when I've laid myself bare to her, in the depths of my most vulnerable times . . . I'm at a loss as to why she felt she couldn't share.

I steer my thoughts back to the present, back to what I need to do to get this all over with as quickly as possible. I'd better get the camera resolution (again, along with my food situation) at least started before I call Gemma.

The weather is warmer than usual according to the app, so I throw on an easy sundress and my favorite denim jacket before I head out. I manage the basics with makeup, but lack the patience to dry my hair, so I leave the windows down in the truck to assist.

I'm relieved to see that both Henry and Charlie's trucks are missing from Henry's place, so I won't need to deal with getting Henry off of my case with replacing the camera.

Just as I'm losing myself to the music in the truck and the warm wind coming through the windows, I see that I'm approaching the big house, and that Grady, along with another boy who looks to be around his age, are standing in the middle of the road, waiting. I inwardly groan, outwardly pound my fist lightly on the steering wheel in frustration. Can't a girl just go get a greasy breakfast and some alone time? It's barely six thirty A.M. and I've already been swept up in this twister again. Pre-caffeine, too.

Grady ambles up to my window with a smile, and since I can't exactly speed off in a cloud of dust without it being glaringly obvious, I return it. I'm sure it looks more like a grimace.

"Good morning!" he says, and is immediately followed by Grace coming out onto the porch and yelling "Breakfast!" before turning around and heading back inside.

"So, how about getting one meal over with, so you can leave the rest of us with something to talk about, but not enough reason for us to keep getting in your way?" Grady says, arms folded on my open window. Wise beyond his years, I suppose.

I laugh through a sigh. "Why not?" I am hungry, after all, and need to regain my footing here. I slide out of the truck and offer my hand to Grady's friend. "Hi, I'm Tait."

Grady chimes in before he can respond, "Oh! Sorry. This is my boyfriend, Caleb." Caleb goes to speak again, but Grady says excitedly, "Come on, we've got waffles!"

I'm not shocked that he's gay, but I am happily surprised that he's been made to feel so comfortable in his own skin—to the point that his boyfriend joining his family for breakfast is no big deal. My heart warms up a degree or two to the family for that. It shouldn't be anything *but* that way, but I've found across the world that it too often still is.

"Hi, it's nice to meet you," Caleb manages, as Grady steps ahead of us. He's almost as tall as him, with the kind of cute face that's reserved for teenage boys and young men—the not-yet filled out look that's both angular and soft. I immediately mentally compare that to Henry's face, one that's nothing but masculine, hard angles and rough edges.

The smells wafting off the porch have me swaying on my feet, but I clamp down on my dignity, and make my steps slow and determined.

I'm hit with a massive wave of nostalgia the moment we step inside, though, and feel like swaying for a completely different reason. The entry is a massive (or so I remembered it, now it seems like a normal-sized) hallway that's filled top to bottom with photos. I avoid lingering and head toward the kitchen behind Grady and Caleb. Things have been updated, but the layout is generally the same. A big built-in dinette has been added off of what is now an open kitchen. The built-in bench part resembles a huge booth, with an oval table big enough for ten between it and the four chairs across from it on the other side. I notice now, so much more as an adult, how there's an abundance of light in each place here, how the windows and large doors are always featuring the outdoors.

Grace smiles warmly and hands me a plate.

"We do buffet style here, so why don't you start us off?"

"Thanks."

I grab a waffle the size of my face, topping it with a berry syrup concoction of some kind, some scrambled eggs, the most burnt bacon I spot out of the batch, help myself to some coffee, and head over to the table.

"Don't wait to dig in, the door will be revolving all morning so just go ahead and eat," Grady says.

Grace backhands his shoulder lightly. "You don't need to rush her, leave her be."

I go for something in-between and methodically cut my waffle so I can eat slowly. I want to get this meal, and any of the discomfort it promises, out of the way, so I want to be sure to get some chat in. "Thank you, this is delicious," I say, and mean it.

"You're welcome any morning," Grace replies with a nod. I smile at her, her expression pinching. It's not pity, nor is it sadness that I see in that expression. It's a tentative nervousness.

Caleb adds, "When the cast and crew gets back you'll probably want to get here earlier though, they clean house at group meals."

"I'll keep that in mind, thank you. I'll probably get to the store today and get some things for back at the cabin since I keep odd hours with . . . lighting and such anyway." Bullshit, but this has already been enough for today. The familiarity slices.

Grady, sporting a cat-with-a-canary grin, says, "Oh, Henry swung by on his way to the stables and told me he has to go to town with you for a new camera today. Hopefully that won't take too long for you."

"What happened to your camera?" Grace asks, brow folding.

I spot Grady chuckling out of the corner of my eye and realize that having a little brother would have indeed been as annoying as I'd suspected. I take a sip of my coffee before I launch into the explanation, but I'm saved as we hear the front door chime.

"Where is she?!" A loud, deep, and melodious voice chimes in. "Where's my granddaughter?!"

"I don't know, Mother, I doubt the girl is even here, the last thing she needs is you barreling in at her. She's petrified as it is." I recognize LeighAnn's voice.

"Bullshit, LeighAnn."

"Jesus, that woman knows how to make an entrance," Grady mutters.

Everyone's paused in their chewing, eyes wide and looking at me when Emmaline Logan and LeighAnn round the corner to the kitchen.

Grandma Logan is the same intimidating woman from my memories. I don't remember being scared of her exactly, just anxious of her lack of fear, and her lack of gentleness. She was always loud, always laughing, or yelling. She was always squeezing us. I remember sensing my mother's tension around her the most, though. She must be over eighty now, and looks exactly the same . . . olive skin, white hair cut in an elegant sort of pixie cut—think Princess Diana in the early nineties—always in blue jeans and boots, even now. She darts her hazel eyes, the same shade as mine, to me, and her hand flies up to rest against her mouth. Her eyes immediately fill with tears and she approaches the table, never once breaking eye contact.

"Well, stand your ass up so I can look at you," she booms, and I jump before I immediately comply. She's all of five-two, but is as straight-backed as I am, and she commands the entire room. Everyone sits up a little straighter, pauses in their eating. I haven't finished chewing the waffle in my mouth, so I hope she doesn't ask to inspect my teeth or anything. She drops her purse abruptly onto Grady's lap and takes my face in her hands.

"Well, look at you. You finally made it."

She seems so genuinely happy, and the gesture, her voice—that damn *familiarity* again. The sense of déjà vu, and the deceptive level of comfort all overwhelm and confuse me. Why now, why after this long? It makes me desperate to return the love, desperate to live in the warmth of knowing that there is a group of people that might drive me crazy at times, but because of some shared DNA, want to love me and have my back. I hate how much I want to return it. I've been to enough therapy to recognize this as something hollow in me, seeking them out to fill a void. I've worked hard enough to build my own life to know that I shouldn't need it, not if it's coming from a place of convenience or control—and what other reason could there be? I'm not some unknown illegitimate; they've always known I was out there. Why didn't they come sooner? I feel like I'd hardened myself into stone; solid, steady, strong. But, in the short time since arriving here, I've been continuously chipped away at from all sides.

I swallow the dry lump of waffle and manage to smile back, feeling my eyes well up in spite of my efforts. The anger is already less sharp, her proximity filing it down immediately, but the confusion and the sadness settle in deeper.

"How is it possible that you look exactly the same?" I manage.

"Oh honey, if you don't use it, you lose it. And I use *all* of it," she winks. Then gestures for Grady to move out of his seat. He rolls his eyes but obliges.

I take that as my cue to sit back down also.

"Well, let's get to it. Caleb, be a dear and go get me some fruit. Tait—" She levels me with that stare again. "Keep chewing honey, we aren't picky about manners here. I'm old and I have no time to beat around the bush."

"Momma, let her eat," LeighAnn pleads.

"Oh shove off, LeighAnn. Tait—I want you to know that your dad forbade us all from you girls. He managed to keep your information hidden from us for years. I love my son, but he's a damn idiot for not standing up to your mother. While

I used my own resources to keep tabs as best I could, I'm sure you can understand that, even as a grandmother, I needed to respect your mother's wishes."

At this, Grace stiffens and interrupts. "Emma, let Charlie." I cast her a grateful look.

"Absolutely not, Grace. I understand that there are parts of this that aren't mine to tell, but I am allowed to speak *my* piece here. Lord knows I've earned it." They exchange knowing glances.

"Tait, I want you to know that we've never stopped wanting to be in your lives. And the moment that you were old enough that it was no longer up to your mom, we did what we could to keep track of you while respecting the fact that you, as a grown woman, knew your mind and didn't want to be involved with us. I thought maybe when you were gifted your wedding present you might reach out, but again, that's water under the bridge—"

"Wait." She looks momentarily shocked to be interrupted, but I need to clarify something. "What are you talking about?"

"The money. The money we gifted you to go towards a house. It was $150,000, dear, I would hope you wouldn't forget."

I search her face for a moment—I received $150,000 shortly after I got married, but was told it was my inheritance from my grandparents—as in, my mother's parents. The only stipulation on it was that it was to go toward a house. We'd used that to buy property and build . . . the house that Cole and Alex currently live in. I suddenly can't be bothered with the rest of my meal, regardless of how good it is.

I stand up, feeling my palms start to sweat and my throat beginning to thicken . . . Mom wouldn't have—would she have lied like that? And why? What would the point have been?

Still standing, all of their eyes on me, skin prickling every place they touch, I say, "The only money I received was from my mom's parents. I was told it was inheritance."

"I don't know anything about that, but I know that *we* gave your mother money from your trust to gift to you as a wedding gift. Are you telling me you never received it?"

"I—I don't know. But, thank you? I think. I need to get going, though." I have a *trust*? Why am I here then? I don't dare ask.

It feels like I'm approaching the top of a rollercoaster, about to see over the edge just how deep the drop is. And I realize that I'm not ready. I start to rush out, but Emmaline grabs my arm. "I need to run errands today, too. Could you give an old woman a ride?"

LeighAnn sighs. "Mom, give her a breath."

"Jesus, LeighAnn, what has giving them space accomplished so far? I'm eighty-two years old, I refuse to die without getting to know her for a bit," she snaps, and gets up to go with me despite not getting a reply.

I throw a desperate look at Grady, hoping he feels like he owes me one, and thankfully he gets it again. Sibling eye language extends to half-brothers, apparently.

"I should . . . run out for a bit, too . . . can I tag along?" he asks.

Grace throws her hands up, but good-humoredly replies, "Alright, well, I guess Caleb and I will get all the chores done ourselves, then."

Caleb grins, clearly unbothered. LeighAnn smiles apologetically, and I take my leave, with my grandmother and half-brother in tow.

FOURTEEN

For some reason, the close quarters of a vehicle always seem to press on a situation, or mood. Which is probably why I love driving alone, most often with music as my only companion these days. Cole and I used to be able to sit silently for hours on a road trip. I was always in charge of the playlists or the stations. He'd occasionally reach across the center console and grab my hand, or squeeze my knee—knowing I hate it—just to draw out a laugh and an eye roll.

Grady and Emmaline Logan are *not* comfortable, companionable passengers.

Before we even get in, they argue over whether or not I should be the one to drive. Emmaline is adamant that Grady should drive, allowing her and I to talk without distraction. Grady is just as adamant that she should, since she's been around the longest *"since she is practically ancient"* and it would be second nature to her, anyway. She eventually agrees, but then Grady decides that is actually *not* the best choice *since she is so ancient* and would likely drive us off the road.

So . . . I am driving, hands at ten and two while being peppered with questions in between being given directions. They start out about my work, about where I live, how I like it, my hobbies, etc . . . then escalate dramatically.

"So, you're not married," Emmaline states more than asks. "When did you split?"

"I guess it's been about three years now. Two since it was official."

"What caused the split?" she asks, like it's a question as simple as *"what's your favorite hobby?"* or *"where did you go to school?"* Not *"what catastrophic event took place that caused you to examine your entire identity and your ability/willingness to ever trust someone again, let alone have hope for a future that includes love and partnership?"*

Blame it on the pressurized atmosphere in the vehicle, or the fact that I'm only able to answer with the bare truth since my mind is also focused on driving. Either way, the answer ends up flowing out of me because my feeble dam has officially sprung a leak . . .

"He fell in love with someone else . . . Well, more specifically, he fell in love with one of my best friends. They are both firefighters and work together. Cole had helped her get on with them—I'd actually pushed for it, ironically. I was traveling a lot to do freelance work. He was ready to start having kids. I wasn't. I had a whole checklist of things that I felt like I absolutely needed to do prior to having them. I guess I thought there would be less chance of me being unfulfilled if I checked off those things, and I'd have less chance of screwing them—the hypothetical kids—up . . .

"And, yeah, I was blindsided. We had what I thought was a really good marriage, despite me not exactly having any good examples for comparison. But, while I was shocked at the time, I look back and realize that I should've had my suspicions. I think I even know exactly when it started."

I can sense them both gauging their responses, approaching me like a wild animal whose trust they've just earned.

"When?" Grady quietly prompts.

"I think it was when I was just starting out in photography. I was doing freelance work, but blogging on the side and really hoping to build a platform based on that. Maybe become a travel blogger of some kind, or something. It was a bit aimless, so I took every job I could. I got an assignment working on a fire that Cole was also on. I surprised him at his hotel before I told him I even had this gig . . ." I clench my eyes shut, blinking away the memories that try to resurface.

"Anyway, it was for this article for a university that was studying how California wildfires had increased so much in the last couple years, the environmental impact, etc., and they wanted their photographs to be something more avant-garde to highlight the devastation. I got this one shot, though, and for some reason, I knew I wanted to keep it for myself.

"It was a shot of this canyon that was split, as in, exactly down the middle. One side completely decimated, the other still lush and green, wildflowers everywhere. I almost missed it at first, but in the corner of the photo, near the top of the canyon on the green side, was a mountain lion. She had her eyes closed and her face pressed toward the sun, sitting peacefully. My guess is that she'd had to outrun the fire, but still, she just couldn't be bothered in that moment to be skittish or scared about it anymore. It's like there was all this unbelievable devastation and her home was ruined, by no fault of her own, but she still knew she could find somewhere safe, green, and warm." I clear my throat.

"I was excited, and just really moved by that shot. I showed up at his hotel that morning and he was excited for me to stay there with him, to be there while he was getting his break at Basecamp. I thought it would feel like being at summer camp together or something . . .

"He'd seen some fucked up things on that fire . . . burnt animal bodies, countless burnt homes. And—and a few people who'd been trapped in their vehicles. One was a kid." I inhale shakily. "I guess he'd gotten separated from his family on a hike. They had barely escaped, but he had made a wrong turn . . .

"People don't realize how fast fires like that can move. Cole used to tell me the noise of them—the roar alone was one if the scariest parts. And he—this poor kid must've gotten into the car hoping it would protect him.

"And then there I was, completely oblivious. I came back and told Cole all about this stupid picture, about what I saw and how I felt about it—probably sounding so ridiculous. So selfish and unaware. I just had to get home, and get it edited and developed as quickly as possible. I remember him being supportive, but it seemed forced, you know? I was so caught up in my own bullshit that I think I just didn't think about his perspective.

"I remember Allie being there, being a wreck. She'd been the one to initially find the boy . . .

"So, I think that I took off, excited about this damn picture I took, and they leaned on each other instead."

They're both silent for a moment. I see Emmaline swipe across her face quickly, before saying, "Well, sweetheart, you don't discount what you do and make excuses for what he did. He could have asked you to stay. He made choices, too . . . When you're married or family, and you need someone, it's on you to communicate that. If you can't, what's the point? You should be able to tell someone when you want to lean on them, or if you just need them there. And before you start,

Grady, and try to tell me that sounds like codependency or some mumbo jumbo—it's not. I'm talking about expression, and honesty. If you didn't let yourself be happy or successful, Tait, because of him, well, *that* would be codependent, plus just a damn shame. Your picture could have inspired a whole other chain of events in someone's life for *good*. Maybe someone saw that and will now pursue a career in environmental studies or preservation, or even firefighting, who knows? A picture, a dream, a story—whatever it is that causes that initial inspiration, that tiny thing is the spark. It is absolutely paramount that you see that, and that you still be proud of pursuing your dreams . . .

    ". . . and also turn left here."

FIFTEEN

The entire downtown hears the truck before we see it. My view is especially front and center, though, from outside the feed store. The truck squeals and fishtails around the corner, then proceeds to creep to its destination; a poor attempt at being inconspicuous . . .

I'm somehow not the least bit surprised to see Tait in the driver's seat. Emma—Mrs. Logan—is in the passenger's, with Grady's face poking through the middle from the backseat. They all offer me a well-timed, singular wave in synchrony, and I can't help but laugh. I tip my hat and get back to loading hay.

I wonder what all transpired to group those three together this early in the day. No doubt Mrs. Logan had a hand in it . . . but I realize Tait is probably here to get her new camera. I'll have to track her down in a bit after I'm done here, before I need to meet Charlie and James up at Duane's to go over the season's schedule.

Duane is the eldest of the Charlie's siblings, and while he is my least favorite, he's been the one to spearhead the most profitable side of the Range, negotiating and managing the production and schedule for *Dollar Mountain*. Charlie is the one who really steered it into a guest ranch versus a working cattle ranch, and evolved the place to something everyone in this family can live with. But Duane has been the one to pimp it out to the big shots. He's had enough remnants of old cabins, areas filled with Native artifacts, and random trees declared historical or protected at this point to keep the land intact forever. This meeting tends to be more of a formality, since we know the overall production schedule, and since the next few months will give Charlie, James, and I an excuse to be gone for hunting season, anyway.

However, we still need to ensure none of our lines are crossed and that they'll remain in their assigned areas so we can still hunt and guide without clashing. Duane thinks that's all second fiddle at this point, but Charlie remains firm—he believes that the land and its history and culture are what draw people of *all* kinds to the place, and will long after *Dollar Mountain* ends. Since the guest ranch is occupied by the various staff associated with the show, we need to maintain the outfitting entity. The Logans (even Duane, in his own way) have a deep respect for their land and what it's always provided. It's just that Charlie and James feel that it's best appreciated in those real, visceral experiences—not via a television.

My mind wanders back to Tait and what *she* thinks of the whole evolution of the place. There's so many years of history . . . Does she think the show cheapens any of it? Does she even know the history and the incredible thing that they've managed to maintain in the first place?

I put away the hay hook when I see her jetting into the grocery store next door, deciding I'd better catch up with her now before I end up being too late. I stuff my gloves into my back pocket and head inside.

It takes me a bit to find her, but when I do she's holding her grocery basket with her jacket in it, staring at chips.

She doesn't give any outward sign that she's noticed my approach, but when I stop beside her, she continues her far-off stare and does a sad sing-song, "Hey, Henry."

"Hey, Tait. You doing alright here?"

"Oh, sure . . . just having my third existential crisis of the day."

I know she's referring to something else, but since she's opting for humor, albeit a little dark, I jump in.

"Yeah, I hear that. Do you go with the Ruffles, or the salt and vinegar Lay's? It's a loaded choice. My personal favorite are the cheddar and sour cream Ruffles, though. They might smell like feet, but artificial cheese is good for the soul."

Her little half-hearted laugh makes something inside me squeeze. She grabs the Ruffles and we move on. I feel stupidly proud of her going with my recommendation.

We both attempt to speak at the same time, "Did you" and "So, what's" coming out a garbled mix. So I gesture for her to go first.

"So, what's on your agenda today? What is it you *do* exactly?" she asks as she throws some popcorn in the basket.

"It's an evolving job, honestly. Aside from the guest ranch and outfitting season, the main jobs revolve around the equine side of things. When the show came in, they brought their horses and their trainers, and I got lumped in with them a lot of the time. Plus, we have our own, still. I guess I sort of represent the ranch's interests by making sure the animals' care is managed while they board with us, and before we have all their people staying on set with us twenty-four seven," I explain.

"I'd guess that that lends itself to having slightly less

people around that way—if they've got you overseeing it?" she asks, seeming genuinely interested.

"Exactly. That was the simplest way we could figure to have less 'cooks in the kitchen,' so to speak. First come the animals, then come the production crew, and lastly the actors, their trailers, their harems." At this she looks at me accusingly, and my stomach does one of those bastardy flips thinking about the little kernel of jealousy I read on her face. "Kidding, kidding. But, by the time the whole swarm descends it'll feel like a music festival in that valley. Thankfully, by that time, I'll get to be far away and on a mountain."

I look down at her basket to see that she's also put in some fruit, a box of cake mix, some fresh herbs, and a rotisserie chicken that is balancing precariously on the edge.

"Plus, there's never a shortage of labor that needs to get done. Fences need mending, fire lines need maintaining. The family tries to keep staff small so I usually do a lot of that. Well, Grady, Caleb, James and I do. Here, let me help you out." I laugh and take the basket from her arm and go retrieve a cart.

I'm not sure why it feels pervy to touch her jacket and neatly put in the top basket, but it does. *Probably because you have pervy thoughts about her, and touching her clothes reminds you of those thoughts, you pervy fucking pervert.*

"Thank you," she says when I return with it. She doesn't go to take it from me, though, so I don't feel like she's anxious for me to leave.

We walk around companionably as she continues to add a menagerie of things. I can't see a connection in much of them, but she seems to know what she wants. I can't help but snort as she appears to have an internal debate over green enchilada sauce versus red—given that I don't see a single other ingredient for enchiladas.

"What? I can feel you judging me," she says, eyes still on the sauces.

"Nothing, nothing. I just was thinking that your grocery shopping reminds me a little of your playlist organization."

She tosses her head back and belts out a laugh, and, just like every other time before it, I can't help but get drawn in. She laughs with her entire face. Her nose scrunches up and her eyes close, like laughing is the best feeling she's had every time she does it. She backhands my shoulder when it dies down.

"I am not saying that your assessment of my playlist making skills is at *all* accurate, but I *am* a terrible grocery shopper if I don't have a list, or specific things in mind. I will be surprised by half of this when I get home," she admits.

"I still take umbrage with the fact that you can transition from Cardi B to Tom Petty back to back," I press on.

"You *'take umbrage'*? Who are you? Who says that?" She laughs again. "You'd probably take *umbrage* with the fact that I eat breakfast for dinner more than not, too, huh?"

"Not at all. That's completely different," I say. "Music is like a filter over an atmosphere. Now, if you were listening to Slayer while eating a crepe, *that* I would take umbrage with."

"Well, I guess dinner's off the table for us then." She shrugs.

"Not to be rude, but I'm not sure I'm interested in the menu at your place." I laugh as I gesture to the cart contents.

She laughs back, but it morphs into a sigh as she looks over the items. "I'll probably come up with something brilliant, and realize thirty minutes in that I forgot the main ingredient. I rarely cook full meals since I got divorced. I *used* to enjoy it, actually."

"I know what you mean. Cooking for one isn't a huge thrill for me either." Her gaze flies to mine.

"Did you used to cook for . . . more than one, then?" she asks, and I hear the real question. My knee-jerk reaction is to change the subject, but before I do, I recall her sweaty, trembling hand as we pulled up to the house that first day, and her monologue on dating later that night, so I compromise . . .

"I have. I did. For a little while." But I can't bring myself to elaborate further. She saves me after a brief pause.

"People always think that when you get skinny after heartbreak, it's from depression. I think a lot of times it's just a matter of convenience," she says with a small snort. I level her with a look and a nod in agreement.

"At least, it could be. Could also be that you're just . . . already full. Of feelings, of questions." And then she adds immediately, "Sorry. I'm not sure why I said that. Cole—my ex—he had an affair . . ." She swipes her hands through the air like she's struggling for more clarification. "He left me for her."

I take a second to decide how to respond. The fury that rises in me at this admission isn't exactly proportional to the amount of time that I've known her, I realize, but it stirs something in me that I usually take care to avoid.

"When someone betrays you, you don't have a chance to lose feelings. You're left with all that leftover love, plus anger right alongside it, with nowhere for it to go and no one to give it to. It's like a phantom limb or something, I guess," I say, and stop the cart when she stops, regarding each other.

"Exactly," she says in a quiet voice, her eyes darting between mine. "I imagine, that, in a way—and I hope this doesn't sound super fucked up—but, I imagine in a way, it's like a death. At least that's how I chose to process it."

She's still looking at me with a mix of shock and admiration, and I feel my expression mirror hers as we just managed to put into words what I've felt for three years. It's amazing how putting words to something, reducing a big, impossible thing to language, makes it understandable.

"I agree. You can look back and try to hold on to the good bits that way, without getting bogged down with the anger. It's harder to be angry at someone who's dead to you," I reply, her expression tripping on a wince.

She turns and keeps walking. Without looking back over to me, she says, "I hate that I still can't honestly say that he's dead to me. Just the relationship, the shared life is. Even though I know that I'm over him, even though in hindsight I can appreciate that being with him led to good things in my life—in spite of the way it ended. I don't *think* I'm bitter, but I don't really *know* if I have closure, you know? How do you know?"

I inhale deeply, carefully weighing my response, searching for an epiphany to share with her as I'm absorbing it for myself. "I guess if you're holding back from anything because of them, you don't have it. I think we learn from experience, so of course you're going to make decisions differently based on your experiences with them. But I think if you are denying yourself anything, or *not* doing something because of them . . . I guess that means you don't have it." I shrug, because fuck if I actually know. I'm still floundering through it myself.

She peers at me sideways, and I'm snared again for a second. We look away and back at the same time and then suppress a laugh. We're both a mess. The silence easily transitions back into companionable, but now coupled with another level of understanding each other. We both have shit, and neither of us is dying to dig into it too deep.

Eventually, we turn down the same aisle for a third time

and she grabs a bag of shredded cheese. I can't hold back another chuckle, and she lets one out, too, and gives me a little hip check. I'm enjoying this version of her that's touching me, even if it's only because I'm teasing her. Childish, or not, I find that I want to find something else to poke fun at.

"I'm going to need to find some takeout places around here, aren't I?" she says.

"Just come by my place if you need anything, I'm sure I've got what you need. I can feed you."

"You think you know what I like? Maybe I need to take a look at your menu."

"I guess it depends on your tastes?"

She smirks triumphantly. "Guess it's not a big menu then, huh?"

She stops and faces me, folding her arms across her chest. A motion which, inevitably, leads my gaze there. I realize what I've said and how she's responded, and how slow I am on the uptake. I drag my focus back up to her face to see if I'm accurately gauging this situation, the fact that a bag of shredded cheese segued into this flirtation, or if I'm just reading into it. I feel my jaw flex at her little eyebrow tilt, and notice the way her mouth makes a little "o" when she sucks in a quick breath.

As much as I want to be a happy distraction (and the current tightness in my lower abdomen is indicating that I *really* want to be distracted back), this would be too messy, I can already tell.

Have I ever noticed the collarbone on a woman? Because all I can think about is running my tongue along it and slipping off those tiny, ridiculous straps on her dress, one at a time. I wonder if she is shy at first when she's naked, or if she gets more confident and bold as she sheds each layer . . .

Her arms fall to her sides and her chest rises in time with mine, her nipples pebbling beneath her dress.

Jesus, man, it's like you've never seen boobs before. Remember when you had the audacity to wonder if they were fake? As if you'd even know or care? Shit, I'm ogling again!

Wait, why the fuck am I here?

"CAMERA!" I practically shout, like the idiot I am.

She jumps, but immediately replies, "Yes, camera. I'm checking out now and am going to go look into it. I promise you, there is no reason for you to come though, I have insurance."

I nod, especially since I realize that I'm already late for the meeting I have seemingly forgotten about, and since her mentioning me *coming* on even that completely unrelated note shot heat straight to my dick.

"Alright, I'll catch you later, then."

BY THE TIME I GET back to my truck, I'm sweating and need to remove my hat and unbutton my shirt. It doesn't feel like it's singularly caused by the heat wave rolling in outside, either.

THIS IS GOING TO BE a long six weeks.

SIXTEEN

TAIT

Emmaline and Grady are already waiting by the truck when I head out with my groceries, violently fanning themselves. The heat feels similar to Tahoe during the peak of summer, probably only ninety or so, nothing *too* intense on paper. But it feels closer to the sun in the mountains, and therefore more powerful. I'm sweating more and stickier than I already was by the time I cross the parking lot.

"Whew, this is late in the year for a heat wave," Grady remarks.

"And hotter than a witch's tit, at that," Emma replies.

I give a noncommittal noise of agreement and proceed with unloading the groceries. I don't ask before making the executive decision to place them around everyone's feet in the cab rather than in the back where they'll be more at risk, when a thought occurs to me.

"Shit, I should have gone to look into a camera first." The groceries will be stuck in the truck for too long now, in this heat.

"Oh, don't worry honey, I called the local Fry's for you. A replacement will be here in two weeks," Emma says.

"Two weeks? What am I supposed to do for two weeks?" I groan. "Wait, how did you know what kind of camera I had?"

"I'm a nosy old lady . . . and asked Henry."

It sets my teeth on edge to have anyone be so cavalier about my privacy, but at least the process is underway. I'll submit the paperwork to Fletcher when I get back to the cabin.

"By the way, the saying is 'colder than a witch's tit', not hotter," I inform her, not without snark.

"Huh? Why would a tit be cold?"

"Not sure, probably because it's implicating being cold-hearted or something? And the heart is right beneath a tit?"

"I thought witches were associated with hell, thereby meaning that their tits would be hot. Are you sure that's not it?"

"I'm positive. I have the dual pack of *Grumpy Old Men* and *Grumpier Old Men* on DVD and have watched them a million times. That is the first and only other time I've heard the saying *colder than a witch's tit.*"

"*ANY* chance you guys could stop saying 'tit'?!" Grady chimes in.

I look over at Emma to find her wearing the same "oops" expression as me, and we shrug. I turn up the music a short while after, and we ride along in relaxed silence.

My mind drifts back to Henry, to his quiet, formidable presence. Sometimes, there's a melancholy in his expressions that doesn't add up. Maybe I just haven't been attracted to anyone in a long time? Most of the sexual encounters I've had in the last couple years have been born out of curiosity and boredom more than anything. I don't really know, but I find myself warming up to the cranky cowboy. It was— dare I say—*nice* to have him around at the store. And I now feel a kinship with him, how he understands my shade of heartbreak.

The jolts of lust that accompany being around him aside, it felt comfortable . . . until that last bit when it didn't. Each time I've been possessed to be a little flirty with him, he's shut down immediately or basically fled like today. Jesus, he practically peeled out the first day I barely touched him, and I wasn't even flirting that time.

Clearly, I need to get my attraction under control. My hormones and baser needs are continuing to betray me as far as he's concerned. I'm somewhat ashamed to admit to myself that if he showed returned interest, I would definitely be willing to explore that lust . . .

The same time that thought occurs to me, anxiety bubbles up and over because it's a terrible, terrible idea. He is more a part of the Logan family than I am. Whatever connection I'm reluctantly building over here with them would get tied up and jumbled up with him, too. I need to tread carefully and not muddy the waters.

I can have a *friend*. If it was just friends with benefits, sure. We are both adults and can keep that separated . . .

At least, I think. I've been able to before, that is . . .

Something tells me that it would prove a little more difficult with him, though.

"Oh my god, you do the *exact* same thing as Dad!" Grady suddenly exclaims.

"What? What are you talking about?" I reply, confused, adrenaline-spiked from being yanked out of my machinations.

"You wear your entire internal conversation on your face!" He laughs, and then mimics some of the expressions I must've been making unflatteringly, cocking his head side to side.

I feel twelve again, annoyed with Ava stealing my clothes, or with her honing in on my deepest insecurities (like only a sibling can). I reach back and smack him in the back of the head, just as Emma does the same thing from the other side.

"Alright. I'm just going to nap then if you two are going to be all in cahoots and shit." He pouts, but closes his eyes to do just that.

Sometime later, I feel Emmaline's eyes on me. I look over to her wistful expression.

"I have a nice Canon you're welcome to use until your camera comes in, Tait."

I feel myself chipped further, that offer so much more meaningful than I could make her understand. I don't want to feel trapped here, forced into this. Being able to do my work will be my saving grace. "Thank you, Em—um, Grandma."

I feel her reach out and hesitate for just a second before she gives my shoulder a squeeze.

THE REST OF THE RIDE home is quiet, apart from one of us girls occasionally humming along to the music, and Grady's soft snores.

SEVENTEEN

TAIT

When we finally pull up to the main house, I find myself easily agreeing to come over for breakfast again tomorrow. I don't recall actually buying anything in terms of breakfast foods, anyway . . . I internally shake my head at myself.

When I pull up to my cabin, I note another truck parked out front. Henry's truck isn't in front of his, so I can't help but wonder whose this is?

As soon as I park, though, I notice Charlie on the porch. He stands abruptly from the rocking chair and bolts down the stairs a bit clumsily.

"I went and grabbed these fans from my mom's place so that you're more comfortable during this heat wave we've got rolling in."

"Oh. Thank you. Won't the eighty-something-year-old woman probably need them more, though?" I say, letting a smile pull up my lips.

He laughs as he grabs a few of my grocery bags. "No, she shouldn't. Her deal with Satan means he keeps her core temperature regular." I raise an eyebrow at him but can't stop a small laugh. "*And,* we installed central heat and air in her place when it was renovated ten years or so ago. Figured we'd get a lot more years out of her if we did," he adds. "She threw a fit at the time. Said all these places needed was heat—never AC, and not even heat since she always heated her place with the wood stove. And she built her own fires, chopped her own wood, yada yada. She must not think we notice that she hasn't had a wood pile there since."

"Or that summers have gotten longer and hotter?"

"Something like that, yeah. But, summers aren't usually *this* hot even still, so the need for central air is rare. Global warming and all that." He looks at me apologetically.

"No worries, my place in Tahoe doesn't have AC. Actually, the majority of houses don't there, either."

"I trust that everything else here is nice and comfortable, though?" he asks.

"Yeah, absolutely. It's a nice place," I say, meaning it.

"Henry did a great job doing the right updates to the old place and building this to match. The plan was to do two more for other guest ranchers, but I think it works best like this."

"Henry built this?"

"Yep. We all helped a bit, but he's the one who was able to translate all the old plans to a new reality. Guy's a bit of a savant, actually."

Unsure why, some defensive feeling crawls into my chest. I hope they really do know how lucky they are to have good help like Henry. And I hope they don't take advantage of him. Building something on someone else's property with no chance for his own profit seems like too much of a stretch to me . . .

"Okay, well, I'll just bring these inside for you, then," he says.

I grab the last of the groceries and set them in the kitchen, only to find Charlie still shifting on his feet, a fan held at either side.

"Tait. I'm sorry I wasn't here to greet you right away, and for—earlier. I'm sorry for a lot of things."

I give it a second before responding, admittedly enjoying his nerves again. Not sure what that says about me, but I'm also not dissecting it much further.

"It's okay. This is all . . . a lot. And honestly, I'm not dying to hash it out quite yet either. As much as I realize that we'll probably have to get it over with."

He lets out a sigh and sets down the fans. "I don't want you to think that I'm upset that you're here, but I just have to ask, Tait. Why now?"

"What do you mean?"

"I just mean . . . Well, is there any specific reason that prompted you to come out here, *now*?"

Ah. There it is. The confirmation I've been waiting on; that this whole welcome act is not quite as genuine as they'd have me think. "You mean besides the job that hired me? I guess I don't understand what you're getting at Charlie."

He flinches at his name, but I'm not sure what else he expected. To be called Dad? I think the fuck not.

"Okay, okay. I just—I had to ask," he says lamely.

No he didn't.

"Who do I need to get in touch with to discuss the scope of work and locations I should stick to?"

He regards me for a second, but accepts my redirect. "Henry has the production schedule and can show you around until cast and crew start showing up."

I nod in thanks and head back in, not sparing him another glance.

* * *

A WHILE AFTER HE LEAVES and after I've nibbled on a few of the grocery items I was most excited (and surprised) to come across, I email Fletcher and his assistant and decide to go ahead and CC Gemma so that she is updated, too. Isabel quickly sends me the appropriate expense report forms along with the insurance forms to fill out. I fill them out immediately and knock them off of my to-do list.

Gemma replies directly, and almost immediately.

> *Taitum. I have some ideas for you to focus on. I think they'll be good jumping off points. I plan to be abstract enough, but I'd really like to know the family's history on the ranch to relate it to the story plot. I'd like photography of more of the place in action, rather than just the scenery. The people, specifically, in action, doing everyday things. I'm struggling through a block on character development and deciding "who" I may be missing . . . Help me find them?*
>
> *Thank you, dear girl,*
> *~G*

I put my head in my hands and feel the dread morph into something else that crawls beneath my skin, a monster trying to take hold. The idea of putting in extra effort to get to know anyone, when they never wanted to know me, fills me with helpless rage. I need to find the divider in my brain that categorizes this as work, the one that might help me separate my own personal emotions about this place and these people. This is what I do—it's what I've done for every single one of these types of assignments.

Capturing pictures of an ultra-modern mansion in the

middle of a forest—something so cold-looking and devoid of life, surrounded by nature. Or photographing an Italian grandmother handmaking her pasta with three generations of women alongside; hands lined up in succession of worn and gnarled, to young and smooth. Sending those photographs with a summary of the conversations that took place during that day in the kitchen. I find the juxtaposition between the laborious work, the time-worn utensils, and the bubbling life that a menial task brings out in everyone.

I just need to get enough material here, and do it quickly. Whatever it takes to get this done, to get me back home and to the life I've worked hard to make my own. Because the resolve I have here is slipping. And why open myself up to this, now? Why open myself up to wondering what life would have been, when it's clear that they never worried or wondered about me?

Before that train of thought gets away from me, I throw on my headphones and change into some workout shorts and set out to get a nice long jog in so I can mentally map out a plan. I start out running circles around the pond since I'm not interested in breaking an ankle on any of the other terrain.

On my third lap, Henry opens his door and Belle comes out and jogs alongside me. I eventually lose track of how many circles I run, the heat stifling.

I even forget that Henry is sitting on his porch, watching us. I definitely don't pick up speed whenever we are passing him, or try to remember my form, nor do I try to not appear winded and ready to quit . . . *I am definitely doing all of that. What is wrong with me?*

"Dinner!" he shouts, and Belle happily picks up speed and bounds for the house. I actually have worked myself into exhaustion, though, emotions replaced with the need to catch my breath. I slow to a walk.

"You too, if you're interested?" Henry calls down to me. I look down at myself, covered in sweat and dust.

"I'm gross, but thank you."

"You're not, and it's already after six, and whatever concoction you planned to throw together would probably take hours based off what you bought earlier. It's up to you, but I've got steaks and salad."

My mouth waters.

And since I need to go over my newly hatched plan of attack with him anyway . . .

I can justify it.

He sees me change directions to the stairs and throws me one of those smiles again. I'm sure I'm already red with exertion, but I feel the heat flood my face further. I'm—the warm-blooded female in me, that is—just a sucker for a good contradiction. And those stupid dimples on his otherwise rugged face are what make my body react. It's a reflex. Like seeing cute, cuddly Jim from the office as rugged, smokeshow Jack Ryan. Eclipsing these images together is . . . effective. He looks freshly showered, in jeans and barefoot, with a white T-shirt on that once again shows off the nicest arms on a man that I've ever seen . . . a vein snakes the expanse of his left one, and my fingers practically itch with the desire to glide down it, to push on it and slide, feeling how much the flesh might give beneath my touch.

I take another appraising look down at myself when he turns to head inside. I don't sweat cute, and the combination of the heat and the desire to run the anxiety out have resulted in a good mess. I do a quick, conspicuous nose swipe towards my shoulder and send up a prayer of thanks that I at least put on deodorant.

I take off my shoes and peel off the sweaty socks, leaving

them outside on the porch. His house is mercifully cooler, but all I see is one ceiling fan. He's got music playing from somewhere, the smells from the grill out back drifting in and making my mouth water even more.

"How is your place so much cooler?" I ask, which makes him wince apologetically.

"I installed an HVAC system in this one a few years back." Damn. Lucky.

"I'm going to go wash up real quick," I tell him, and he nods, grabbing two beers from the fridge and tipping one my way in offering.

"Sure," I say before I pad off to the bathroom.

The temptation to stay in the bathroom of dreams is immediately real, but I hear Grady's voice through the door.

"I rang Tait's doorbell a couple times to bring her some of Em's cookies. I forgot about the Diana Ross by the way—and I forgot how funny Gretchen thought she was—sorry, any-whoooo, Tait didn't answer but the truck's there."

I cover a flinch at the mention of my ex. "She's here," I tell him regarding Tait.

"Ooh, I see. Interrupting date night?"

"What? No."

"You know, you *can* date. Everyone knows that you go off the ranch and get laid once a month. Since we never meet any of these lucky gals I'm guessing they're one-offs."

I can practically feel Henry's glare through the door, even when it's not directed at me.

"Alright, alright. I'm just saying is all."

I choose that moment to head out and feign mild surprise at seeing Grady.

"Oh, Tait! Hey, you look . . . sweaty. Been exerting your-self?" Grady says with a wiggle of his eyebrows.

Henry sets down the knife that he's using to chop up vegetables with an exasperated sigh and throws Grady another look. I brush past it.

"Did I overhear something about cookies?"

"Ohhh yes. These are Em's BTS cookies—just wait until you try one."

"BTS? Like, the band?"

"Better Than Sex—but, color me impressed."

"Ahhh, that makes more sense. And sounds like her." I laugh before I grab one and take a bite.

"Holy shit," I say, still chewing.

"Right?!" Grady says, nodding like he knows the tastegasm happening in my mouth. "There's something to do with brown butter and chocolate and oats. Henry's the only other person in the family who she's taught the recipe to."

I turn around and frown at Henry, who shrugs at me innocently. For some reason he's never struck me as a dessert kind of man. And imagining him using those biceps for baking makes my brain short circuit.

I inhale the rest of the cookie, a moan escaping me when I bite into a second.

A crash sounds from behind me and I turn to see Henry picking up a tray and some BBQ tools.

"Steaks should be ready. Don't spoil your appetite," he grumbles, annoyed, and then stalks out to the patio.

Grady throws me a conspiratorial look. "What is with you guys?"

"Nothing at all. The guy barely started being cordial to me."

"Lies. You look at his face how I look at these cookies."

"He's like seven feet tall. I'm not even convinced that I've seen his face."

"Uh-huh. Anyway. We typically convene down here on

Wednesday nights for dinner and game night. You should join us while you're here!"

"Who's we?" I ask warily.

"Me, Emma, Lucy when she's in town, Caleb when he's not working. Sometimes Auntie LeighAnn. Wednesdays were always my mom and dad's date night growing up."

I nod and smile, grabbing my beer from the counter. It's, again, an unidentifiable feeling imagining a family unit—one that I might've belonged to once—with traditions and game nights and marriages with date nights . . . noise and laughter and annoyance. Love and companionship . . . I shake it off quickly.

"What games?" I ask.

"Anything, really. We usually stick to cards. When it's nice out we'll do yard games. Tonight I've brought Yahtzee."

Henry walks in with the steaks and lets out a groan.

"If you're trying to get her to come back I would save Yahtzee for another time," he says, setting down the food and grabbing another cookie. He manages to toss the whole thing back and there's something explicit about it. My stomach dips.

"Yahtzee? Really?" The game that takes no skill whatsoever.

THE GAME THAT TAKES NO skill whatsoever is apparently the one that brings out the worst in everyone because Grady has won every round, and it's clear that Henry and I both are hating it. Dinner was delicious—the cookies are all gone but one. The combination of full bellies, sugar highs, and mild buzzes have us all turning the volume and competition up.

"Where's Mrs. Logan?" Henry asks Grady.

Grady looks down at his phone. "Huh. I guess she isn't feeling great." He continues to frown after he puts his phone away. "Okay! How about 'Impossible Questions' since Grandma can't join us?" He then pivots, rubbing his palms together menacingly.

Henry grunts. "Grady, aren't we too old for that game?"

"You know that we're absolutely not. Okay, Tait, you up for a drinking game?"

"Ummm, sure? Anything beats Yahtzee," I say with a shrug. Fucking Yahtzee, stupid, useless, mindless game.

Grady claps once before he gets up and goes to fetch something from the buffet, vibrating with excitement. Henry looks at me in a way that can only be described as "you asked for it" before Grady launches into his intro.

"The game is only fun if *you* are fun. It's very similar to 'Do or Drink,' but with our own spin on it. The object is to ask an impossible question in one of three categories: 'this or that,' 'yes or no,' and 'vote.' You'll draw a card and depending on the category, pick a person and a question that fits in that category. You have to come up with the impossible questions for 'this or that' and for 'yes or no,' but the 'vote' cards have pre-written dares on them. Example round." He picks a card. "I'll pretend this is a 'this or that' card. Henry, Belle or Murphy? You have five seconds." He mock whispers over to me, "Murphy is his horse."

"That's not even—how am I supposed to pick?" Henry complains.

"Five seconds!!!" Grady shouts.

"They serve completely different purposes—"

"DRINK!!" Grady roars.

Henry throws me a wink, one I am very unprepared

for—my hand actually clutches my chest before I cover it with a feigned scratch. Then he takes a long drag from his cocktail glass, licking his lower lip to catch an errant drop.

"See? Fun, right?!" Grady laughs at my expression, oblivious, but proceeds to line up fresh beers, and fills up three shot glasses with tequila . . . Good Lord.

"Also, terrifying," I add. But the competitor in me doesn't want to turn down the challenge. " 'Yes or no' seems straightforward, but what's 'vote'?"

"If you draw a vote card," Henry says, "you need to read it out loud, and immediately after say 'shot' or 'vote.' So, either take a shot yourself, or risk voting for someone at the table to do whatever is written on the card. If you—the person who drew the card—end up losing the vote, by everyone voting *for* you, you have to finish everyone's drink at the table, *and* do the dare. If someone gets voted for and does the dare, everyone else drinks. Keep in mind that Grady wrote these when he was a teenager."

"When I was in love with you, apparently didn't care about our extremely distant shared lineage, and tried to invent ways to make you kiss me and change your entire sexuality. See?" He hands me the cards he retrieved from a cupboard in Henry's bar area. "I made copies and laminated them for all the regulars."

"As we've gotten older and wiser, we usually just take the shot," Henry offers, trying to comfort me as I look over the cards.

" 'Kiss the person to your left,' 'streak around the house three times,' 'send a dick pic to someone at the table'?! You play this with your family members?!" I laugh, horrified.

"We have varying versions, okay?" Grady explains. "Note

that the kiss doesn't say where or with tongue or anything, and most are up for interpretation if you're smart." He taps his temple. "I once sent Grandma a picture of Dick Cheney when I pulled *that* card. This version at Henry's place is admittedly the nastier, less family-friendly one because he never plays. The one we keep in the bunkhouse is by far the worst, though." He beams with pride.

I look across the table at Henry again who gives me a challenging, single brow lift. So much communication from that face, with so few words.

"Let's play," I say.

"I'll go first," he replies, without breaking eye contact.

He draws and seems to exhale when he reads the card. "This or that. Tait. California or Idaho?"

It's not as easy as I make it sound, but I quickly respond. "California, duh."

"BOOOOOO!!!!" they both shout at me simultaneously. "DRINK!" Again, in unison.

"What?! I answered in less than five seconds!" I slam my fist down on the table before I can rein myself in, indignant.

"Oh, did we forget that part? If we don't like your question *or* your answer, you have to drink. So, don't hold back." Henry tosses his head back and laughs, his hand in the middle of his ribs, delighted at my display.

UH-OH.

EIGHTEEN

TAIT

It's obvious within twenty minutes that the parameters for this game are constantly evolving and are not meant to be confined, or therefore limited by, being inebriated. Apparently, the game is also dependent on how seriously the players take the questions. Henry pulled a 'yes or no' and asked Grady "Harrison Ford, yes or no?" Which put Grady into a panic. "That depends, are we talking Indiana Jones, Han Solo, or old Harrison like the one where the one-armed man kills his wife?"

"YES OR NO?!" we both shouted at him until he drank. Then he stated, "Who am I kidding? Yes to all."

I attempted to challenge when Henry asked me if I'd rather have no arms or no legs, because, really? But my challenge was squashed. We've only come across two 'vote' cards so far, the first of which Grady decided to put to a vote, a gamble that ultimately paid off for *me* when they both pointed at me. I had to sing the opening line to "I Will Always Love You" by Whitney Houston at the top of my lungs. It wasn't news to me that I am a horrible singer. They both drank.

Henry pulled the second vote card, and we earned one vote each. Grady declared that this meant we all had to do the dare.

"'Share your most embarrassing story,'" Henry reads, but his jaw immediately tightens, all traces of humor lost.

"Ehhh, maybe we don't all have to do that one, actually," Grady says.

"What?! Uh, yeah, we most certainly do," I argue. But then I take in the truly miserable look on Henry's face and decide to try and recover. "Since it's split three ways, it's diluted. Just share a top three level embarrassing tale. I'll go first."

Henry's glance meets mine, the corners of his mouth not tipping up, exactly, but relaxing. There's heat in that gaze, unabashed. I lick my lips, suddenly in need of a drink despite the constant sipping I've been doing.

"So?" Grady prompts.

"What?"

"*So*, Tait, you said you'd go first. Top three embarrassing story?"

Oh, shit. "Oh! Okay. Ummm. Well . . ." I sift through an admittedly lengthy mental catalogue before I decide. "Well, this one involves my sister, but she's not here anyway, so screw it. When she found out she was pregnant, she had an ultrasound early on in her pregnancy that I went to with her, since her husband had to work. In the early weeks they do transvaginal ultrasounds, which means that there's a wand that has to go up your hoo-ha, not the kind that just roll around the outside of the belly.

"Nothing medical embarrasses me, or grosses me out, really. It's why I originally went to school for nursing. I can deal with that sort of thing. Ava, on the other hand, cannot.

She is horrified to be naked in front of a medical professional in any capacity, even as an adult. So, I am sure you can imagine her excitement, then, when her sonographer walks in, and it's her ex-boyfriend." Henry and Grady start to laugh, and damn, I love how Henry splays his hands like that, this time interlocking his fingers across his abs as if the laugh is trying to burst from him, as if he wants to hold it and keep it close.

"So, they catch up. Ava is sitting there with her bits out, a paper sheet between them. This guy was still so completely hung up on her, even with another man's child inside of her. He just kept chatting away, completely oblivious to her discomfort. I was dying in the corner, trying to keep in tears as her face just got more and more frustrated. And then she snapped, and she screamed at him. 'Are you going to stick that thing up me or what, Anthony?!'" I die laughing all over again, remembering, and fight to get the rest of the words out. "He just looked at her with the wand held out, already lubed, and said, 'Actually, you insert the wand yourself. I thought you knew that and just needed to stall, or to be distracted.' Her face was *stricken*. Death by mortification. So, I couldn't resist, and needed to put this idiot back in his place on her behalf. I piped up and said, 'Oh, *Anthony*, that's right. You just like to watch, huh?' Ava picked up on it immediately, stuck the wand up her crotch and said, 'Different Anthony.' When I tell you that this man's face was so miffed. Ah! It was glorious, you guys."

Grady swipes at the tears of laughter leaking from his eyes. "Okay, that one isn't actually embarrassing, it only makes me love you more, but it's better than either of ours so, next."

I avert my eyes away from that comment, because how is

it possible that I already love him, too? Is there really some scientific, DNA-related thing that inexplicably binds us? No, I know that's not the case, more than most.

I draw a card. Another 'This or that.'

"Oooh. Can I do more than two items?" I ask Grady since he, obviously, acts as the judge and jury here.

"Sure." He burps.

"'Kay—Henry. Breakfast, lunch, or dinner?"

"Can't answer that one." He laughs and drinks.

"Seriously? That's not even a hard one!"

Grady hiccups and then laughs. "I know whyyyy." I feel myself roll my eyes. Do we really need to take these questions *this* seriously?

"You forgot the best meal! Dessert," Henry explains as he takes a sip of his drink.

"That's not a *real* meal." It comes out higher and whinier than I intended. I'm drunk.

"Dessert is absolutely the most important meal. I don't go a day without it."

"You're a liar. You don't look like that and eat dessert every day."

"Look like what?" He smirks and folds his biceps on the table.

I roll my eyes again at his feigned ignorance. "You know what."

"I think you need to expand on that for me. *Deliverance* here doesn't pick up on innuendos."

"I think your ego is expanded enough and doesn't need any stroking from me. How about *that* innuendo?"

"I think you both need a room," Grady says, head tipped back, eyes closing slowly. He hasn't developed a tolerance like the big kids, apparently. "Go again, Tait," slurs out of him.

"But I drank!" Henry says, and now who's the whiner?

I stick my tongue out at him and draw a card. My stomach drops. 'Vote' is scribbled in big red letters. I read the card. "Skinny dip in the pond." I look up as Grady's head snaps back to attention. "VOTE!" I yell, "Three, two, one." Grady and I both point at Henry, sitting wide-eyed, no vote cast.

"No," he says flatly.

"Then drink, bitch!" Grady replies. "Sorry, I'm just kidding, love you."

I look down at all three of our fresh cocktails with a wince. There's been a lot of consumption in a short amount of time.

"Maybe we've all had enough," I say, suddenly full of reservations. Henry's expression narrows at me.

"Oh no you don't," he replies. "Don't you try to back out of it now."

"Then *you* better decide, big guy. Drink or strip," Grady says.

"Or, we could just stop playing the game. We *are* adults," I say and shrug, shoulders jumping, suddenly feeling quite sober.

Henry studies me then, and I feel my face scowl under the scrutiny. He comes to some internal conclusion before saying, "We don't quit or chicken out on anything, here. If we did, what would be the point in ever playing anything?"

I start to say, "I don't think that drinking games are the arena in which we learn life lessons," but then he stands up and takes off his shirt, and my mouth goes dry. I dart my eyes to the table before I can get caught studying the details.

"Let's go darlin', I need a witness." He turns to march out the doors to the deck.

Grady tips his head back, and closes his eyes.

"What are you doing?! You better go out there with me!" I hiss at him.

"Ew, no. He's distantly related to me, remember?" He closes his eyes again.

"Grady. Come on."

No response.

"What if I'm uncomfortable going out in the dark alone with a naked giant lurking in the water?"

He cracks open one eye and somehow manages to roll it. "Something tells me that's not the case, but if so, don't go. He'll come back inside and that'll be the end of the game. No skin off anyone's back either way." Then, "Heh, not sure how that's a pun in this moment, but it must be, somehow."

"Shit."

"Sorry Sis, this is your moment, your call. I really am down for the count, anyway."

And with that, his eyes fully close and his mouth falls open in a small snore.

I act quickly, and go snatch a towel—two, actually, because I guess drunk me has lady balls. I catch my reflection in the mirror. The remnants of the mascara I hadn't already sweated off earlier are smudged beneath my eyes, I'm flushed, my ponytail has migrated, and the look in my eyes is a bit wild, but alive. I take a big breath before I head back out and proceed onto the deck.

I call out, "Henry, Grady's asleep, you don't have to—" but the rest of the sentence dies as I turn just in time to catch a pair of strong ass cheeks dive into the pond.

The rest of the big body disappears underwater along with those cheeks, the only light coming from the patio, illuminating the dock and a small area around it, the rest of the pond encased in darkness. I continue to stand awkwardly holding the towels for what feels like hours before he resurfaces, rests his head on folded arms at the end of the dock, and looks up at me curiously.

It's muggy outside, the air *just* this side of stifling.

"Hi," I say. He smiles a half smile.

"Hi back."

I stand there for five seconds, painfully awkward, until it's clear that my lady balls have vanished—castrated by my own neuroses. I go set down the towels by his elbow.

"Why two towels?" he asks, almost too quietly for me to hear.

It's usually easy enough to be attracted to someone and to act on it. I am not one to deny myself when I want something simple anymore. I did the whole lead-up, the slow burn with the happily ever after. I did all the steps before, and where did that land me?

Now, when I want to do something, to be with someone, I do it.

I have to admit to myself that those encounters have typically left me wanting, while not actually wanting anything more from *them*. I suppose that I'm a ball of nerves over just how intense my physical attraction is to Henry without knowing much about him. And, despite living far enough away from one another, there's too much common ground that we share. Ground that feels more foreign to me than it does to him. Old insecurities creep in, making me wonder— no, making me, again, *suspect*—that this attraction is more one-sided. Reminding myself of him flinching under my hand, and running away at my silly pick-up line, I deduce that it must be. That isn't something I'm up for. I sigh, realizing that he's still looking at me expectantly.

"You're a large man, I thought you might need two."

He laughs through his nose, then looks down at his knuckles. "I guess I won, huh?" He doesn't say it victoriously.

"How do you figure? I think I ended up with the most cards collected," I say as I take a seat next to his arms and dangle my feet in the water. A sigh escapes me. The pond is on the cool side of tepid—perfect.

Henry tilts his head on his folded arms to look up at me. "I'm sure Grady knows of a bylaw that states how many cards one of these dares is worth."

We both laugh, because he's probably right.

"God, I really can't remember it ever being this hot here," I muse, wiping my forehead with the back of my hand.

"It never is. How old were you when you . . . moved?" he asks. It's a jab in the stomach, the reminder that Charlie really never even spoke about us, but it's not surprising to me.

"I was seven."

"I'm sorry about your mom. I remember the family talking about it when she passed away . . . ," he says, and my heels dig in to that bitter place.

"I find it shocking that they even gave my mom a second thought."

He frowns sternly at that. "Why?"

Exasperated with this line of questioning already, I snap, "Because they didn't care all that much when she moved multiple states away in the first place. About her, or us, Henry. I understand that you might see a different group of people than what I knew, but that's just the truth. I'm sorry to tarnish their reputations for you." I go to get up, but he wraps a big hand around my ankle and stops me.

"Hey, I'm sorry. I don't know what all took place or anything. I shouldn't have gone there." He sounds completely sincere, but flinches slightly before continuing. "But, are you sure *you* know everything, Tait? I know it's easy as kids to see things a certain way, and to just accept that as reality."

"The reality is that my father barely put forth a modicum of effort to have a relationship with my sister and I, Henry. I know you mean well, but that's just a fact."

His palm is still wrapped around my ankle, and he traces a circle with his thumb, considering his words carefully before continuing.

"You're right. And even though that makes no sense to me, and isn't the Charlie I know, I just know what it feels like when you don't get another chance to have things be better— to at least have the *chance* to mend things."

I consider him, again, and am struck with wanting to know *his* story. I'm failing to reconcile this man, who looks like Avenger-lumberjack, but says things like "nefarious," and "takes umbrage" with me, and who can read this situation pretty clearly even as an outsider.

He barks out that husky laugh again, and I realize I've said this last part out loud, slightly less than on purpose (though who are we kidding, I feel like I'm getting the equivalent of a gold star each time I manage to make him laugh).

"I'll have you know that I read. Real books and everything. And I have a degree in environmental sciences. Even know a few big words and how to spell them, too."

"Nerd," I deadpan.

At that his hand shoots up to the back of my knee, and with one arm he shot puts me into the water.

I come up laughing, relief flooding my senses at being cooled off finally. I can't even feign irritation, splashing water in his general direction once before floating onto my back and closing my eyes.

I hear him swim closer, and feel him watching me,

somehow. Gripped by the need to fill the silence, I say, "Thanks for that, saved me from having to take a shower."

"Oh, so you don't mind the leeches, then?" he says, which results in me practically levitating out of the water and losing all semblance of calm.

"WHAT?!" I panic dog-paddle back to the dock in great, big splashes, and latch onto the ladder when his hands go on my hips, digging in pleasantly.

"I'm kidding, I'm kidding. I'm sorry." I turn slowly and level him with a glare. He's laughing silently, eyes watering. Bastard.

"I'll have you know, I don't do bugs. I am not prissy, typically." I feel my cheeks heat.

He struggles to regain composure, and I struggle not to look down. The water is too dark to catch a peek at anything, anyway.

"I'm sorry, I owe you for that one," he says, and then takes his hands away with another, quieter, "Sorry."

"A bath."

"Huh?"

"You owe me a bath. I want to use the tub and shower of dreams."

"Right now?" He looks almost afraid, which *almost* endears me to him again.

"No, that's okay. I'll call it in at some point, though." I reach out a hand while my other grips the ladder. I know I'm setting myself up again, but can't seem to stop. He shakes it, nods, and predictably pulls me back into the water. As soon as he does, he swims a few feet away, giving me distance, it seems.

"So, environmental sciences, huh?" I say, needing to fill the silence once more.

"Yep. I stretched the truth, though. Never finished my degree. I was a few months shy."

We circle each other now, moving around like magnets, an opposing force between us.

"What stopped you?" I ask, though I can tell he was hoping I wouldn't, which disappoints me more than it should. He stills, regarding me with gold, hooded eyes again, visibly struggling with his next words. He tucks his bottom lip in and runs his tongue back and forth over it a few times before deciding. "Family drama."

I laugh through my nose, humorless. What a perfectly vague response. I swim toward him and his eyes widen a fraction. I clench my jaw, knowing I'm probably hurting myself more than him in doing it, but still I let my chest graze his as I reach past him to grab onto the side of the ladder. I'm not prepared for the jolt of sensation that zaps through me at the contact, though. The workout top does little to shield the feeling of my nipples sliding over his warm chest. I manage to bite back a moan. Up close I can see his lashes, stuck together with water droplets. His lips are parted and glistening, softness surrounded by scruff. His mouth closes and a muscle ticks in his jaw, and I realize I'm staring.

I try to pull myself past his shoulder quickly, awkwardly careful to avoid further contact. But when I get my first foot on the rung of the ladder, his right hand closes over my left one, his other hand gripping my hip and flipping me around so I'm abruptly sitting on the top rung, him floating between my legs. We breathe like we raced here, his eyes wide and intense on mine for only a moment before they go to my mouth and he leans in.

"Tait," he whispers.

"Yes?" I say, and the breathy tone makes my cheeks heat again.

"Can I—shit." He shakes his head a little, but I'm already nodding mine. "I'm going to kiss you now," he says, his voice a low rumble. And then he does.

It's painfully sweet, him lightly tasting my bottom lip first, before moving to my top lip. I'm gripping the ladder to keep my hands from running through his hair and pulling him to me. He moves away slightly before he uses the ladder and my hip to pull himself closer through the water, up. His eyes slide up to mine before he kisses me again, this time without a hint of hesitation. I open for him, tongues gliding over each other greedily. He tastes like cookies and tequila and so, so good.

I nibble on his lower lip, and his gruff hum of approval makes me thrust my chest out to his, wanting to get closer, to melt and to fuse against him, but refusing to grab at him with my hands, keeping them wrapped firmly on the rungs of the ladder. He's too big to get any closer this way, the sides of the ladder restricting how far I can part my legs to make room for him. But when he trails kisses down my jaw and neck, I lose a little of that control and scoot my butt off of the rung, legs floating further apart of their own accord. When he runs his tongue along my collarbone, I sigh, letting my heels hook behind his bare thighs to pull him closer to me. I'm quickly dissolving into a mindless, needy thing. The boneless feeling of floating heightens every other sensation. I feel the rough hairs on the outsides of his thighs grazing the insides of mine, his thumb hooked around the front of my hip, his hand so large that I feel his other fingers pushing into my lower back. He's moved over to the other side of my collarbone, beard scraping cruelly over the area he'd just soothed.

It's too much, and not enough all at once. I give up, peeling one hand off the ladder to wrap around the back of his neck and into his hair. The motion throws off my balance and I react by trying to right myself using my legs, the action bringing his very, very naked hips to mine. His choked sound is drowned out by mine, the hardness of him giving me friction right where I need it most. He pulls back and looks at me, a combination of heat and shock in his eyes. I'm panting, heavy-lidded and too wound up to care or consider being embarrassed as I grind against him, our gazes still locked. A smile reaches my lips and I close my eyes, not wanting to see his intense stare, not wanting to come to my senses. I can't remember the last time I dry humped someone. Is it still dry humping if you're in water? I bite my lip to stifle a laugh and let my head fall back.

"Sexiest smile I've ever seen," he says, and when I open my eyes I want to return the compliment.

His lips are swollen from kissing, his dimples maddening. But, he appears completely in control even as he stares. I want to make him as desperate as I feel, dipping momentarily into self-consciousness again. Before I can fully descend, though, he lays his palm across my chest, thumb brushing the hollow of my throat reverently while he slips a large fingertip under the strap of my tank top, slowly pushing it down, down, down my arm.

Before I can second guess myself, I wrap one hand around the wrist on my chest, and grab his shoulder with my other. I think he must do some of the work for me, since he's a behemoth and I likely couldn't flip him around using my own strength alone, but I somehow manage to smoothly turn us and push him into the ladder. I float a few feet away and hook my thumbs under the straps of my top, sliding them off without hesitation. He gives up our eye contact to look his fill, color blooming on his cheeks and his jaw clenching with restraint. He licks his lips and reaches around in the water until he finds the back of one of my knees, then the other. He keeps my body suspended half out of the water as he drags me back to him, my arms floating slightly behind me, and I laugh thinking of those mermaids plastered to the fronts of ships.

He smiles back, but as soon as I'm within reach, he bends his head to pull my nipple into his mouth, and a moan-gasp flutters out of me. It's not a slow or gentle lick; he sucks me and then keeps my peak wedged in an almost-bite, while he flicks his tongue back and forth. My hips grind shamelessly against him again, and I hazard reaching down between us to grasp him. "Of course," I let slip out as I slide my hand up and down. Of course, he's perfect . . . ly huge, and I shouldn't be surprised by his size, but I am. He lets out a small chuckle that's nothing short of knowing, male pride, then hisses around my nipple when I squeeze him. He lets me out of his mouth, planting a chaste kiss there before moving to my other. He flexes in my hand and I feel that familiar tugging, throbbing sensation start to build in me. Jesus. I haven't been given an orgasm by anyone other than myself since Cole, and even then I normally take a lot more work and time. I'm so keyed up I can practically hear the buzz of my blood rushing.

And then I really do hear buzzing, plus the crunch of tires on gravel.

Henry releases my other nipple with a small pop, and

looks up. One side of his hair is gorgeously mussed where I've been gripping. The look on his face is pure panic, though.

"Fuck, I'm so, so sorry," he says, right before I see the beam from headlights shine on the dock and the side of his face, and right before he promptly launches me out into the pond.

NINETEEN

HENRY

The horror and acute shame I feel at having literally thrown a half-naked Tait away from me makes everything in me (and on me) instantly deflate. Thankfully, the pond beyond the light is pitch black, so although there are ripples, I doubt I'll raise much suspicion when I exit and wrap the towel around me.

Charlie and Grace come around the corner as I'm walking up the dock, and I send up a prayer of thanks that I didn't chance it after all.

"Hey guys," I say, voice coming out a pitch higher than normal.

Grace quirks a brow at me. "Taking a dip?"

"Yeah, heatwave, you know." I do a weird hand shrug and try to herd them to the house. "Can I get you a drink?"

"No, thanks. We figured Grady couldn't drive and we'd grab him and take him off your hands," Charlie says.

"I'll go drag him to the truck. Night, Hen," Grace adds.

Charlie studies me for a second longer than is comfortable.

"Did you see Tait tonight?" he asks.

"Uhhh, yeah, she came by and had dinner with Grady, and I. Grady and me—and I."

"Don't hurt yourself there." He chuckles. "Did she bring you up to speed?"

Oh, fuck me. Why does that sound dirty? Shit. Shit. Shit. "On what exactly?"

"I told her you'd show her around and go through the production schedule with her."

"Oh, okay. Yeah, of course I will. Are you sure she's ok with that?"

He frowns at me. "She didn't take an issue with it when I told her earlier. Why wouldn't she be? You guys seemed . . . friendly?"

"Yes—yeah, totally. We're good. Is Duane going to shit when I can't be around for all the pre-production setup, though?" I'm not sure why I'm trying to find reasons not to, but it's clear that Charlie wants her to be looked out for, and all the plans I had for her a minute ago were not exactly what I would call *nice,* making me feel like an utter piece of shit at the moment.

Oh, God . . . I *threw* her across the pond.

"He'll be fine. He doesn't even know she's here yet. How is she?"

Probably spitting mad and ready to gut me. "She seemed good."

"Good. Good. Okay. Thanks."

I start walking to the house when he steps around me toward the end of the dock.

"Charlie, uh—"

"You forgot your other towel." He bends down and picks it up. Then he looks over at me, then out over the pond with a frown. He remains there for a second, contemplating. But if he has any suspicions, he lets them lie, walking back and handing me the towel with a look I can't decipher.

"Goodnight, Henry."

"'Night."

"Henry?"

"Yeah?"

"Don't let this heatwave get to your head . . . .People always seem to get stir crazy when they're overheated."

I nod, feeling my face tighten.

Oh God . . . I fucking *threw* her across the pond.

As soon as the truck is out of sight I slip my feet into boots and rush over to Tait's cabin. The light is on now at her place, so I know she must have snuck back. I almost burst through the door, but figure it'd be prudent to knock first.

"Tait?" I call when she doesn't come. Finally, I hear footsteps, and the door swings open. She leans against the doorway casually, if not a little awkwardly, blocking me from coming in, and says, "What's up?"

"Uhhh—I'm sorry about . . . back there. I just didn't want them to see you. I didn't think *you'd* want them to see you."

"Probably for the best." She looks right at me with a shrug. Ah. I see. That's how we're going to play this. I suddenly feel stupid standing here in my towel, flustered and panicked while she is so unaffected. I let myself take her in again—she's changed into a Willie Nelson T-shirt that reaches mid-thigh, each of which has a cute freckle in almost exactly the same spot, I'm now noticing. She's taken down her wet ponytail and washed her face, which now wears a look of icy indifference instead of the undone one I was losing myself to just minutes ago.

"Did you need anything?" she asks, pulling me out of my reverie, away from the freckles I'd veered off to again.

Did I read things this wrong? I must have. But no way did I read her sounds, her returning kiss, or the way she grabbed me wrong . . .

"Are you going to just stand there and brood or do you have something you feel you need to say?" she says, shrill now.

"I am picking my words carefully. It takes me a minute sometimes, okay?" I say, and it's the truth, but I repeat my apology. "I am sorry. I didn't think before I did it, I just registered that you were half naked and probably needed to hide."

At this, I see a blush creep up her neck and her hand ball up in a fist. It's an odd combination of adorable and terrifying.

"My tank top was around my waist. Wouldn't have been hard to pull up really quickly and it's a pond, people swim in it when it's hot. It was *you* who didn't want to be seen, Henry," she says, and holds up a hand when I start to inter-ject, to remind her that I was naked and that it would've been hard to explain away that.

"I meant what I said. It is probably for the best. I am only here for a few weeks, and that was . . . well . . . too intense for a few weeks." She looks down her leg and watches her foot as she traces circles on the floor. I let her words sink in and real-ize that she's right, it was intense. Her honesty leaves me feeling hollow, though. Too intense, but not worth it?

Of course not. Not to her.

"You're probably right," I manage, trying to mask the sour feeling in my stomach.

She looks up at me, something passing over her face—something like regret—before she smiles a half smile.

"Would've been fun though," she offers, and we both let out a quiet laugh. Sex would ultimately complicate things and bring our messes to the forefront, which neither of us wants.

Still. "Oh, I have no doubt about that."

I also have no doubt that mixing family and my love life will risk disaster again, and the last thing that Tait or I need is drama. That kind of intensity blows the door wide open to drama.

"Friends?" she asks, holding out her hand for another shake, and fuck me if she doesn't take my breath away in that moment again. One of her eyes has more flecks of brown than the other, but they're such an interesting shade of green, the irises lined with gray. At first, I thought they reminded me of Charlie's, but up close I realize they're all her own.

"Friends," I confirm, switching the hand that I'm holding the towel with so I can shake hers.

"Sorry you have to escort me around some more, but the quicker we start, the quicker I can get out of your hair, so, how about tomorrow?" she asks, all business.

"Tomorrow I have a meeting that had to get rescheduled, and I think your uncle will kill me if I bail again. How about the next day?"

"Sure." She grins and leans off the doorway, signaling the end of the conversation.

"Okay. Uhhh, goodnight, then?"

"Goodnight, Henry."

I turn to leave and start walking down the steps when she says, "Oh, Henry?"

I turn back to see her expression pulled into a smirk. "Since we both know you owe me. You know, since I had to sneak through a dark pond with my tits out, army crawl up a bank and slip in through my own back door . . . drop the towel. It's the condition of my friendship."

I laugh, but when she doesn't, I realize she's not kidding. Fine, I owe her a bit of embarrassment on my part. But I'll be damned if I act fazed. I unwrap the towel and fold it carefully over my arm, not rushing. I then walk it over and hand it to her. She doesn't take her eyes off of mine; the only indication that she's affected at all is the blush that's spread to her cheeks.

"Sweet dreams, honey," I say, and take all the care I can to turn and march slowly away, down the porch steps and toward my place, her laugh following me.

"Sweet dreams, sweet cheeks!" she calls when I finally make it to the dark part of the road.

TWENTY

TAIT

It started as a night of tossing and turning, nothing seeming to cool me down or let me get comfortable. A cold shower and a sleep aid I keep for emergencies eventually did the trick. Despite waking up drenched in sweat the next morning, I wake up in the best, or at least the most determined, mood I can recall being in in days.

I guess I am fired up. This is what fired up feels like. It feels good to feel determined and fired up about something.

I am happy to have parameters now, in regards to Henry. This feels like the best case scenario for that anyways. I'm here temporarily, and last night, quite frankly, was too intense for temporary. Neither of us seems to be in a place where we are willing to concede much of ourselves, so at least we did the adult thing and nipped it quick. Go me. Go Henry.

* * *

GOOD.

   Great.

   Grand.

WONDERFUL!

NO YELLING ON THE BUS!

I QUICKLY DRESS IN SOME shorts and a tank top after brushing my teeth, swipe on a bit of mascara, and throw my hair in a ponytail, before I head down for breakfast.

There are no extra trucks out front when I get to the big house, though, so I call out when I get inside, "Hello?"

"Hey, Tait, in here!" Grace says.

When I round the corner she continues, "Hey there—I saved you a plate."

"Oh, shoot, did I miss breakfast?"

"Yes, but we figured you needed the rest, so don't worry." She smiles and I look at the clock as I realize that I left my watch and phone back at the cabin in my haste. It's already past eleven.

"Holy shit," I exclaim, and then immediately say, "sorry, I just can't remember the last time I slept in this late."

"A day with Em and Grady takes a lot out of anyone, let alone all of us and all of . . . this. Really, you didn't miss much, I promise. Henry grumbled, Grady annoyed—it'll be the same way tomorrow." She grabs a plate of biscuits and gravy from the microwave and slides it across the island to me. "There you go."

No need to tell her that the portion of my day with Grady and Grandma was the least of it. "Thank you, my favorite."

"Your dad said as much." She turns before I can meet her eyes, surprised, then hands me a coffee as well.

"I have to go take care of a few errands, though, sweetie. You ok if I head out?"

"Of course. Not much I can do today anyways except wander around," I say with a full mouth of food.

"Oh, speaking of that—Em brought you this." She grabs the camera off the counter behind her and slides me a piece of paper along with it. "Charlie will be up at Duane's today if you want to go find them. They need to go for a run to try to steer that herd of horses away before they tear up the place and push any of the elk off. He left you these directions. If you can get there before one you should join them. Just, you know, for work." She awkwardly shrugs and smiles before turning to head out.

"Grace," I say before she gets to the door.

"Hmm?"

"Thank you . . ." And I hope she knows that I mean for more than breakfast. For being gracious, kind, and welcoming, without an ounce of pushiness.

She looks at me, sucks in a breath as if to say something, but decides against it; instead, she smiles and nods before heading out the door.

May as well check the uncles off the list, today, too. Baptism by fire and all that. I inhale the rest of the biscuits and take off, some of my pep gone and replaced with a returning surge of worry, eclipsed with the hope that this won't be so bad, either.

HENRY

"Cast and crew start arriving in two weeks, which is why I wanted to meet on this and finalize it two weeks ago. You can't expect shit to run smoothly if you can't show up to meetings when you say you will," Duane fires at us, and by "us," I mean me.

"The meeting is a formality, Duane. We approved each other's schedules over a month ago. Pending some extreme weather, nothing will change," Charlie replies.

"I'm just saying . . ."

"What? What exactly are you saying Duane? I told you, something came up," I snap.

"Then you should've given a couple hours' notice, Marcum. I have other stuff to do besides waiting around on you." Duane makes a point of using my surname, a conscious effort to remind me that I'm not part of this family. "Besides that, *you* were the only one who couldn't be bothered to show up yesterday," he adds, and I look at Charlie to try and ask permission with my eyes to backhand him.

"Duane, relax," James says. "It is all covered. Charlie's right, this meeting is a formality to double verify something we have already verified. What we need to worry about is getting the herd out of here before they tear up the valley for your show's pretty shots."

"Fine," Duane sighs irritably. "Let's go."

"Um, let's wait until one if you don't mind?" Charlie says.

"What? Why?" Duane asks, and we all look at Charlie, confused. He's usually the one anxious to get back out and on the ground.

"I left Tait directions to come here in case she wanted to join," he says.

Duane continues to get redder, stuttering for a second before regaining composure. "Tait's here?" he asks, more quietly than I would've guessed, judging by his face.

"Yes, she is. And you are to treat her to the warmest and kindest version of yourself, do you understand me? You owe us that, at least," Charlie spits with surprising venom. Even more surprising is Duane's downward look and nod, not putting up any fight in return.

At that moment, we all hear the truck coming up the driveway. Something somersaults in my chest.

"Well, at least she knows how to show up on time. Early, in fact," Duane says in my direction. I roll my eyes. I was on time after the morning chores, but he just enjoys lashing out at me.

I INHALE DEEPLY THROUGH MY nose and step out the front door behind James, who is practically running to greet her. He picks her up in a hug and shakes her back and forth a few times before setting her back down. Grady's lack of boundaries may not come from Charlie, but clearly they stem from somewhere in the Logan bloodline.

"Holy shit. Look at you, kiddo. The last time I saw you, your teeth were as big as your eyes and pointed in different directions!" They both laugh, and James turns to me and says, "Her teeth, not her eyes."

I can feel her looking my way from behind her sunglasses, so I nod in her direction. Duane shoulder checks me as he passes.

"Tait. Look at you, all grown up. What brings you here after all these years? Is your sister joining you?" he says, putting unnecessary emphasis on the "all these years."

She picks up on it, her body language stiffening. I'm not surprised by the sass in her tone when she responds, "Well, I'm here to take some photos, Duane. I was hired. And uh, no, Ava isn't joining me." She frowns.

"Hired by who?" Duane asks quietly, more to himself than anyone else. Charlie shoots him one of his death glares, so he doesn't press.

James laughs and throws his arm around her again. "Looks like we don't need an extra body after all, Duane. You're off the hook."

He rolls his eyes. "Perfect. I've got a shitload of actual work to take care of anyway. Someone has to. Tait, it's lovely to see you. I'm sure we'll all get together soon." He turns and takes his leave.

"You can ride with me in the rig!" James says, looking down fondly at her. Charlie and I simultaneously reply "NO."

"What? Why not?" James whines.

"Because you've flipped that thing three times. You're on your own. We are all going to stay on horseback," Charlie states.

"Fine. Let her at least ride with me in the truck down the road so we can all catch up with her a bit?"

"She's here for six weeks, James," I say when I see that Tait's face has gone from happy to nervous in an instant.

"That okay?" Charlie asks her.

"Yeah, I just—haven't ridden a horse since I was a kid. I love them and everything, but I'd imagine this kind of ride requires some speed and skill in that aspect." She toes a pebble with her boot.

"Ah . . . I didn't think about that," Charlie says, and proceeds to do the same thing.

I see these two are going to need a little coaxing, so, mentally setting aside the irony in it being *me* to do it, I offer up a suggestion . . .

"Charlie, why don't you take her in the rig, and James and I will keep up on the horses? There's an extra helmet and a headset in the trailer. That'll be better for taking pictures, anyways."

Tait and Charlie both nod emphatically, as if relieved.

I load up the truck hauling the horse trailer while James follows with the toy trailer.

"What's the need for driving these horses out of the valley, exactly? Wouldn't they typically avoid groups of people, anyway?" Tait asks when we're all in the truck, quickly avoiding any awkward silence.

"It's less to do with the show and being concerned about them, and more for the horses' sakes, actually," says Charlie. "It's a small enough herd that we've grown somewhat accustomed to them, but you still have to encourage them to rotate areas before they decimate one in particular, plus it's just better conditions for winter. Eventually, we'll have to push them onto government land where they'll most likely be driven to auction, but I haven't felt the need to yet."

"Auction for what?" she asks, concerned.

"Just for pets, really. The ones that aren't bought usually end up in a comfortable sanctuary, with plenty of hay and shelter. Nothing sinister happens to them. Actually, horses that would have otherwise died because of the state they were in often get saved that way. And we—by 'we' I mean LeighAnn—end up with the rest."

"I had no idea that was even a thing, still. Or that there were still herds of wild horses out there—anywhere."

"Yeah. In a lot of places, even in California, they get large enough that they'll use helicopters to drive them out."

"You guys don't though?" she says, and Charlie snorts a laugh.

"No, I still do some things the old-fashioned way. I figure I've got my ancestors rolling in their graves enough as it is . . ."

"He's full of shit. He just likes them," I say.

At that, the energy shifts into something more pensive

until I can practically feel them both grasping for something to talk about next.

Tait's the first to be successful. "Does LeighAnn not do anything with the equine center anymore? I remember she used to be great at all that . . . Teaching and training for all the Western themed events and such . . . She even started that breeding program and hired trainers for cutting horses and everything, right?"

She says it so excitedly, with such admiration . . . and the familiar, nasty pit of dread and guilt opens up in my stomach.

"Not anymore. We closed down that entity and sold most of our personal stock about three years ago . . . before the show started production. We needed the room for them, the show's horses and all that. She's filled up her personal barn with rescues, now," Charlie replies, smiling. Covering for me where he shouldn't have to, making it worse by laying it on further. "It's simpler that way, anyway. When we got away from traditional cattle ranching, we were going in a bunch of different directions trying to make money. Keeping the property intact and keeping it a simple dude ranch, inviting outsiders to come, stay, and experience the outdoors and this life, is what really matters anyways."

Thankfully, we roll up to the edge of the valley, and my torture ends. I accidentally slam the truck door and head to the back of the horse trailer, ready to be deafened by the wind, to clear my head.

"Henry, can you get Tait set up with the helmet and headset? I'm going that way a bit to see if I can glass them," Charlie calls out, holding up the binoculars in explanation.

Tait grabs her camera and waits as I unload and ready the horses, while James backs the rig out of the trailer. I look over at her expression, expecting to see a hint of worry. It's like a dune buggy on steroids and mean—if a machine can look mean.

Instead, she's got a wild, excited look in her eye. She chews her lower lip and smiles a little. That's when she turns my way and catches me staring again.

The issue here is that I now know how good those lips taste and feel, and I'm just supposed to forget the little noises she makes, too. She must be oblivious to where my thoughts have veered because her smile grows.

"Suit me up."

I laugh and gesture for her to go into the trailer. The first helmet I place on her head is way too loose. The second one too tight . . .

". . . and this one is juuuuuuusssst right," she says in a cartoon voice when the third one fits.

"You excited?" I ask, my fingers fumbling around for the buckle underneath her chin.

"It looks fast. Is it fast?"

"Yes, but you'll be able to communicate with Charlie through the headset the whole time when you push this," I say, guiding her hand to the button. "Let him know if you need a break or anything."

"I'm sure I'll be just fine." She bats my hands away and buckles the helmet herself before she marches over to the rig.

Charlie coughs behind me. He definitely does not see me looking at her ass from behind my sunglasses, but I whip around anyway and head over to the horses.

"Nice to see you being friendly for a change," Charlie says to my back.

Heat. The heat is stifling, and I am ready to move and to get some damn air.

TWENTY-ONE

TAIT

I fling myself into the machine, and I have to swallow a yelp from the seat burning my ass. The heat feels like it's increasing by the minute today.

Charlie climbs in on the other side of me and immediately sets to turning knobs on the radio until I hear his voice come through the headset. "Can you hear me?" he asks.

"Yep." I push down the button under my chin and repeat it, and he nods in response.

"Henry?" he asks. Henry rides up next to us and grabs a walkie talkie that's strapped to his chest.

"Yup."

"Same here," comes James's voice.

"Alright, let's roll. They're still out on the eastern ridge area, so coming at them from over here will push them closer to the house and southeast, away from the main hunting areas."

"All shit that we know, Charlie," James drawls, making me laugh. It's obvious Charlie is trying to do an overview for my benefit.

"If you push this button here before you speak, it'll stay between you and I," Charlie says as he shows me another button on the inside of my helmet. He points to the one Henry showed me. "This one goes out to everyone."

I push it before I say "Okay" to let him know we're good to go, and that I'm ready. I'm anxious to take off, to feel myself flying.

Henry and James speed off ahead, and Charlie floors it. I let out what I'm sure is a delighted, but very girly squeal as we propel forward, the rig gliding across the field. Every time we approach what looks like a huge divot, I'm shocked at how smoothly we skate over it. It takes a while, but eventually I stop tensing up for each bump and start laughing at the sheer delight of it all. The speed, the music blaring—90s country to be exact. Charlie is a Shania guy, apparently, a fact that delights me. I'm singing along at the top of my lungs without the bummer of having to hear myself, the roaring engine blocking out the sound. I haven't felt so much pure, simple bliss in forever. The heat is intense, but the speed keeps it off of us and morphs it into a pleasant, breezy blanket that pours over my skin continuously in waves.

I'm aware that the impending awkwardness of whatever this rekindling is will be intense, but I feel an easy contentment settle on me, despite the chaos that carries us across the valleys and over hills.

Sometime later, as I'm singing along to Brooks & Dunn, *"Mariiiiiiiiiiiiiiiiiiiiieeee, Oh, my Marieeeee—ieee—aaaaahhhhhh!"* loud laughter booms in my earpiece from three male voices as Charlie lets off the gas. I see Henry and James ride up, holding their sides, trying not to fall out of their saddles.

"Tait"—gasp—"your radio button is still on," Henry's voice gets out in between bouts of laughter.

"Honey, you cuss like a sailor on HBO," comes Charlie's reprimand.

Oh, God. *All* the sound effects. *"How long was it on?!"* I ask.

Henry snorts and starts dying again. "The entire time," says James.

Cool, probably forty-five minutes of me saying *whoop, whoop* at every little hump, and singing directly into their ears when I couldn't even hear myself. That had to be gold.

Oh, God—the *singing*.

"Were those Muppet impressions?" James asks.

Kill me now.

"Alright, alright. Why don't we take a beer break here for a bit? Probably some good spots for pictures."

Bless Charlie's heart . . .

We pull over on the top of a hill, and it takes me a beat to get my bearings when I look out over the other side. It didn't appear to be a large or steep incline from the slope we crawled up on, but the dive down is a monumental canyon.

It's an odd combination, looking over and seeing the places where fall has begun to take over, viewing it through ripples of heat. It makes it feel like I'm looking at a well-done version of the valley: sunbaked, overcooked—not one on the verge of autumn.

Charlie and I remove our helmets, and he goes to undo a tied-down ice chest in the back when Henry and James ride up. A pang of sympathy rings through me for Henry's mount. He's probably 250-ish pounds, a veritable mountain of a man. The mare herself is sturdy, though, probably close to sixteen hands. I share my observation out loud when Henry dismounts in an easy swoop, and he replies, "She's pushing seventeen, actually. This is Murphy girl."

His movements and mannerisms are so swift, easy, and natural on him . . . an exhibition in contradiction—like watching a buffalo sprint, or a bear scale a tree, and watching him does these jumpy things to my insides. Unfortunately, I now know firsthand what's he's working with, and remembering the feel of his mouth on me has a fresh layer of sweat gathering above my lip. I track his hand as it slides gently across her hide before doing a leisurely circle. Enormous hands, large knuckled and calloused, fingers thick and long.

He snaps off a quick swat of appreciation against Murphy's rump and I visibly jolt at the satisfying *thwap* that it makes, squeezing my thighs together. He catches me, lips pulling with suppressed laughter again. Bastard.

Really on a winning streak here.

I groan and turn in embarrassment, anxious to get a cold beer in my hand. Charlie tosses me one, and Henry's giant hand jets out and grabs it before I can catch it.

"Don't worry, I'll get her a beer—*All she's gotta do is just gimme that wink,*" he offers, singing the line with an actual wink that doesn't help relieve my situation. Ugh, that Neal McCoy song is a classic and it is officially ruined forever. I feel my face flush, which really annoys me further since the last thing I need is more heat in my face when I feel like I'm already stuck inside a toaster.

I snatch it from his grip without a fight, his expression a playful challenge. He's dust-covered, sweat pooling through his shirt, but according to the sparklers currently being set off under my skin, there's nothing gross about it. I can't come up with a snarky reply, so I turn to retreat back to the shade. He snakes an arm around me and flips me back around before I can, starting in on an off-key rendition of "Any Man of Mine." I cover my face in embarrassment, but let it melt into laughter as they all three continue on. *If I was awful, they are horrendous . . .*

"Okay okay, I guess I'll pay more attention to the radio tutorial next time," I let out.

"Hey, I didn't mind." James shrugs. "We don't normally get to hear the music from horseback real well, so that was a treat as far as I'm concerned." I smile at him gratefully.

Henry takes his arm off of me, along with the weirdly pleasant smell of his sweat/dust/deodorant/man combination. He heads out of sight, presumably to take care of a bathroom-related need, since the other men disperse in different directions and James declares, "Piss break."

I decide to chug my beer before I'll break the seal myself, and I find a tree to settle under.

I'm almost finished with my first beer, refreshing and crisp, when I catch Henry hiking back up the hill out of my peripheral vision. The juxtaposition of him, someone so vast and looming, being dwarfed by everything around him, compels me to snap a picture. He looks up from under the brim of his hat right as I do, directly through the lens, right through me. His plain green T-shirt is good and soaked now. A bead of my own sweat tracks down my chest between my breasts as I lower the camera and continue taking him in. Even from a distance I make out that vein snaking down a substantial bicep, and my fingertips twitch. He doesn't break eye contact as he marches up, up, up, until he comes and settles down against the tree with me. Then, because I'm feeling idiotic, an awkward chortle coughs out from between my lips.

The bubble burst, I get up to get another beer.

"Need another?" I ask him over my shoulder, before I see James and Charlie walking closer.

"I've got 'em. And sandwiches," Charlie says, flipping open the chest.

He tosses Henry and James theirs, but walks mine over to me, looking at it in his hands.

"I realize that I don't know what you like, now that you're grown up. But I remembered . . . I know you didn't like mayo, didn't like mustard, and only liked lettuce and white cheese." He chuckles mournfully before continuing, "Hopefully it's not too plain." And hands me my food.

I swallow down the emotion that rises, and respond, "It's perfect. I'm still picky. Thank you." It's a sandwich, but it's also tangible proof that I took up space in his mind, that I existed here. It's proof that he knew some insignificant part of me, and that maybe he understands—or cares to understand—some of the bigger parts, as well.

And *that*—that thought right there is what I need to avoid. That is what I need to keep in perspective. I can't fill a twenty-year void with a fucking sandwich.

"You know, I can't tell you the last time I saw him smiling and laughing this much," Charlie says with a nod in Henry's direction. "It's nice to see that he's made a . . . friend." I don't miss the question implied.

"Sounds like someone did a number on him too, huh?" I say, and immediately regret casually prying into his life and word-vomiting a bit of mine in one sentence.

It's usually easy to get others talking about themselves and those they care about, so it's a habit I haven't entirely shaken since being here. The problem is that, no doubt, *these* people will expect me to reciprocate.

"Yes, and no. I think *he* beats *himself* up more than anything, and doesn't trust himself anymore," he responds, leaving me bewildered.

I don't see a way to keep up this particular line of conversation without him having to divulge too much, and it doesn't feel right, so I search for a subject change.

Charlie proceeds before I can come up with anything, though. "He brought someone he loved into all of our lives, got her on with the ranch. The short of it is that she ended up embezzling a pretty huge sum of money over time, and we needed to dismantle the whole equine center. We were looking at having to sell a portion of the land or something—I had already quit ranching, and we had taken on too much with trying to build up the other businesses. We all had stretched ourselves too thin at that time, and it made it easy for someone to take advantage. That's when Duane came in with the offer for *Dollar Mountain* that let us hold on to the place. There was no way Henry could have known. We weren't exactly organized with the finances at the time, until Duane caught everything up and then *he* caught it. But Henry still blames himself. I'm just saying that it's nice to see him try, though—to try and open up a bit, I mean."

He talks about Henry's betrayal and shame—something that obviously affected his business more than he's letting on—casually, as if it wasn't a big deal to him either way, and I realize that this was always one of the things that drove Mom crazy about him. He let things go *too* easily. He let everything go too easily. When Mom left, she wanted him to chase her. But he didn't, and didn't pursue us by extension.

Why did you stop trying?

It's there, on the tip of my tongue to ask. Asking is admitting, though, isn't it? And if I hadn't been forced to come here, I'd have been *fine* not knowing, fine with his absence, long since forgotten.

I catch a glimpse of Henry again, right before he disappears over the edge of the ridge; and for reasons I'm not fully cognizant of, I want to head in that direction right now, and away from this conversation. I'm up and moving before I think on it too long.

TWENTY-TWO

HENRY

I hear Tait before I see her; her steps somehow manage to sound agitated as they crunch behind me.

"I want to show you something," I say, the thought escaping before I could consider trying to be smooth about it.

"How'd you know it was me?" she asks, catching up to my side.

"You stomp your feet like the ground pissed in your Cheerios. I noticed it the first night I saw you in the woods. It's probably why I mistook you for a Sasquatch," I tell her, and immediately lose the hold on my expression when I see her affronted one. I blow out a quick laugh, and it draws out her smile.

"Ass. I guess that explains why you tried to mount me, then. You finally saw one of your kind and went into rut?"

The word rut, husky and hot from her lips, grabs onto that invisible chord between us and fucking yanks, sending fire through my core. "You give me whiplash, you know that?" I say, and I don't bother to temper my tone.

She smirks, fucking wicked—triumphant, even. "What do

you mean?" And she doesn't sell me on her coyness, doesn't even try.

I scoff, frustrated in more than one way, and turn back to the trail, only now noticing that we'd veered from it. This time, *I'm* determined to stay on track, to stay on the path of least resistance. The path that, ironically, *is* resisting her.

"Hey, don't get too far ahead. One of your strides is like four of mine!" she whines.

"Something tells me you can keep up just fine, Tait."

"Speaking of piss in Cheerios . . . jeez. What's your deal?" She laughs.

I grunt in response.

"Henry?!" She grabs my belt loop from the back to stop me. When I turn around, she's looking up at me through her lashes, challenging, searching. She wants to be distracted, even if it's by a fight. Fine.

She steps onto the raised edge that lines the side of the game trail, an indiscreet effort to size up, and this is the gesture that breaks me down.

I've always been hyperaware of my size. Not just because most people have a propensity for reminding guys like me about it all the time, either. The assumptions that I played elite sports are flattering, but there's always been an edge of . . . not insecurity, per se, but wariness about it. I am wary, knowing that my size means that I don't have the freedom to simply get into a bar fight without restraint, because I am automatically a target and a liability. I could kill someone without meaning to. I always hold back to a degree.

So, when it comes to women, I have traditionally preferred tall ones, not for the physical aspect, but because of how they carry themselves. I can't stand simpering, or diminutive, because I don't need to be made to feel like a big man. I already am.

So, when this woman, at least a full foot shorter than me, steps up, almost like she's trying to make herself bigger . . . it fucking *works*. I don't admire it in a condescending way. I admire it because she's a force. So, I give her what I think she wants.

I place my palm above her head on the tree behind her, crowding her space, meeting her challenge. "Hey, *you* dismissed me last night, remember? So, don't go acknowledging it and making me remember it, and definitely don't flirt with me unless you want me to do something about it."

The look in her eyes wavers—she didn't expect me to say it out loud, I guess. She probably expected me to just act; fight her or make out with her, I can't be sure. Our breathing's the only thing audible between us, now, and I can see the pulse jumping at the base of her throat. She swallows, and I notice the dust that's collected where the helmet and goggles didn't shield her face.

"You have—" I take my arm back and swipe at the area on my own face to show her, sparing her from responding. She blinks, then lifts the hem of her shirt to wipe it away. I turn quickly, but not before I catch sight of her smooth skin, along with another fucking freckle to file away in my brain—on her rib cage, right below the underside of her breast. Below one of her perfect, sweet tits.

I grind my teeth as I walk away, as I refuse to acknowledge the silent laugh I feel from behind me. She likes games, apparently. While I'm up for them if they help create some common ground, I'm too damn overheated to play right now.

"Here. Up over this ridge." I point with my free hand, a beer and my sandwich held in the other. I pop the lid off of the bottle on my boot, too impatient to wait until we reach our spot.

Tait hisses a breath behind me. "Are you okay?" I ask, looking her up and down to see if she rolled an ankle or something. Besides the strange look on her face and her hand on her chest, she looks fine. I feel my face pull into a confused frown.

"Yeah . . . just. Hot," she replies.

"No kidding." I continue on, only a few more yards left. "I promise, we typically get four seasons."

"Yeah. The weather," she says, dully.

"You good?"

"Yep. Good. Great. Grand. Wonderful."

"O-kay?"

She smiles and shakes her head, entertained by her own inside joke, I gather. Sometimes she is easy to read: clear and open. Right now, she's a puzzle.

"Oh my god," she says when we crest the ridge, finally, and I feel smug at the look of happy awe on her face.

"Figured we could have lunch with a view."

"The water is so *green*. I don't think I've ever seen a lake that color. I've seen turquoise water, cerulean blue, blue so dark it's black. Then, you know, *regular* green pond, lake water. This is totally its own."

"I always thought that this little valley itself was the cool part. If I would've known the color of the water would be this exciting I'd have bought you some crayons and really blown your dress up." I chuckle.

"No, it is. The valley is cool, too, definitely. But I've just seen so many different bodies of water. I mean, I *live* in Tahoe. So, this is . . . it's really beautiful."

The valley that surrounds the little lake is entirely rock.

Little bumps and ridges that lead and indent down to the center, to the water. The perimeter of the granite valley is made up of grassy hills.

"Do you want me to ruin it for you?" I ask her as I sit.

"Ruin it?" she asks, still standing and looking out.

"Yep. I'll tell you what Grady used to call this spot when we were younger, and you'll never look at it the same again."

"Well, now I *have* to know, obviously."

"He called it 'the Dinosaur Butthole.'" I smirk up at her and take a bite of my sandwich while she looks back out over the view and cocks her head to the side.

She closes her eyes and laughs through her nose. "Okay. I see it." She sits down next to me and starts to unwrap her food, giving it a funny look before she begins to eat.

We continue this way for a bit, eating and sipping our beers, until curiosity, and some kind of nosy feeling—one that's completely unfamiliar to me, because I normally just don't give a shit about other people's business—prompt me to ask, "So, what were you guys talking about back there? Things going ok with you two?"

She pauses in her chewing, hazards a glance my way.

"Not a lot, actually. We haven't exactly gotten into the meat of things." She lets out a frustrated sigh. "I'm worried that his answers will leave me more angry, will make me bitter over something I didn't even know I missed."

"Well, do you feel that way now? I mean, did you already feel a little sad or bitter about not having a relationship with him before you came here?" I decide to elaborate at her skeptical look. "I just mean, maybe assess the risk, and decide if it's worth it to you to bond again. You'll have to go through some of the negative crap, sure. But if you were fine before you got here, then maybe you'll be just fine when you leave, too.

Regardless of whether or not you want your father in your life. Do you think you have any unresolved bitterness?"

She thinks for a second, raising her eyebrows when she answers, "Honestly, no. I don't think I do. I think when I was a kid, sure. But it's been so many years, and I have a great life, in spite of the messy parts. I don't love to dwell on what I don't have." She shrugs. "If that sounds calloused, I'm not sure. But I've had adventure, excitement, and I have my sister and nephew and her family. I don't think it'd be fair for me to sit back and mourn or be deeply angry over missing some Father–Daughter dances."

"Jesus, Tait, you are way more like him than you realize." I shake my head. Stubborn asses, both determined to plow forward and tell bad feelings to fuck off.

"What do you mean?"

"I mean, to me at least, it sounds like you have an impressive ability to let shit go. Or to convince yourself that you are over things, even if you're not."

Her face drains of color at that, her mouth dropping open a bit before she recovers; and then she starts gathering up her trash as she stands.

"What did I say?" I ask, panicked that some part of that was so upsetting that she's *not* arguing, not even attempting a sarcastic comeback.

"Nothing that isn't true, Henry. But I don't want it to be. I don't want to let shit go." And she starts her march back.

TWENTY-THREE

TAIT

Henry's observation sets my heart racing at a new rhythm. Because, when it comes to Charlie, I fucking deserve to know why. I shouldn't have to move forward until I get some goddamn answers to things, shouldn't just be expected to be happy because of some obscure scale of blessings and hardships I've built for myself in my head. Because I *haven't* let it go. And if I did, then I want it back. I want to know why he didn't try to stay in our lives, and I want to figure out if I want the Logans in it going forward.

I let my husband go. Let my friends go. Let my mom go, taking her as I could when she'd be good to us, but *always* letting it go when she wasn't. I let my damn house go, didn't even take a piece of furniture with me.

"Why did *you* stop trying . . . with Ava and I?" I say as soon as Charlie's in front of me.

He sucks in a quick breath, but the look on his face says he knew it was coming . . . Grady was right—he wears his internal conversation on his face. Another thing we apparently share. I see the tilt in his brow go from embarrassed discomfort, to irritation, and settle on something in between.

"You're ready to start this now?" he asks.

"I think it's as good a time as any . . . I mean, I'm here anyway," I say, and try to shrug, not wanting to bulldoze him before I can get some answers. "I guess I want to know why the split even happened in the first place."

He takes a deep breath before continuing, his eyes scanning back and forth like he doesn't know where to begin.

"Did Viv—your mom—ever tell you how we met?" he asks.

"No, but I don't see how that has anything to do with this?" I feel my face frown.

"Tait. I won't claim that I was a good husband when it came to your mother. Young, stupid . . . We couldn't ever get on the same page, it seemed. I feel like it is important for you to know how we began, though. Can you let me tell you? It's important, I think, for you to understand." He is talking to the ground, but I can hear the emotion in his voice. I nod, and he must see it out of his peripheral, because he proceeds.

"Your mother and I met for the first time when Duane brought her home with *him* for summer break in college." My mouth falls open in confusion, but he trudges on.

"He was very clearly smitten with her, but she wasn't nearly as much with him. Still, I knew how he felt about her, and I didn't care. It felt . . . out of our control. I can't explain it. It was like love at first sight, and the more we got to know each other just felt like confirmation of those feelings."

A ball of sadness and anger rolls in my stomach . . . the words "out of our control" are so similar to what Cole once told me.

"Duane and I were constantly at odds with each other. He had the brilliant business sense, was a walking calculator, and was—is—still good at everything he puts his mind to.

But, he hated it here. Ranching was never for him, and even now I think he would rather be in charge of his own separate thing. Your grandfather wasn't gracious about it, which pitted us against each other constantly . . . and . . . well, your mother and I weren't exactly proud of what we were doing, but . . ." He sighs shakily. "We were in love. And then . . . then we found out about you." He shrugs.

This is news to me, too. I'd never thought to ask about my conception.

"Our plan was to give Duane time, to stay a secret until the sting wouldn't be as bad. But I knew . . . I knew how he looked at her. I knew it wouldn't help. Your mom, though. She didn't want to constantly live under the umbrella of being known as a cheater, or the one who broke Duane's heart. We had every intention of doing things as right as we could so that we could have the best future together as possible. When we found out about you, our plan went to pot, obviously, and we needed to come clean."

"Was Grandma awful to her?" I ask, unable to stop.

He looks at me quizzically. "No, not at all. Not then. But your grandmother *is* a bear. She was determined to steer the whole family in a direction that she deemed fit, and she bulldozed everyone else. But she and Dad really never held it against her, or me for that matter. I think your mother couldn't forgive herself, though, Tait. We married, and I needed to work, and to feel like I could provide, and could make her happy in this situation that I felt I put her in. Dad had his first stroke right before you were born, and I ended up taking on more responsibility at the ranch, but your mom wasn't having it. She was angry that I couldn't go out and do something—anything—else, and that I didn't want to. I should have listened to her, should have seen that she was starting to become truly unhappy here. I guess I was willfully ignorant . . ."

He takes another deep breath, then looks over at me. "Do you remember anything about the split when it happened?" he asks.

"Not specifically. I remember Grandpa passing, living on the ranch for a little bit after that . . . then when we moved with Mom . . . she kept saying you would be coming soon."

"Well . . . Your mom didn't grow up in a volatile home or anything. Your grandparents were great people, but they also never fought, not even the good kinds of fights. They were passive aggressive at best. So, your mom *hated* fighting. I say that in the hopes that you understand all that came next. A part of me thinks that she didn't feel like she had a choice other than to leave . . . that she wanted to force my hand, maybe?

"When I needed to take the ranch over, I needed time to figure out how to change things, and I did—I wanted to change it all so that I could make her happy, wanted to make it into a thriving business so that I wouldn't be stuck running cattle and be gone all the time, never able to take vacations. I truly tried, Tait. But I got swallowed up in running the place and her fears probably all seemed like they were coming true. I didn't know how to expand when I was drowning as it was. She asked me to move countless times. She wanted me to leave it to James and Duane to run. But James wouldn't have changed anything, which means he would have eventually forsaken work for fun, every time. Duane . . . Well, I'd be lying if I said I didn't want to compete with him a little. I liked that this was mine, that it became my identity. It's probably why I was throwing myself into it harder when he got involved. He came home from his big shot job and took an interest in

investing in everything to help facilitate some of the changes
we wanted to make.

"By the time things were starting to run smoothly, I had
let Viv down in so many ways. I was already so sure that I had
been too shitty to her to ever make up for it, and that is what
she started to tell me. She never seemed happy when I was
around, but was angry with me for being gone so much . . .
And all the while she was pulling more than her share of
weight at home and with you guys. But, suffice it to say—I just
seemed to be the cause of her unhappiness, and it got easier
to stay . . . away.

"Eventually, she had enough of not being one of my pri-
orities. I thought that the work I was doing was to set us
up—thereby making her my priority." He stops here and
seems to consider something for a while, his foot shaking
anxiously.

"Is that when you met Grace?" I ask.

"It is. And while nothing happened until after the divorce,
I realize now that I was having an emotional affair, even if
Grace herself thought we were just friends. For that, I am
sorry . . . No explanation justifies it."

I nod, appreciating the blunt honesty.

"And then, everything else just happened. There was already
so much distance that by the time she decided to physically
distance herself, I didn't have the fight in me, anymore."

He sighs a few times, agitated, before continuing.

"So . . . yeah. When she ultimately decided to leave, I
was . . . angry. And I wasn't exactly helpful. I was angry at her
and refused to beg her to stay, or to at least stay near—to help
me stay close to you guys.

"And, when it became clear that neither of us *could* compromise . . . she was afraid that the life she could give you

guys wouldn't compare to what we all had here, and she
didn't *want* to compete. I realize now that we were young and
making our decisions based on us, and not you guys. I can't
tell you how much I regret that, or how sorry I am. Each time
I did call, it seemed like it made it worse for you guys, too. By
the time I grew up and pulled my head out of my ass and realized that years had passed, you really were happier without
maintaining ties, it seemed.

"And, Tait . . . I need to be clear. I don't feel like it is right
for me to speak to her character when she's not here. It seems
too easy for me to say whatever I want to now, to make sense
of it. So I won't do that, and I won't make excuses for myself.
I thought I was doing the right thing by your mom, and I still
don't know what the right thing to do was. I can't say that I
wish I would have picked up and moved with our family
when I had the chance, because I met Grace, and God, I love
her, and don't deserve that woman . . ." I can see him struggling and bouncing around mentally, so I stay silent and wait
for him to wrap it up.

He is looking at me, his eyes so similar to mine, but
brighter and tear-filled, and I feel some of the anger in me
deflate. I *know* how easy it is to get lost in ourselves, even in
a marriage. I know he's leaving pieces out, but this feels like
an honest start.

I can see how it might have been, between them, laid out
before me. Charlie with his huge family, loud and boisterous,
affectionate and playful, with a mass of history and tradition
between them . . . and Mom, subdued, mercurial, with two
similarly dispositioned parents but no other living relatives,
and the quiet, suburban existence they led in comparison. I
could see how it *could* become an insecurity, because I lived
it. I just went the opposite direction and decided to brand

myself onto Cole's family, ignoring the less desirable history of my own. I trudged on, headfirst, and abandoned them all when I had something else to look forward to. I was a kid, sure, but I abandoned even the notion of wanting to reconnect with my family. It was born out of self-preservation, but I bore it nonetheless.

"I met your ex-husband, Cole. I'm sorry to hear that things didn't work out with him . . .," he says.

"What? When?" I ask, incredulous.

"At your mother's service . . . I came to the church first and ran into him outside. I wasn't planning to go in, was still in my car."

"Why wouldn't you come inside?" Something I've held on to with righteous anger is the fact that he didn't bother to show up to Mom's funeral. I'm having an internal crisis trying to process this information.

"Because I didn't want that day to become about me. I wanted to give you girls the space to grieve . . . And I didn't . . . This is going to sound juvenile, but I don't know how else to put it. I didn't want it to *seem* like I was only there out of convenience or something. I didn't want to show up and have you think I was going to pressure you for a relationship now that Viv wasn't in the picture. I didn't want that day to be about me." He looks away, radiating shame.

"He—Cole—knocked on my window. He must have recognized me or something because he introduced himself as my 'daughter's husband,' and then asked me to respect your privacy. I told him I intended to, and that I would like to attend the burial as well, but would stay unseen. I waited until everyone was gone to say my goodbyes."

I nod, not trusting my voice to speak, but wanting him to know I understood.

"I have probably recited this next part to myself a million times over the years, so I'd like to get it out now if you're okay?" he says, and I nod again.

"When you were born, Tait, and when it came to you girls . . . it was like Vivien found what she was put on this earth to do. She was so enamored with you guys, amazed. We both were. But we stopped paying any mind to each other, except to hurt each other by what the other did or didn't do. It's really not a unique story, I know." He takes a deep breath and looks at me nervously, like he's approaching the part that he knows he'll lose me on.

"Our marriage died the death of a thousand little cuts over time. I had to carry on this family legacy that I wasn't ready for, that I knew she resented me for—but it was what I knew, and what I *wanted*, I just didn't have the balls to tell her. I was a selfish bastard, because I was so busy being wrapped up in myself that I didn't make sure I prioritized *you*." He takes a deep breath again.

"I think as parents, we think of our kids as a kind of extension of ourselves, and don't realize that they are their own human people . . . at least not right away. I think your mother and I had become too wrapped up in our bitterness toward each other to see you guys there in front of us. But Viv desperately wanted a family that stayed together, and when we failed, she felt like she failed. I hated the idea of making anything any harder for her, and yet I was so angry at her at the time. I know this sounds like a cop out, but I felt like I was giving her what she deserved when she asked for it, the chance to be the best mom she could be to you . . . because, when I did come around, or when I called, all I did was disappoint her and I could see it bleed into her other actions. And Tait, she was so amazing with you guys. When she asked for full custody, I felt I owed it to her. I was so stupid . . . I wasn't considering what I owed *you*. There's no excuse for me allowing it to go on as long as I did. I should have tried harder for *you*."

I feel my face, wet with tears, hot and swollen. I don't know what I expected to hear, but the simple and honest explanation makes the kernel of sadness, the one typically wrapped in anger, bloom. I always expected him to blame her . . . to say that she kept us away. I expected him to keep things surface level, maybe to blame work and then distance. The fact that he is owning up to what it all boiled down to—selfishness, hurt, and bitterness—has rendered my carefully considered responses to be useless.

I can't help but wonder how I would have felt if I had been in my mom's shoes. Cole's family was fun, wonderful, loving. How would it have felt to have kids with Cole, before the split? To imagine the fun holidays with them, the new siblings they'd get with their other side of the family . . . to constantly be compared to Allie, to swallow my personal rage and devastation so that my children could go enjoy their holidays guilt-free, to then come home to a quiet house, and a broken-hearted Mom barely keeping it together, scraping by, trying to hide any unhappiness from them. It's so similar to what *still* took place in my upbringing that I lose my breath. I am suddenly so grateful that I didn't have a baby with Cole. That I didn't take that decision lightly. Because I know that kids aren't an accessory to marriage, they're not an extension of us. They just *are* . . . and I don't trust that some of my own selfishness wouldn't seep out onto them. I don't know if I'd have the strength that so many parents have.

"Thank you. For sharing all of that with me," I manage.

"I think I'm glad that I ended up here. And, even though I don't think I'll ever be okay with all the years we missed together, I am still glad that I am here, now."

Charlie's eyes fill, and he says, "Your mom did an amazing job from what I can tell. And I'm glad, too . . ."

James saunters over to our tree finally and asks if we are ready to go. We gather our things and load back up.

I feel Henry's eyes on me, but I don't glance his way. Too raw and exposed as I am.

We take off again, but this time I feel nostalgic, lost in memories, coming to terms with the fact that maybe, just maybe, everything did happen for a reason. After all, if Mom hadn't moved us, I wouldn't have met Cole. And even though that ended in disaster, without him bolstering me, I never would have pursued the career that I now love. I can stack the blocks of my life and make sense of them, this way.

A Garth Brooks song comes on the radio, and I smile as a memory surfaces . . .

I pull up in my Jeep to our little L-shaped house and immediately see Mom through the window. A smile plants itself on my face. It's a good day, she's in a great mood.

Mom is in the kitchen with rubber gloves, music blasting. As soon as I walk in the front door and toss my keys on the hook, she whirls around, singing into her dish brush with abandon. I join her and we share the mic, screaming a ballad about being shameless.

We laugh hysterically, hug and dance in the kitchen . . .

Mom and I that same night, going through wedding plans, looking over the timeline we printed off of an online wedding planning How-To page. I quickly Sharpie over the Father–Daughter Dance, and anything alluding to being given away.

"Tait," Mom gently rebukes.

I look at her in confusion. "What?"

"I just don't think . . . Well, I want you to know that I will be okay if you want to invite your father to be a part of this," she says, leaving me stunned . . . I think that she must be saying this in an effort to check off some kind of Mom guilt-reprieve list she has going on, so I don't toy with feeling that out more, and respond with as much levity as I can.

"Why would I invite him to my wedding? To meet my husband for the first time? That's silly, Mom. I don't need him there. I've told you numerous times that I don't even need this whole wedding. I'd be happy doing it at a courthouse."

"I think you should send an invitation out that way. Who knows, maybe he'll send a gift at least?" she counters, and I see right through her forced levity, too.

"And why would I want that now? He's been perfectly happy to just pay you your support for us. He hasn't pursued more, at least not for a long time, not really . . . so why should I be the one to try?"

She looks at me sadly, then, and her eyes start to fill with tears. Shit. Wasn't it twenty minutes ago that we were dancing and laughing in the kitchen as we put away dishes? Now I've made her feel guilty, like I'm some angry, unadjusted young adult with Daddy issues. Look at me! I'm happy, I'm great, I'm marrying my best friend, and he's as crazy about me as I am him. Ava is happy, she's great. She's got a new boyfriend, is away at college. She did good, we are enough, we made it. The three musketeers, all for one and one for all.

"Mom, I . . ."

"I have you guys. They let me have you guys. That's all that matters to me. I just want this day to be about you, babe. I just *want you to know that I support whatever you want to do. Don't worry about me. I can face the music whenever you are ready."*

Easier said than done . . .

I SPENT SO MUCH TIME worrying about determinedly and decidedly being fine for her sake, that I never considered that she might have *actually* been fine, then . . . and been genuine about trying to bridge the gap. Was she feeling sad that she hadn't encouraged us earlier? Did she feel guilty over keeping and moving us, for us missing out on something? I had assumed that was what she meant by facing the music. Or did she feel sad for him, and what *he* missed? I had made that call, along with many before that, in closing him out.

TWENTY-FOUR

TAIT

The silence in the truck for the ride home morphs into a comfortable, if not slightly melancholy one. Shortly after we took off a second time, Charlie discovered that they'd forgotten to pack the extra fuel for the rigs. So, rather than chance it, we turned around and headed back.

I find myself agreeing to dinner the following night, accepting hugs from James and my father, a distant wave from Duane, and an encouraging nod from Henry before I bid them farewell and head into my truck and back to the ranch.

I GET TO WORK AS soon as I get back to my overheated cabin and start to upload the material from the day. I'm only a tiny bit embarrassed to find that I didn't actually capture much. Too often, being a photographer means you're forced to miss the beauty, because you immediately auto-analyze the lighting and angles of a landscape, rather than soak it in. Today was understandably distracting, reconnecting to this place that once was home, and it forced me to be present rather than work-minded.

Nevertheless, when I start uploading what I did capture to my laptop, I can't help but fall in love a little bit with the terrain. Dry, dusty fields peppered with sage in one series fade into lush forests, mountainous views in another, then change back to what looks like endless flat meadows. Just a small section of Idaho looks like it could instead be three different states altogether. And this isn't even my best work.

AND THEN THERE'S THE SHOT of Henry . . . I loose a sigh and then shake my head to clear it, kicking myself for sucking face with a stranger so soon into this trip. Wishing I could just take the edge off of . . . this . . . whatever all of this is.

MY PHONE JOLTS ME OUT of my trance, but I ignore Ava's call again.

THE REMINDER OF THE OUTSIDE world makes me take pause, and I suddenly feel a bit spooked about the developments of the day. I should remind myself to remain cautious. Regardless of what all took place, actions speak louder than words, and at the end of the day, no one in this family has shown through *action* that they gave a rat's ass about having a relationship with Ava or me.

BESIDES CALLS THAT TURNED INTO letters.

Besides a large sum of money that I never even knew came from them that they didn't even care to follow up on to get credit for.

Besides the fact that you now know that many of the details surrounding the split were kept from, or misconstrued to you, and probably still are.

Besides how welcoming and genuinely kind they've all been since you got here . . .

I ROLL MY EYES AT that inner voice and set aside those details to continue to process over the course of the trip.

On the heels of that feeling, there's guilt over continuing to ignore Ava. All other family aside, we have always, and will always, have each other. I'll need to get over it and quit icing her out soon.

I OPT TO TEXT:

Me: Had it all out with Charlie today. I'm smoked and about to pass out. It's all good . . . better than I would've thought, I think. Promise to call tomorrow. Love you.

The text bubbles go up and disappear a few times before she ultimately goes with:

Ava: Okay. Love you, too. Miss you.

I do the bedtime routine thing then settle in, and ultimately end up on *top* of the covers with my laptop, making some (pathetic) "people notes" for the day to send off to

Gemma, when my phone dings again. I sigh, expecting a demand from Ava, but am surprised to see:

> **Henry Marcum:** Breakfast at my place or yours? Thinking mine if that's cool. Rotisserie chicken doesn't really hit right until noon or later . . .

I snort, and then look out my window like a dolt, as if I could see him all the way across the pond . . . and, *oh*. I can. His light is on, and he's pacing in his room, bare chested, looking down at something in his hand. His phone?

Warmth floods in my chest at the sight. Crap. I feel the stupid, traitorous smile plaster itself, too.

> **Me:** I can be convinced to forgo chicken . . . depending on the alternative offered, the time I'd be expected, and whether or not you're a coffee drinker?

Oh, Jesus. He's smiling at his phone.

> **Henry Marcum:** Omelettes, at 7:00 a.m., and absolutely.

> **Me:** Tits a plan, then. Sweet dreams!

> **Henry Marcum:** Well, now that you've brought them up, I'm sure my dreams will be.

> **Me:** OMG. TITS.

> **Henry Marcum:** Yeah . . . I got that.

> **Me:** IT'S, OR EVEN TIS!!!! ONE OF THOSE.

Me: You know what, I'm good with chicken. It's going to go bad soon anyways.

Henry Marcum: Lol . . . Bring it and we'll pack some for lunch. See you at 7.

TWENTY-FIVE

HENRY

I tell myself if I just don't open my eyes, I'll be able to sleep in. Instead, I toss back and forth for thirty minutes (I know because I keep checking my phone), and give up and roll out of bed at 5:30 A.M.

I busy myself after showering with some cleaning, then debate for a few minutes on shaving before the doorbell rings at 6:15. I open up the door to a sleepy, grumpy looking Tait— rotisserie chicken tucked under one arm.

"I saw your light on. I slept *maybe* an hour," she huffs before letting herself in.

"Coffee?" I ask, adding as much cheeriness as I can into a single word. She plops down at the counter and nods.

"Why couldn't you sleep? Nothing *sweet* to dream about?" This earns me a glare.

"It's a billion degrees upstairs, so I tried to sleep downstairs on the couch, but I roll around too much . . . Here, hand me something to cut, I'm starving."

I give her the peppers and leftover steak. She easily finds a knife and a cutting board, and we work side by side in comfortable silence—which seems like the safest option before her coffee kicks in.

"What's got you smiling like that?" she says grumpily, leaning a perfect hip on the counter and eyeing me suspiciously over her mug.

"I don't think I'm smiling," I say, feeling my grin grow. "I just think I'm a morning person, and you're not."

"I'm so glad I continue to give you material to laugh at me with."

"Honestly, me too."

At that, she snorts, but finally cracks a small smile.

"I can only imagine how funny the mental image of me being hurled across the pond would be," she says, giving me a light shoulder punch before reaching to refill her mug.

"Trust me, *that's* not what I think of when the other night comes back to me." Oops.

Her shoulders tense, but she looks back up at me sideways before we break into an awkward chuckle.

Determined to refocus, I plate our omelettes and go over today's plan.

"I thought you might want to see some of the more functional parts of the ranch first before exploring more of the property, and I need to help out over at the garden today anyways."

She shrugs merrily, the caffeine's effects visible. "Sounds good to me. You like to garden, too? Is there anything you don't get roped into doing around here?"

"It's one of my favorite parts, actually." And I can't help but feel a little self-conscious, suddenly unsure about whether or not she'd find my love of growing things particularly manly.

She slowly cocks her head in that studious little way of hers, and the gesture is so similar to the turn of her head before she kissed me back that night, that my jeans immediately feel tighter. God, I love the little seam that divides her bottom lip, the one that makes it into two pillows stuffed together.

I break eye contact to precisely cut an oversized bite of my omelette to hoover up. I feel her assessment while I do the dishes, studying me with a look I can't make out. I told Grace I'd pick her up, but we've got an extra hour before I'm supposed to, and the thought of killing time fills my head with ideas that I grind my teeth to stomp out. I feel everywhere her eyes land on my body.

"Ask me something?" I say before I can change my mind.

"Huh?"

"Well, I feel you ogling me, and we've got time to kill. Ask me something if you want."

I expect her to deny it, or to make some sarcastic and cutting remark about my ego, so she surprises me with her response. "Can't be helped. I'm a sucker for watching a man clean. Especially one who does it well." She shrugs again and bends down to scratch Belle.

Damnit, my whole chest feels like it fills up with air bubbles and a laugh barks out of me. "You should see my feather duster." I waggle my brows, at which she puts a hand on her chest in mock surprise and bites her lip with an over-the-top "Oh my."

Nope, nope. Abort. Can't play-pretend flirt with her when I remember the taste of her mouth and skin. Yesterday I was prepared for her to call me on the bluff, but this early into today I can't.

My face must look horrified, because she tosses her head

back and starts laughing in victory, holding on to the counter for stability.

And, yet again, I get tunnel vision. Tait looks so damn beautiful in this moment, laughing with her entire body—the one that has no rhythm or predictability, tinkling out of her in chaos—that it hurts. I suck in a breath at the sudden realization that I, someone who is not inherently funny, want to be the one making her laugh like this, for as long as I can.

She wipes a tear from the corner of her eye as it settles. "Sorry. But I actually do know what I want to ask you!"

I swallow and try to pull myself together. "Go for it."

"Can I see your playlists?"

"What? Why? No." I scoff and clutch my phone through my back pocket like she's going to try and rob me of it.

"Now, now. I think it is only fair. You were incredibly rude about my taste in music. I want to know what you're into." She holds out her palm. I can think of a lot of things I'm into that don't have a fucking thing to do with playlists.

I try to remember what songs are on there, not thinking of anything particularly weird or embarrassing. It's music, not like I actually made any of it, but it feels intimate anyways.

"Alright," I relent. "I gotta load up some stuff and will pack some lunch while you scroll."

FIVE MINUTES LATER I HEAR her bellow . . .

"HENRY. GET OVER HERE." I take the steps a couple at a time and burst in to a very red-faced Tait.

"What? Are you okay?!" I look her up and down.

"You honestly made fun of my playlist choices when you are rocking with THIS?!" She holds out my phone to me and breaks into a massive grin.

Fuck . . .

"*Mamma Mia!?!!!* You're into MUSICALS?! Come on, man. I'm trying not to judge here, but you've got both albums on here from *both* movies. And you judged me first! Explain yourself!"

"I . . . I . . ." I struggle for a cool explanation and come up empty. "Fine, okay. Yes, I like it. It's Grady's fault, though."

"Uh-huh . . . sure, Abba man." She is way too delighted at this.

"No, I swear. He got a bad case of something called hand, foot, and mouth disease when we were younger. I was old enough to watch him and the only other person who got it, so they quarantined us together . . . Basically I got stuck on babysitting duty while sick with him. He was a tyrant even then, and made us watch the movie and *Grease* for a week straight while we alternated between ice cream and soup."

I can't keep the smile from my face when I remember us both from way back then. I was sixteen and still felt like an outsider most of the time, but it was after that week that I knew I had a brother in Grady.

She hands me my phone with a flourish and a smile. "I am delighted more and more by everything I find out about you that is clearly so off-brand. You contain multitudes, Henry. I'm sorry to have ever called you '*Deliverance*.'"

"Well, now I know what I want to listen to today."

WE FINISH LOADING HER CAMERA equipment and spend the ride over to the house blasting the *Mamma Mia!* soundtrack in hysterics. Her enthusiastic air drum solos are Oscar-worthy, and despite the bruise still left on my self-esteem from her dismissal, I find myself wanting to enjoy her presence more than worrying about my pride.

The ride ends too quickly, and I drop her off at the house to get the rest of the group while I go check on the horses. By the time I head back, I can hear Tait's laugh above the rest all the way from the porch.

That smile falls when she sees my face, though, and the rest of the room goes awkwardly silent.

"Uh . . . Good morning?" I say with a frown at everyone.

"Morning, Hen. Muffin?" Grace quickly brushes over the weirdness and hands me a plate. That's when I notice Jake Lockhart, producer (and asshole) extraordinaire. Ah, that explains it.

"Henry Marcum, speak of the devil!" he bellows. And fuck, I hate not being in on the joke.

"Jake." I nod, friendly enough. "You're back early."

"All for you, too, my man. We've got some new extras, and Sadie will be riding this season. I need them to look like naturals. And I'd like to go over some of the scenes with you and Charlie to get your suggestions for locations. Figured we could get a head start," he says, leaning on the counter like he owns the place. He's wearing his overpriced, perfectly clean cowboy hat indoors, and doesn't go to remove it even as he drags over a stool to sit on before diving into his breakfast. I share a glance with Charlie, who seems to be noticing the same thing, grinding his jaw before stabbing a bit of eggs.

"I thought you guys already went through all of this with Duane? The locations, I mean," I reply, carefully monitoring my tone.

"Indeed, but you know how these things go. We've had

some rewrites. Nell mentioned some sweet spots *you* took her too, actually, that she thinks would be ideal." The meaningful look he throws me from under his stupid fucking hat is smug. I'm tempted to tell him that his ex-fiancée (Nell—aka Sadie Dollar—a fan-favorite who he fucked around on constantly) actually followed *me* out one day during filming last year, put herself in my truck, and asked to go to my place—claiming that the bathroom options were all taken. Nothing happened while we were there, but the illusion she wanted to create was solidified when she continued to flirt shamelessly and aggressively the rest of the season, always turning it up a notch in Jake's presence. I'd never taken the woman anywhere else on this whole damn property, though, but I didn't know if I should tell Jake that and sell her out ... We'd become pseudo friends over our shared enjoyment at pissing off Jake, after all.

"Uhhh . . . sure, Jake. I'm busy today, though."

"Already got it covered. The lovely Tait can join us. Nell and the extras get here next week and we'll make up the time during production as long as we get a plan together," he proclaims, smacking around an overly large bite of eggs. My eye twitches and I feel my lip curl, but I let out a grunt of agreement.

I catch Tait's watchful eye as I sit down across from her with my muffin clenched a little too tightly in my fist, something in my face making her flinch. She must read me too well, already, and feel guilty.

She confirms it by speaking up next. "I figured we could all go, two birds with one stone, you know. That way you're not stuck carting me around extra, on top of advising for the show. I'm sure your time is stretched thin as it is." She throws in a few casual shrugs, but I don't miss the apologetic note.

I feel my jaw clench, but I quirk an eyebrow at her and shrug back.

"Sounds good to me." I quickly finish off the pastry, catching Charlie's shrewd look before he pipes up.

"Actually, Jake, why don't you go over the rewrites and the scenes with me today so we can have a solid game plan together. I'd rather be efficient with our time instead of wandering around in this heat. I need Henry to stick to some scouting today before our hunting trip."

My face pulls into a frown, because Charlie knows damn well that in this early season heat wave, the elk won't be moving around at all, and he can't stand Jake just as much as I can't. He has never treated me as anything less than a son, but we've got an unspoken agreement that when it comes to *this* side of the business, it's typically on me to grin and bear it.

"Alright. Well, ready to get started, then?" Jake asks, not doing a great job at hiding the disappointment in his tone.

"Yep, I'll meet you out front," Charlie dismisses him.

"It was great meeting you, Tait. I look forward to seeing you around," Jake says before waving the rest of us off and heading out front. Asshat.

Charlie scoffs as soon as he's out the door.

"Well, I know you'll get good pictures next week on set and behind the scenes and whatnot," he says to Tait, flourishing his hands agitatedly, "but you should take this time to get some better material of this place outside of the show. Lord knows our website needs updating."

"Of course, Henry seems to have a good plan," she replies with a sweet smile and a sidelong glance my way.

It catches Charlie off guard, his stare lingering a little too long on her face before he squeezes her shoulder, reaches over to kiss his mother on the cheek, and heads out. Grace walks him to the door.

I might not understand his angle, but I'm not going to look a gift horse in the mouth on this one. I nod a confused thanks and glance from Tait's quizzical face over to Mrs. Logan's beaming one. She sips her tea and gets up, slowly for her, before gathering the empty plates and starting the dishes. Tait gets up silently and heads toward the bathroom. I wonder if she is cognizant of knowing where it's located.

"Emma, please don't, damnit," Grace says as soon as she returns. I chuckle at the familiar dance they're entering into.

"Oh, stop. I'll do these, and you put away the leftovers. I'll bring them over to Grady and Caleb on my way out," Mrs. Logan replies.

"Where are Grady and Caleb this morning, by the way?" Tait asks when she gets back, and an unsure look passes over her face, like she's mad at herself for being comfortable. Jesus, I need to dial back on being tuned in to this woman and her expressions.

Grace chimes in, "They're already at LeighAnn's starting on the garden work. We're getting a late start and with the heat I don't have high hopes, but . . ."

"But Grace is the MacGyver of gardening. Between Henry and Grace, they've made this place almost completely self-sufficient." Mrs. Logan throws her a loving look. Color drains from her face suddenly, though, and she grips the edge of the sink with white knuckles. I jump up and over there, but only hover, knowing better than to call Mrs. Logan out on any kind of frailty. While she and Grace share some silent communication, Tait, oblivious to the moment, starts piling things into the Tupperware containers on the counter.

I catch Grace's eye and do my best meaningful look towards Mrs. Logan and back.

"Shoot, you know what—I just remembered. I have an appointment in town and need Em to drive me." Grace nods. Mrs. Logan gives us both a resigned look, some color returning to her face.

"No biggie," Tait says, looking at us all suspiciously.

"Tait—I'll meet you at the truck. I uhh . . . gotta use the bathroom," I say, and wish I could punch myself directly in the face. *Nice one, Henry. Great seduction tactic, letting her wonder about your bowel movements.*

She nods my way, then looks to Grace and Mrs. L, saying, "Thank you for the muffin." She smiles warmly, awkwardly (adorably) waving a hand before she goes.

GRACE WAITS A BEAT AFTER hearing the door shut before turning to me.

"She needs to go to the hospital; she's needed to for days now, but I can't get her to."

"Don't speak about me like I'm not goddamn here, Grace. I'm fine, just old," Mrs. Logan says, but it's lacking her typical venom.

"Mrs. Logan. You know I would never insult you. But you went from Helen Mirren to the crypt keeper in half a second. I think Grace is right," I say.

She squeezes my arm, giving me a glassy-eyed look.

"Tell him, Em," Grace says quietly, earning a defeated look from the woman I consider my grandmother.

"Tell me what?"

TWENTY-SIX

TAIT

Henry's presence proves to be more distracting than I'd like. And not just because of the pangs of lust that surge each time he does some small, inconsequential, purely masculine thing (e.g., throwing his arm over the back of my seat and looking over his shoulder to back the truck out, scratching his beard, doing the *dishes* for fuck's sake), but also because something is . . . off.

Despite the other day, and the playfulness since, I keep expecting a bit of coolness from him—maybe even some detachedness after the other night when I sent him away. Instead, he's been suspiciously nice. Doting, even.

After an oddly silent car ride over here—a stark contrast to the ride before that—he's been overly attentive. He hovers over my shoulder, checking out shots on the little screen and smiling and complimenting. It's disorienting, to put it mildly.

Plus, the man is just obscenely large. Watching him deftly haul around my lighting equipment like a sack of feathers rather than the cumbersome load it is puts my libido at odds with my feminist ideals. My mind continuously wanders to how those large hands felt splayed across me, fingertips pressed into that spot on my spine right above my ass. RBG help me, even remembering how easily he tossed said ass has a giddy feeling building in my solar plexus.

As aware as I am of the man, this garden setup *is* impressive.

"Eventually, we'll build a more permanent greenhouse structure around all of this, but this will do for now," he says, hauling me out of the mental gutter.

"Henry should show you the whole system and what everything is. He designed it," LeighAnn offers.

I look up at him to find him practically bouncing on his toes. *Oh, he's really into this.* Gardening. Of all the things.

"Well, like I was saying, eventually I'm sure they'll put a more permanent structure around it, but this is just easy to add to for now, or adjust later," he says, walking me over to the area where I've been informed the fall garden will be popping through. Sure enough, there's a pumpkin patch sprawled out around a corner.

They've had the foresight to build it under a massive hanger-style building, with greenhouse sheeting in panels that are easy to rotate and remove for more or less sun exposure. It's the length in total of a football field, if I had to guess, complete with a composting area, a chicken coop, a massive indoor potting bench that's got numerous labeled fertilizers, feeds, and tools neatly organized and labeled. There are even rainwater collection barrels that are piped in from both ends. It's brilliant—at least, to someone with no experience in this, it sure seems to be. He's seemingly thought of everything. The pride on his face, mixed with his thinly veiled excitement, is contagious. I find myself asking about each area and plant, mooning over him wax poetic about how he wants to attempt this chili or that squash, or the cobbler he and

Emmaline made with a mix of the berries they grew over summer . . . his eventual hopes of having an orchard . . .

Hoooooboy, I've got the hots for a farmer. Farmer? Cowboy? I don't know which, or both, but I'll bet he's one of the few men on planet Earth who could rock the hell out of a pair of overalls. I bite my lip to stave off laughing at the mental image.

"What?" he says sternly. He thinks I'm laughing at him.

"Nothing. I'm just a stereotype. I feel like every other bitch."

He frowns in confusion. "I haven't known you long, but even I think it's safe to say there's only one of *you*, Tait," he says before getting distracted by an errant weed. He jerks it out of the garden bed like its very existence offends him, and I wonder if he realizes that he's just paid me such a weighty compliment.

I'm not unique, and while I know that's perfectly fine, feeling as though I'm special to someone again is . . . causing me to have a moment.

The man is just so damn *helpful*. I can't help but notice how easy it is for LeighAnn, Grady, Caleb—hell, even the other employees in this place—to all ask him questions or for a hand without hesitation. And while I couldn't categorize Henry as someone eager to impress anyone, it's all too obvious that he cares about every aspect of the place.

And yet . . . this is all just outside of LeighAnn's house. He helps with the Range's animals and horses. Even *his* house is James's old one.

What does *he* get for all his loyalty and dedication, I wonder?

Belle chooses that moment to lick my hand like she's aware and happy that I'm noticing this about her guy, and I look up to catch Henry's eye. He flexes his hands and shifts uncomfortably, grinding a muscle in his jaw, but not breaking eye contact.

I'm aware, all over again, of the tiniest sensations under that stare—wishing so badly that I could read the thoughts on his face like he apparently can mine. I feel the beads of sweat trickling down my tank top as he strides my way. I slowly pull my camera up higher as my shield de facto, and he smirks.

"Got enough here?" he asks.

Not nearly. "Yeah, I think so."

"Feel like a swim? Grady and Caleb want to go to a swimming hole," he says, including the last sentence for my benefit, I'm sure, so that I know this is a G-rated swim adventure this time.

"Absolutely. We'll stop on the way to unload the equipment and grab suits?"

"Perfect. I'll load up an ice chest and some dinner."

TWENTY-SEVEN

HENRY

I'm apparently a masochist for suggesting the swimming hole, but here we are.

We could've easily hiked from mine and Tait's pond, but we all decide to hop in the truck for the AC. When we get as far as we can in a vehicle, it's only a small walk over one ridge to my favorite spot on the entire Range.

It's really a collection of two pools, one smaller one up top, looking out to a view of a valley stuffed full of trees. A short waterfall starts off to the side of the upper pool and trickles down a smooth face of rock into a larger one. There's one massive tree trunk that spans the width of the larger one, over the deepest part, making it ideal for jumping.

I say I'm a masochist because *of course* I fucking knew Tait would wear a swimsuit, and that swimsuit would direct my attention to all the parts of her I am desperately trying to ignore. I want to be a good friend to the woman, really. I'd love to get extremely friendly, in fact. I want to get so fucking friendly that I lose track of where I stop and she begins.

Fuck.

But I know that if I pursued *that* now, it would be easy to make whatever it is between us all about sex, and I know that that's not what she deserves. Not in the midst of reacquainting with her family.

So yeah, I mean it. I want to be a friend. Which means that I should tear my eyes away from how her swimsuit bottoms have migrated, one cheek much more exposed than the other. I absolutely should stop wondering what it would be like to be on my knees behind her. To slide my hands up the back of her thighs, kneading them as I go, until I could sneak my thumb in and slide those bottoms all the way to the side, to see just a peek of her pussy.

That is probably a bit too friendly.

Thank God for Grady and his ability to monopolize a conversation. He's been yammering on, asking about what Tait's seen and taken pictures of so far . . . I've been unable to contribute much to the conversation. I'm darting between my attraction and the knowledge of just how much Tait needs a friend, how much I want her to take this time she has with everyone. I feel the need to show her the best of this place, in the hopes that she sees the best in the people here, too.

Her smile is beatific as she takes in the view, ignorant of my warring thoughts. She snaps multiple photos, some including me, but she thankfully doesn't ask me for any poses or faces. Eventually she lets out a little satisfied sigh, gingerly stepping over to her bag to put her camera away before she joins me in the upper pool.

"I never knew this was here," she says, quietly, and I notice how she can't seem to suppress a smile despite some obvious effort.

"Mmm? Yeah?" I say, because my brain lacks any more duality at the moment.

"Yep."

I nod, grateful for the water's cool temperature. Any other year, this would be far too cold for comfort. It's pure relief in this heat.

When she gets back up, my eyes snag on the crease where her upper thigh meets the front of her hip, and for the life of me I can't remember what that's called. Does that part of a woman even have a name? Hip cleavage? It's fascinating. And I'm tempted to punch myself in the balls so I can focus. I should feel sobered by today's information. Instead, I feel more urgency, and it's all centered around the woman walking across the tree trunk, laughing as she cannonballs into the pool below, splashing Grady and Caleb.

That's when it finally clicks in my thick skull. I really do need to hold off. To be a friend in the capacity she needs, but, regardless, in a non-distracting capacity. She needs the space to get to know this place and her family and I need to keep my dick in check. I blow out a breath when she gets out again, the sun throwing shimmering ripples off the water and making her seem even brighter than everything around her. I grind my teeth when I notice her nipples pebbled beneath her black bikini when she slides her thumbs down the sides of her bottoms to right them. I should probably get a medal for the effort it's going to take.

I get out and grab my phone, coming up with an idea that will provide both a buffer for me and an opportunity for her. Charlie texts back right away, freeing me to join Grady, Caleb, and Tait for a few more hours of fun.

We swim and float and mess around like kids, completely separated from the adult, outside world. We start a harmless game of Impossible Questions. I tell her about my friends on the Range, Duke Wade being the most recent, and a surprising one at that. A real, true-blue Texas cowboy who also acts.

Then there's Marshall, an advisor for the show, and also Duke's cousin, the far rougher of the two. We make loose plans to all go out sometime when they get back on set.

Grady falls asleep, lying on his towel as Caleb sleeps with his head resting on his back. I'm splayed against the warm stone and would be slipping off to sleep myself if Tait weren't here.

Her presence is a laser pointer; I am the cat. As much as I'd love to curl up in the sun for a nap, I can't seem to resist her pull.

"Do you mind?" she asks me, holding up a bottle of sunscreen.

"Seriously?"

"Uh, yeah. I take the UV index *very* serious, in fact."

"That is the most 'California' sounding thing I've heard you say." I snort. She laughs and sits in between my spread legs with her back to me, lifting her hair.

I swallow forcefully, squirting the sunscreen into my palms. It spurts out way more rapidly than I'd have guessed, and I end up with a small mountain of it. My hands hover above her shoulders helplessly, feeling the warmth radiating off of them even before they meet her skin.

"I didn't ask if you were serious in regards to the skincare aspect, Tait, and I think we both know that." *I meant are you seriously asking me to put my hands on you, knowing what it will do to me.*

We make eye contact over her shoulder, just as my hands land on her and I begin to rub. It would take nothing to pull her back to my chest, to curl my neck around hers and taste her lips. For a brief moment I see it on her face when she registers this, too. I think I hear the hitch in her breath.

And then I recall who she is, why she is here, and I reel it the fuck in, knowing that she will have to take the reins for this to go any further. I tear my focus away from her and put it to my hands, kneading and stroking and massaging. It takes way too fucking long—sunscreen mountain and all—so I'm not surprised when she jumps up and away as soon as I'm done.

"I'm starving, aren't you?" she practically yells, scaring Caleb awake.

"I could eat," I reply with a smile.

TWENTY-EIGHT

TAIT

Charlie rides up over the hill just as I've finished the last of my chicken and broccoli salad. I had been blissfully content: full, warm from the sun but easily cooled by the pool below, calm settled over me like a soothing blanket, despite the frenzy of sensations that had surged under my skin during the sunscreen application.

I only had myself to blame. I knew what I was doing to myself, finding a reason for Henry to put his hands on me like that. I'm certain he was on to me, too.

It'd taken a full meal, along with about twenty yards of separation for me to calm my senses. I was just settling back in to these new, warm, *comfortable* feelings, thinking about the other parts of the day, of the laughter and conversation, when Charlie's silhouette came into view.

He's on horseback with another horse tied at his side, saddle empty. The calm leaves my system because I can guess what his intentions are, and this feels bigger than it should already.

"Hey!" he calls out warmly as he dismounts, and I'm

putting my shirt and shorts on because no matter what, this obviously signals the end of our time here.

"Hi." I look back and forth at both horses' faces and wonder how you can feel elation and dread simultaneously. I *loved* horses as a kid. The feel of their soft, nuzzling, fuzzy lips on my palm was what I imagine my dementor-fighting, patronus-summoning memory would have been. I have never had the opportunity to ride or even to be near horses since we left here. It's simply never come about again.

"I figured we could take the chance to give you a refresher tonight?" Charlie asks, holding up the reins.

Have you ever thought about just how terrifying it is to ride an animal? First off, who had that thought initially and just went for it? Second of all, there is some manner of control in any motorized vehicle, no matter how fast or dangerous or powerful. There are brakes that are controlled by a driver. A steering wheel.

With horses, there are commands. Your safety is entirely dependent on that creature's willingness to abide by those commands. It's quite terrifying once you step outside of it and truly consider this.

And yet, I'm already lacing up my boots, because I know that I want to. Once I finish, I reach up and slide my hand down the horse's nose, letting him open and close his lips against my palm, letting the wistful feeling wash over me. I nod to Charlie and proceed to climb on . . . something I'm suddenly aware that I remember.

Once I'm settled, I look down at Henry. He's holding the reins with a poorly suppressed smirk. "Shit. I forgot to grab those on my way up, didn't I?" He just nods and hands them to me.

"I'll grab your camera and bring it back to your place," he

says, squeezing my calf before he turns away. I wave to Grady and Caleb before I look over to Charlie expectantly.

He gives me the quick refreshers on how to tell the horse you want to go left, right, forward, stop . . . "What's his name?" I ask, feeling rude and like I should offer an apology to said horse for hoisting myself onto his back before even making his formal acquaintance. Charlie laughs, seeming to understand my train of thought.

"This is Ace."

Ace is buckskin in color, with dark markings at the base of each leg, a dark muzzle, and a black mane. Gorgeous, powerful. And, even with that voice in the back of my mind reminding me that he might not be so impressed back, I feel . . . peace.

We slowly turn and climb, side by side with Charlie and his mount, my weight rocking gently back and forth with his steps, until we crest the top of the hill and I look down. Behind me is a view of the forest, below the safety of the pools, the river flowing off and into it. Before me is a vast valley, the pond with the two cabins off in the distance, the rest of the Range behind the ridge just beyond that. The few clouds cast peppered shadows all over the hillsides as the whole thing is bathed in golden hour light.

Charlie spends the time asking me questions. He asks about my time in high school, in college. He asks about the places I've been to for photography. He asks about Cole and about everything that transpired. Ace's steady steps create a rhythm that I fill with simple, truthful, and honest replies, never once feeling the need to hold back, or to check myself. I ask him about turning this into a guest ranch, about raising Grady. In turn, Charlie never holds back when I remark on how that would've been nice to have—a father so loving and invested. He just apologizes, again and again. We laugh at shared memories, and when each of us shares a new one that the other missed.

Hours later, when dusk has settled and we are back at the Range, after we've unsaddled the horses and put them in the stables for the night, Charlie hugs me again and tells me again how glad he is that I'm here.

"I'll never get the time back, I know, but I'd be honored if you'd let me be a part of your life going forward, Tait," he says.

I nod, smiling in agreement, because it's all I can manage when I feel as jumbled as I do.

I mentally promise myself, more than him, that I'll try.

Henry is outside the stables with a truck when we leave, ready to give me a ride home. We do so in silence, dark closing in rapidly. He doesn't ask how it went, not even how I liked riding again—which, I realize later, was likely because we didn't do any sort of challenging ride.

When we pull up to my house, he gets out and walks me up the porch, though not quite to the door.

"Breakfast again tomorrow?" he asks.

"Sounds good."

TWENTY-NINE

TAIT

This becomes our routine for the next two and a half weeks. It's eighteen days of golden hour.

HENRY AND I BREAKFAST TOGETHER at his place followed by him taking me somewhere for a few hours of shooting, each day with a new family member in tow—if not a few. Charlie and James alternate keeping the producer busy, and almost all of us manage to have dinner together every night. Emmaline retires before dinner on the days she hangs out, or comes for dinner on the nights that she doesn't. Duane is notably absent from almost everything. We all complain under the heat, but thankfully the evenings and mornings get progressively cooler despite the afternoon's refusal to relent.

The tension with Henry remains—I know he's caught me letting out the odd sigh when he does something particularly forearm-y, and I'd be lying if I said I haven't seen that jaw muscle tick whenever I wear my cutoffs, or feel his gaze when it wanders and lingers.

I've decided to let go of feeling suspicious of his kindness and have accepted his friendship with the view that goes with it. Every night, I make arrangements for whomever we plan to join or bring along the following day. It feels a *bit* like arranging for my own chaperones. And while each anecdotal story about him growing up lessens my resolve, I know that there was originally a good reason, at some point, to have needed those buffers.

On night one at the swimming hole, we start an ongoing game of Impossible Questions—sans the drinking and dares. I think we call it a game so we have an excuse to ask each other ridiculous questions, one-upping each other with their specificity. One of my personal favorite prompts comes from Henry; or rather, a radio show he heard once that asked listeners to design the seven circles of hell, made up of only inconveniences. So far, we've determined six, with some honorable mentions that we haven't nailed down.

In no particular order:

1. Watching SPCA commercials on a loop.
2. Filling out those "I'm not a robot" picture grids online, when the traffic light/bicycle/crosswalk has a tiny corner in another square and you can't tell if it counts or not.
3. Your car forever stuck next to a bad parker in the lot (apparently this is *huge* for Henry and happens a lot with his size. He often has to crawl through the passenger side).
4. Mosquito bites. Self-explanatory. An itch that can't be scratched is the *worst* kind of torture, after all.
5. Autocorrect and "ducking" (it is NEVER ducking).
6. Forever getting the feeling of needing to sneeze, but losing it right before. This was my proudest

contribution. He agreed this would be the most hellish misery we could come up with within these guidelines.

Honorable Mentions:

A) Ill-fitting shirts. Apparently, it's hard for him to find shirts that are long enough, while wide enough on the shoulders, but not TOO wide for his trunk area. I think this is a Henry problem and not list-worthy. *(Yes, yes . . . I did let loose a crack about how he could just go without, which earned me a wink that made me need to cross my legs aggressively.)*

B) Working up the courage to kill a spider, only to miss it. Henry was disappointed in my fear of spiders, but promised to come relocate the beasts should I find any at my place during my stay.

AT TIMES, THE QUESTIONS TURN more serious. He tells me about his mother's passing and his dad's incarceration—something he doesn't seem to have much, if any, resentment about. When I comment on that, he says, "Why would I? I got to grow up here. I've had more opportunities and privileges than most people get in their entire lifetime."

I want to remind him that letting go or setting aside something when he's not actually done with it might not be good, but then I realize it's different for him. He *can't* do anything else about his dad, can't form a new and better relationship with him when his father doesn't even want one; when their relationship prior was, objectively, shit.

I also want to tell him that he doesn't owe the Logans militant allegiance for his life. That he doesn't owe Charlie his *entire* life. That if he wants to find his own thing, seek his own way, he can and should . . .

But then the thought occurs to me that, when I did that, when I decided to go after something for just myself, it led to the dissolution of my marriage. I loathe myself for thinking it, because, logically, I know that's not all there was to it. I know that Cole made his choices, knowingly. But those feelings and insecurities that I've smothered rear up, telling me that maybe if I'd finished nursing school, not sought a career with travel and adventure and art . . . a career to define myself by . . . maybe if I'd stayed the girl that I was when we married, who'd *only* wanted family, stability, and calm, then maybe he wouldn't have fallen out of love with me.

Though, I don't mourn it, I realize. I don't wish it was any different, anymore. Henry's done that for me.

THE MORE MORSELS OF INFORMATION I get, the hungrier I am to know more about him—hell, about everyone.

I spend more time with Emma, and she brings me a series of articles she used to write for a local section of their newspaper. They were always about the ranch: the seasons, events they'd hosted here, recaps from town meetings, cattle and horses and even rodeos. I'm incredibly impressed with her writing—her ability to make even the mundane seem so interesting.

"Guess maybe the art genes run in the family, huh? Your photography is so good because you love it, too, you know," she says.

* * *

BUT WHEN IT COMES TO Henry, I can't seem to ask a weird enough, or random enough question, which he typically follows up with a more normal-adjacent one.

I THINK IT'S ON DAY four that I ask, "Who would you want to narrate your life in a movie?" To which he instantly replies, "Matthew McConaughey, you?"

"Leslie Jones. Do you want to work here forever?"

He quirks a brow at me, but responds in an obvious tone, "Yeah, I think I really do."

HE ASKS ABOUT AVA AND Jack, and I ramble on story after story.

He doesn't pry into my past, so I decide to leave his alone, still feeling a bit dirty for knowing the pieces that I do.

GAME OR NOT, IT'S THE most fun I've had in forever.

ON DAY FIVE, MY COUSIN Lucy shows up, declaring that she is taking the remainder of the semester off. LeighAnn supports it without argument, and my warmth toward her increases anew. Having Lucy here is as close as it could feel to having Ava here with me. She's a fast friend and ally, especially when it comes to ribbing Henry, and getting a rise out of Emmaline. She's convinced everyone to throw us a joint birthday party in a few weeks, for which she's booked a DJ, a full bar service, and a lighting company faster than I could say "whoa," and has resumed planning on a level more suited to a wedding than a family barbecue.

On day six, Duane asks me:

"What is it about photography? Don't get me wrong, your stuff is a different caliber, I'm sure, but isn't everyone their own photographer these days?" He holds up his phone in explanation. Emmaline and Charlie throw him such venomous looks that I immediately go into peacekeeping mode, answering without considering being offended.

"I get what you mean. And I actually think the premise behind professional photos and taking a selfie on your phone is kinda the same. It's wanting to stop time for a second and capture it, preserve it, make it something tangible. I guess for me . . . I've always felt a little like an observer. I think I've always been painfully aware of the fact that I'm not the main character?" I realize how bad that sounds, so I flail my hands and quickly continue, "Or at least, not the *only* character. What I mean by that is in no way belittling myself, but it's made me feel very watchful of what's around me, rather than always feeling like I'm the one being watched . . . if that makes sense.

"Taking a picture of something is my way of having my own bits and pieces of all kinds of things. And sure, it can make you cynical about lighting and angles and all that, but at its core it's being able to notice and see something that might otherwise go unnoticed or unappreciated. I think having a camera in my hand lets me find even the most mundane, suburban existence beautiful. Even people's daily grind and routines are beautiful, when you think about it; people just doing whatever it is they have to do to take care of themselves and each other, not for the recognition of it, just for what it is. We take pictures to preserve and stop time. So, I guess in a roundabout way, photography also helped me find myself, by shining a light on my own strengths and character. Pictures do a great job of making the ordinary come alive."

Henry's face is the first my eyes are pulled to, and I can't interpret his expression.

Lucy, being a gem, cuts the tension with a resounding, "Fuuuuuuuuuccckkkkkk. Welp, I'm going to need to take pictures of everything, now."

"How'd you get your 'big break' though?" Duane presses, finger quotes included.

"Luck, really. It was all luck." I shrug.

I don't miss the looks exchanged between Duane and Em again, and I feel bad for the man and the verbal whipping he's sure to receive later.

That night, Charlie asks if he can give me a ride back to my place. When he drops me off, he reaches across the truck to grab my hand, and says, "I am so sorry that you had to grow up thinking that just because you were observant enough to see what other people needed, that it was *your* responsibility to be considerate of that, or to ever put yourself second, Tait. I hope you can . . . I hope you can see yourself through our eyes, sometime, and see how beautiful and incredible you are, and see how much you have to be proud of—not just your work, although you should be so damn proud of what you do, sweetheart—but be proud of yourself, of *your* life."

In a wobbly voice, I say, "I really, truly am. I promise, Dad."

ON DAY NINE, HENRY INTRODUCES me to The Teskey Brothers, The New Basement Tapes, and vows to organize my music into *appropriate* playlists. I introduce him to Kacey Musgraves, *8 out of 10 Cats,* and make him promise to watch *Star*

Wars with me (since he has never seen a single movie). I talk too much about my air fryer.

For someone typically stingy with his words, I learn that he's easy to get babbling when it comes to gardening, desserts, and music.

ON DAY TEN, HE AND Grady bring me to meet the llamas that they use to help carry out equipment on hunts, and I understand why loving the creatures damn near becomes a personality trait for some people. I even let Henry take a few photos of me with them when he asks. He surprises me when he does so using his phone.

WE SPEND A FEW DAYS dedicating photography to all the animals in residence, as well as the wild ones.

We *finally* see the wild horses.

We see herds of elk, wolves, even bighorn sheep out across the land.

When I cry watching a barn cat give birth to kittens, Henry asks me why I don't have any pets. I brush it off with the explanation that I travel too much. When he continues to frown, I admit, "I look at dog shelters online when I'm back at home, every single day. It's my 'not porn.'"

His expression turns downright frightened. "Please unpack that sentence a bit for me, Tait."

"Everyone has their 'not porn' . . . a certain type of video or thing they have to look at online—something that's not porn, but still addictive—because it makes them feel something. Like, videos of soldiers coming home and surprising their families, or pimple-popping videos. I just don't think it would be fair for me to do the rescuing if I'm going to turn around and leave all the time."

ON DAY TWELVE, I ASK Henry what his favorite dessert is.

"I think it might be creme brûlée," he says with a smirk, but before I can question him further, he asks me what my favorite show is, which leads to discovering our shared love of *New Girl*.

ON DAY THIRTEEN, EM ASKS me to go with her to the nursery to buy some plants for around the property for fall. When we get back to my place, she startles me by jabbing into the bottom of the plant with a pair of shears and slicing through the dirt and roots. At my dumbfounded expression, she explains:

"When you buy a new plant, you often have to cut the roots when it comes out of the pot. That way, when you put it into the ground, the roots will reach outward, and it will thrive. If you left it in that plastic pot, in that compacted shape it's in, the roots would grow around and around in a tangled mass until it'd choke the life from itself. It would become too rootbound to grow."

CAST AND CREW START ARRIVING, with filming scheduled to start the following Monday. This is also when Charlie, James, and Henry are set to leave for ten days for a hunting trip.

I tell myself it will be good for me to have some distance from the attraction, to gather my wits like I haven't been able to since arriving here. But the truth is, I'm not really fooling myself: I'll miss him. I'll miss Charlie and James, even. Charlie and I seem to understand one another now at least, and whenever certain comments trigger my resentment, he takes his lumps in stride.

IT'S DAY SIXTEEN THAT THIS cozy little slideshow of moments I've been mentally compiling (probably set to something by The Beatles, complete with snapshots and slow-mo clips, if we were to get specific) comes to a screeching, skittering halt.

IT'S THE FIRST DINNER THAT Henry and I are left to on our own. Everyone else has plans—something I did not account for when I made enough taco meat to feed twenty. I don't know how to quantify portion sizes to begin with for cooking for more than one, but I stupidly assumed everyone would be free to join, being that it's a Friday night, and with the birthday party coming up on Sunday. I've only just finished shredding the meat when Lucy's text comes through.

Lucy: Sorry, meeting up with some friends in town tonight. Thanks for the invite, though!

Shit. I should just text Henry and tell him I'm not coming.

But, he was probably planning on tacos. I talked up my crockpot game already. It'd be an obvious cop-out at this point.

It's fine. We manage just fine during breakfasts, after all, and we've had so many conversations where the others fade to the background, anyway. It really should not matter.

Still, my chest starts to hollow out and feel like a windy

tunnel—of anxiety, nerves . . . excitement? This thing with us has begun to feel . . . inevitable.

My phone jolts on the counter and I jump, but answer when I see that it's the man in question.

"Hey," I say, overly bright, breathless.

"Hi. Just making sure you're not going to come up with an excuse to cancel on me." Even his stupid phone voice is full of that warm, deep timbre.

"What? Why would I do that?"

"Because you'll actually be alone with me again."

I suck in a deep breath, swallow. She must've let him know she was cancelling, too. "I'll head over in a few."

I hang up without a goodbye.

I TAKE EXTRA CARE WITH my appearance because damnit, if I'm going to be tortured, then so will he. I throw on my olive sundress because I like how it looks with my hair and skin tone. It's a wrap style, with short sleeves and vines in a pattern all over. It's a midi-maxi, but it opens up along the leg all the way above my mid-thigh, and the neckline is nice and deep. Sexy, yet understated. It wraps around my waist in the best spot.

It's only when I get there and knock, crockpot tucked unsexily under one arm (because how does one carry a crockpot without looking overly eager? Yes, this is how much I've worked myself up), that I realize the effort was futile compared to the raw sex appeal Henry has, *without* having to try.

He opens the door, looking freshly showered, in a solid black tee, soft-looking jeans, and yes, his damn bare feet again. His beard/scruff combo looks like it's been trimmed, but I thank Jesus, Mary, Joseph, and all their carpenter buddies that he didn't cut it entirely.

I wonder what that little beard burn he left on my chest weeks ago would feel like on the inside of my thighs . . .

Thankfully, his expression is also a bit wide-eyed, which gives me the confidence to stride in. He clears his throat behind me as I start setting things down and immediately go for a glass in the cupboard where I've learned he keeps them.

"New boots?" he asks, roughly. And I try not to squirm as I feel his eyes travel over me.

"Yeah, since you and LeighAnn have both pointed out that I needed some better shit kickers, I got them while I was out with Em."

"Attagirl."

Oh, fuck. I'm tempted to grab a tortilla from the package nearby and slap myself with it. An "attagirl" has me practically preening; I think one of my knees caves a little.

"Here, let me. Margarita?" He reaches to grab my glass from me as I turn around, unable to meet his eyes, yet.

"Y-yeah. That sounds perfect." *God, get a GRIP, WOMAN.*

"Tait?" He waits until I finally look at him. "You look beautiful. I really like your dress." He smiles. It's not his full, crinkly one; this one is a little more searching, those gold eyes assessing.

His hair already looks longer than when I first got here, a piece falling forward to rest along his jaw. I reach up to tuck it behind his ear before I can think better of it.

"Thanks," I say before grabbing my hand back with my other since she's apparently gone rogue. I scuttle out of the kitchen and around the island to put something between us.

"Sleep Walk" by Santo & Johnny is playing from somewhere, and though the melody doesn't take the sex out of the air, I desperately will it to calm my nerves.

He passes me my drink and says, "Question time?" Then, after I nod woodenly, "Why'd you get dressed up tonight?"

I scoff, instantly annoyed. He knows why. "You know why."

"Maybe I need you to say it out loud, though, just to be sure we are on the same page."

"Well, why don't you say what page *you* think we are on and I will confirm or deny."

He takes a gulp from his drink before setting it down a little too hard. "Tait. Please?"

I close my eyes. "It felt like this was . . . a date."

I open them to see him twitching that hard jaw again. "Honey, they've all been dates to me. I've just been waiting for you to catch up."

Oh.

And, instead of taking that opening, I jolt out of my chair, shove a tortilla chip in my mouth, and say (around said chip), "I—I gotta go to the bathroom." Damnit.

He smirks, but gallantly tries to hide it. "You really do have a thing for bathrooms, don't you?"

I stutter step down the hallway, ready to throw myself in. I fling open the door, and step into . . . confusion.

A hospital bed. An oxygen tank. An end table with a basket full of pill bottles.

The bathroom isn't in the same location as the one in my cabin. This is the converted room.

My mind starts spinning before I can stop it.

"What the fuck?" I say out loud.

"Tait?" Henry calls, and I hear him heading this way. I can't force myself to move fast enough to close the door and pretend my oversight never happened.

He comes to stand beside me, putting his hands on his

hips and looking down before I feel his gaze on the side of my face.

"Henry, when you talked about getting over someone by having them be dead to you . . . did you . . . um . . . did you mean that you have an ex that *actually* died?"

"Tait, no—"

"Because that's pretty fucked up. Were you just, like, mocking me mourning my cheating ex the whole time, meanwhile you actually *lost* someone?"

"Tait, what? No. I wouldn't compare loss like that anyways. Being left by choice isn't necessarily *easier*." He has the good grace to wince when he says that, at least.

"Jesus, Henry, are YOU dying?"

"TAIT. Let me explain this to you. Calm down."

"It's just weird that you never mentioned any of this, and that you kind of hid this room. Is this going to be some weird *Jane Eyre* thing? Do you have a hidden wife?"

He must realize that I'll continue to spiral out loud, so he shakes his head "no" to my badgering and approaches me like a skittish horse, eyeing me gently, silently, waiting until I breathe.

"Jesus, I'm insane," I say, starting to calm. "You don't owe me an explanation for any of this anyways. I—I'm sorry."

"Can we sit?" he says with a sigh. He looks so forlorn that I squeeze my hands into fists to prevent myself from reaching for the poor man and holding him.

Especially since that would directly contradict the self-righteous badgering I just subjected him to. I feel my face wince in embarrassment.

"My mother," he says as his intro. My eyes meet his. ". . . I know I told you she died. And she did. But I never told you . . . She left when I was three. Took off where no one could track her down, or at least my dad never tried to. Abandoned us to escape my father."

I think I hear my heart crack for him—this kind man, who probably seems like a cranky asshole to any outsider, but who *lives* for the ones he cares about. Grump he may be, but I'd love for him to be *my* grump. He's already become my favorite friend.

I have a friend again—friends, plural, I realize.

"I have to do this in bullet points and just fill in the blanks later, okay?" he says, and I nod. "Well, she—my mother—was dying. Ovarian cancer. And her caregiver, Gretchen, decided to track me down. Gretchen and I became close. She'd had a hard life, had grown up in foster care. She basically lived a parallel life to mine, but more the cautionary tale of what mine could have been if not for *your* family. Mom and Gretchen moved into that—your—place, but then we all started getting close, and Gretchen was staying here so much that we just decided it would be easier to spend the rest of Mom's remaining time together here. So that's when I set up that room. Remodeled so that her view was of the mountains. And my time with my mom . . . Our time was so short, I still am angry at myself. The first half of it I wasted, still resenting the hell out of her for leaving in the first place. And Gretchen . . . Gretchen bridged that gap. By the time my mom passed, seven months later, Gretchen and I were . . . engaged. I asked Charlie to find her somewhere on the ranch to work then, and he did for me. And . . . well, she . . . God, she fucking stole a ton of money from them, Tait. And, I should have picked up on it. I think she tried to tell me what she was doing, talking to me about where we could move, always talking about travelling—because she knew that was something I wanted to do, too—but she wanted to actually live abroad, move to another country, at least another state—someday."

"You do?" I ask, sad that I didn't realize this.

He frowns, confused. "Do what?"

"You want to travel?" I ask, sheepishly.

He sighs, running a palm over his face. "I'd love to see new places, but this is *home* for me, Tait. I need that to be clear. I . . . I love this place." He searches my eyes, waiting, so I nod my acceptance.

"And yeah, then she left. She either was setting up for the long con the whole time, or building her own parachute, knowing she wouldn't get me to leave. Charlie and Grace and the family wouldn't press charges or go after her without me, and I fucking couldn't do it. I didn't want to drag that shit out for a moment longer, and it was honestly fucking embarrassing. I'll never know if any of it was real, but I do know she helped me get that time with my mom.

"The only thing I was hung up on was that I wanted to make sure she wasn't some grifter trying to take advantage of other families with ill relatives. I hired a PI a few years back to make sure, and no, I guess she's part owner of a diner out in Rhode Island and used the money to set herself up with a hunky-dory life," he finishes.

"Henry . . ." Jesus, I really don't know what to say. I feel indignant for him. How could someone do this? Especially to someone with more loyalty and generosity in his pinky finger than five average adults put together.

"Sometimes when you ask things, I can see you pitying me, or thinking that I am oversimplifying my life by doing what I do here, Tait. The truth is, I've done my penance to myself for my choices, and while it's simple work and a simple life, I love it here. I love doing work with my hands, in beautiful country, and I love my family and friends. I love that it's not always the same.

"It's not experiencing an ancient culture, a castle in Scotland or the Dolomites. But it's my home, and I see you falling in love with it, too, Tait. Someone who's seen so much—even you can still appreciate it here. You might not be ready to admit that, but I'll be here when you are."

It's not this *place* I'm falling for, I want to tell him.

"I'm sorry that happened to you, Henry. I'm sorry that people can be so shitty," I say, instead.

"Do you think I'm pathetic for not pressing charges?" he asks after a pause, eyes searching again.

"I doubt I could ever find anything about you pathetic, Henry. But no, I definitely get it. I . . . I *gave* my ex our house because I wanted to flee the scene," I admit bitterly.

He smirks. "I guess you got taken for *way* more than I did, then." He chuckles, and I move to slap his chest. His hand closes over mine, holding it there. He takes a deep breath before continuing.

"I wish you could see how you glow. How you brighten a room every time you enter it. I can't imagine anyone, ever, losing sight of that with you. And I'm glad you're here, and that you're not wasting your time with anyone like I did. I hope . . . I hope you'll continue to."

And with that, I decide to waste no more time. I move in to kiss him, but he blows out a frustrated breath against my lips, cutting the kiss short. He plays with the ends of my hair as he stands, then walks to the other side of the table, smiling in the face of my frown.

At my puzzled expression, he says, "I think we both need to go ahead and eat and finish our drinks before we continue." And it's now that I can see the tension in his shoulders, his hands opening and closing on either side of his plate when he sits.

"We can eat and still sit by each other," I say, and I wish I could take back the needy tone to it.

He smiles, taking a massive bite of a taco. He chews methodically, and when he swallows I wonder if anyone else has ever found an Adam's apple so fucking sexy before. "You smell better than dinner, and I'd rather have you, Tait. So if you want to eat, I think it's best if I stay over here."

And there it is. Because who are we fooling at this point but ourselves? I want him, and I plan to have him.

The New Basement Tapes are playing now, singing about *when I get my hands on you* . . . The rhythm plucks in time with the building, nervous desire pumping in my belly.

I breathe in through my nose and out, slowly picking up my drink, finishing it in three gulps before setting it down thoughtfully.

"I think we might need to take the edge off first, Henry."

At that, he bolts up and kicks his chair back, and I follow a half second after. He stalks around the table, a predator covering the distance in three of his large strides, before we collide.

His hands grip under each of my ass cheeks and he lifts me, my legs wrapping around his hips at the same time that my hands fly to his hair, yanking his face to mine.

His lips and tongue crash into mine and it feels like I can finally breathe, despite him stealing my air. He makes a sound of relief when my hands fist against his scalp. When he separates an inch I bite his lower lip in protest. He hisses, then drags a ridiculously large palm up my side, sliding his thumb over my nipple through my dress, then into my hair to move my head and give him access to my neck. I catch his gaze when he looks down, falling forward a step. The slit in my dress has given way to one whole leg, up to one whole needy part of me crudely exposed, and pressed to him.

"Tait, are you not wearing underwear?" His dilated pupils fly to mine, black.

"What does it look like?" I say, not recognizing my own voice.

A deep, choked sound—maybe a growl—falls from him.

"Fuck. I want to see you." He swipes the vase off the table behind me and sends it flying, shattering against the nearby wall. I think I hear a small sound of alarm from Belle and hear her pad away as he leans us over, disentangling my limbs from him as he lays me on the table, and stands.

He looms over me, hair jutting out in different directions, lips swollen and wet, and I feel practically feral taking him in. I make no attempt to adjust my dress, knowing there's no turning back now, especially as I notice the wet spot on his shirt.

No more thinking. No games right now. I part my knees and let him look his fill. His grip on my thighs tightens unbearably for a moment before his eyes find mine.

"God, look at you."

"It's Tait, actually, but feel free to worship all you'd like." I gesture down the length of me, because I'm apparently incapable of not injecting humor at the worst times. He smiles, though, and I might just become *his* zealot in that moment instead.

"This dress makes you look like a present just for me, honey." He slides his hands slowly up my thighs, up my ribcage, palming my breasts appreciatively once before meeting in between. He slides his splayed fingertips under the edges of the fabric, eyes still locked with mine. "Can I unwrap you?"

"Yes, please."

He slides the sides apart, those rough fingertips just barely grazing the tops of my breasts as he reveals them. He groans painfully, then floats that same light touch over my nipples. I'm panting at this point and biting my lip with the effort not to squirm.

The cadence of my breathing should feel embarrassing, but Henry unwrapping me peels away the veil on my desire, on his, every warm moment between us stoking this heat that's broken loose.

"Now, ladies. You'll have my attention again soon enough, but I have been thinking about this pussy for far too long, now," he says to my chest, staring at me like I'm something miraculous.

Wait—"Are you talking to my tits?"

"Shhhh, we're in the middle of something," he admonishes, placing a finger over my lips.

I bark out a giddy laugh, the motion making me bounce, and his playfulness disappears. He swallows once. Twice. Then clenches his jaw and closes his eyes.

"Fuck. I am overstimulated."

"I'd like to be," I tease, and it has the intended effect. He smiles again and huffs a laugh. I feel the warmth of it in my very bones.

"I got you, honey." He slides his palms over my tips one more time, making them impossibly harder, tighter, causing me to groan once before he quickly plants a sucking kiss on both. He then drags me down the table, kisses the inside of my knee, and hooks my booted foot over his shoulder, exposing me entirely.

"Fuck, Tait. This pussy is so pretty." He runs the backs of two fingers up my seam, and I whimper, wondering how long he plans to make me wait until he touches me where I need it most. The answer is not long. He splays his palm across my pubic bone and thumbs my clit lovingly.

The way he watches, studies, and marvels as he touches me is filthy, perverse . . . like he is getting as much out of it as I am. He dips his thumb and drags more wetness up, circling, moving back and forth lightly across the tip, my nerves flooding with sensation at every swipe.

He twists his hand then and slides a finger into me slowly as he tears his gaze back to my eyes. His stubble scratches the inside of my knee. He shakes his head ruefully even as he gives me another crooked smile. "Ah, honey. This is gonna be a tight fit."

I feel heat surge to my face and gather, then ripple out through my core. Oh, God, I fucking hope. "Yes."

My eyes roll back in my head as he puts my foot back down on the table and hooks a second finger into me, thumbing my clit all the while, kneading my thigh with his free palm. My many daydreams of his massive hands pale in comparison to this.

"I can't count how many times I've thought about this, Tait. Is this really happening?" he says, echoing my thoughts. His free hand squeezes my knee and I realize he wants me to respond.

"Fuck, if it's not then it's the best dream I've ever had." I moan, long and hoarse as he drags his fingers down my inner wall along a sensitive spot.

"Good girl, there it is." Shit, that mouth on him sends a fresh wave of lust over me, and then that same mouth licks my clit as his fingers continue to pump and drag.

My back arches off the table and I prop up onto one elbow so I can watch what he does to me, winding my fingers in his hair with my other hand and grinding against his face shamelessly. That feeling begins to build, each lap of his tongue in time with that drag against that inner sensitive spot, piling on one another until I'm gyrating and trembling with need to come.

I register his arm at the corner of my vision, forearm muscles working as he adjusts himself then, absent-mindedly rubbing himself to what he's doing to me, and my blood sings, rushing.

I whimper, cresting that edge but not falling time and time again. "I'm sorry, this—this is taking too long."

He doesn't chuckle, just meets my gaze with his hazy one, and says, "Baby, I'm determined to finish a meal once tonight, I don't care how fucking long it takes." My eyes shutter, but fly back open to his impaling gold ones as he sucks the whole bud of me into his mouth, the effect like pulling loose a lever that frees my orgasm.

The wave crashes over me, sensation exploding down my limbs, and then thumping back up and through me. When I try to pull away, over-sensitized, he places a perfectly pressured kiss to my apex while pushing that button from the inside again, and it crashes anew.

I scream out as the second orgasm pumps out of me brutally.

I come back down to earth to find Henry cradling the back of my head, planting tender kisses to the corners of my panting mouth, to the tears that have leaked out of the corners of my eyes to slide down my temples.

"God. Oh . . . Oh my god," I whisper.

"It's Henry, actually, but feel free to worship all you'd like." And his smile is everything, all dimples and stubble and wet beard, swollen lips and flushed cheeks.

I laugh like a cartoon mental patient again, sated beyond sanity. "I might have to," I say, and I might mean it. It's the reverence on *his* face that ignites me again, though, so I drag his face back to mine and kiss him deeply. "Take me to bed?" I ask.

"You don't want me to feed you first?"

"No, Henry, I want you to fuck me."

I swear I see his pupils dilate again. He drags my body off of the table and tosses me over his shoulder, my dress barely hanging on to any part of me, and I can't stifle a giggle as he runs us up the stairs.

THIRTY

HENRY

There's a race going on inside my chest. That's the only explanation for this feeling. It's a marathon, one I began running the moment I watched Tait Logan descend the escalator at the airport. One that's picked up the pace over the last few weeks, galloping to a finish that I hope is just a beginning.

Just being in her atmosphere is addicting. She's funny, she's smart, witty, moody. Hell, she's got a labyrinth of a mind and working my way through it is how I'd like to spend my days.

She pulled back before on us physically, sure. But now, instead of just knowing I'd love to get in her pants, to be her friend . . . Now I fucking *know* I want into her soul. She's crawled beneath my skin, tattooed herself onto me with her wacky laugh, her kindness, her damn goofiness. She feels inevitable to me, and I have the desperate need to make her feel the same. To prove to her that this, whatever the hell it is between us, is worth seeing more of.

I hurry us up the stairs, taking them two at a time, and into my room. I note how small she feels compared to me, thrown over my shoulder like this. Yet every moment she's come to mind over these weeks, I've realized how very abundant she has always seemed, in so many ways. A force in the form of curves and edges, humor, warmth, and heart. And *that* poetic thought has me pausing a step.

Back to the business at hand, Henry.

I've paid special attention to her gorgeous tits finally, but damnit if her ass hasn't made me want to put my head through a wall for the last few weeks, too. I feel like an evil pirate, hauling my wench away with despicable plans, fucking giddy at the prospect of unraveling her further. I indulge myself with a smack on that ass, earning me a squeal.

When we get to my room, and I settle her on her feet, I have to remind myself to breathe again. Take this slow. Drag it out and savor it.

I take a step back to take her in, her pretty dress entirely open and hanging from her shoulders. Before I can move to do it, she steals my breath by sliding it off completely, letting it pool around her feet. Damn, I love that confidence. I clench my fists at my sides, desperately wanting to be everywhere at once. Her eyelashes flutter, the same desire reflected in the flush on her cheeks. The gold glint of her earrings matches the flecks in her eyes and in the eyeshadow stuff she's put on her lids and—fuck—I'm noticing her eyeshadow now. I'm a goner.

She keeps her eyes locked on mine when she slides her hands under my shirt and up. I'm too tall for her to reach to pull it off, so I finish that for her.

I watch her, chest rising and falling, as she undoes my jeans—the sound of the zipper sliding down blaring through the room. I thank God that the moon is full tonight, shining through all the windows and casting her in enough light for me to see her so clearly.

I'm vaguely aware of Eric Church singing from downstairs, and I smile because I can't think of anything more accurate than wanting to rock some sheetrock and knock some fucking pictures off the walls with this woman.

My jeans slide down, and her wide-eyed expression at the strained state of my briefs makes me feel like a Neanderthal. No more games. I don't feel self-conscious over my physicality, no matter how perfect she is. Determination surges, and I walk her backwards toward the bed, refusing to break eye contact as I lay her down.

Before I can drop to my knees in front of her, she surprises me by placing one booted foot on my abs, giving me a front row peek of her glistening, swollen pussy, causing an actual growl to rumble out of me.

"Take these off?" she asks with a naughty smile, flicking her eyes to the boot.

I apparently can't manage words yet—Neanderthal-mode firmly engaged—but I oblige, peeling it off with the accompanying sock, nipping her ankle before she drops it and props up the next.

I let myself take her in briefly as she comes back up onto her elbows, her wavy hair floating wildly around her shoulders. She looks at my briefs and licks her lips, and it feels like my dick literally jumps, carrying me to stand between her legs.

"Tait . . . fuck." I reach for the nightstand drawer, pulling out a condom when she traces a hand up the outline of my cock, and says, "I'm on birth control, haven't had sex in a year, and am clean."

My eyes fly to hers. They look vulnerable, and I'm gutted by the expression. "I'm clean. It's been about six months, despite what I know you overhead from Grady. I can show you my bill of health if you'd like."

"I trust you."

THREE WORDS.

Three fucking words and my world is changed. She could have said those other three words in that moment and I don't think even they would have been as impactful. Trust is a conscious decision . . . the heaviest decision in my book.

I bend to push my forehead to hers, her hands holding mine as I stroke the sides of her beautiful face.

I nod, swallowing past the lump in my throat, then straighten, cupping her jaw to have her look in my eyes. "Thank you. I trust you, too."

She beams at me, then slides her hands to my waistband, swiftly pulling down my briefs and freeing me.

"Jesus Christ!" she exclaims.

"There you go, again. Woman, it's Henry. Hen-ry."

She smirks, but before I can laugh at my own joke, she squeezes me, running her hand up and swiping her thumb through the precum beaded at the tip that I can't bring myself to be embarrassed about.

Before my vision can get a chance to clear, she leans forward and swipes her sweet tongue between my balls. The world goes white, and I let out a choked, very smooth, "Ahfuckshit."

A few moments and inches in her hot mouth tell me that this won't be conducive to me lasting long, so I cup her jaw and bend to kiss her again.

"Honey, I gotta come in you for the first time."

"Who says that wasn't my plan?" she says up at me. Lust blackens my vision for a second.

"Keep talking like that and I won't be able to go gentle, Tait."

"Promises, promises."

"Fuck."

I tip her onto her back and guide myself to her entrance with trembling hands. I push in a few inches, and fuck. She's hotter, tighter, wetter than anything I could have dreamt of, and I tell her as much. Her hands slide up my chest as I retreat, hooking her knee around my hip before I push in further. She lets loose a sigh, and smiles in that way that stops my heart. She steals the words from my mouth then, saying, "You're beautiful."

It overexcites me, and I thrust harder, just shy of all the way in. Her face looks pained for a second before she relaxes around me. "God, Tait. Baby, it's the best. It's so good, love. So tight." I kiss the corners of her eyes, holding as still as I can so I can get my bearings. We rock and grind, push and slide until I'm fully seated, eventually pulled all the way by her as I have been in all ways.

I murmur to her, all the things I love, eating up every sound and sigh and whimper, grinding against her until she's moaning incoherently. I can't look away, willing her to read my mind and every thought, willing myself to memorize every expression she makes. She keens out my name and I become an animal, sliding us down the bed to the edge where I can stand. I fling her leg over my shoulder and slide a pillow under her, propping one of my knees on the bed to angle the way I notice elicits little grunts of need.

I see it play out in slow motion as her eyes roll back, her hair fanned out across the bed, her tits bouncing, body covered in a sheen of sweat. Her wrists are bound by my one hand above her, my other splayed across her belly as I touch her. She says my name when her pussy starts to contract around me, and I have the clear thought that this, this right here, is what I pray plays through my mind when I kick the bucket. I want this to be the last thing my mind remembers before I die.

The realization unravels the last of my control and I start pounding into her, the sounds of our bodies smacking together echoing. I come on a strangled sound that I can't withhold, my orgasm starting from the top of my skull, shooting through the base of my spine and taking a piece of my soul with it.

I STARE DOWN AT HER in awe, petting her lovingly as I pant. She turns to kiss my palm, and I don't know why, but it chokes something in me. I cover my expression by bending down to kiss her, sliding out of her regretfully. I can't manage words yet, so I go get supplies from the bathroom and tend to her, cleaning her up with a warm wet towel before wiping everything with a dry one. The sight of me on the insides of her thighs brings out the caveman in me again, and I wonder how long she'll smell like me, and I like her.

We can't seem to stop touching after that, but I worry that sharing what I'm thinking will just scare her at this point, so I tuck her back to my front after a bit, putting her safely under my chin.

"Impossible question?" she asks me, quietly. I nod against the top of her head. "Was that the best sex of your life, or . . . ?"

I push her shoulder down to turn her to me. "Tait, I'm

back here writing sonnets in my head about it. Yes, that was the greatest sexual experience of my entire life." *Also, how do I keep you? Is it way too soon to feel like this? I think you're my soulmate and I never thought that was a real thing before I met you. You've turned my thoughts into an endless stream of cheesy romcom lines that are somehow applicable and understandable now. You had me at hello.*

She laughs, and I laugh back, both sounding worn.

Outside, it begins to rain.

The last thing I remember before sleep takes me is kissing her shoulder, smelling her jasmine scent.

SOMETIME IN THE NIGHT I wake up to her mouth and hands and the curtain of her hair dragging down my front. My cock surges, hard to the point of pain. My eyes find hers just as she takes me in her mouth.

She peppers kisses along my shaft in between words of praise. "Sweet. Sexy. Beautiful. Generous man."

"Stealing my lines, Tait . . ."

SOMETIME LATER, SHE SLIPS BACK to sleep easily, but it evades me. I stare at her peaceful face, mentally walking myself through the last few weeks until we got here, stifling the odd laugh when certain moments come to mind.

She's here, wrapped in my sheets, peaceful, beautiful. An angel, so sure of herself in so many ways, except in this—in trust, in letting herself be seen and loved, in letting herself love something back. The woman won't even let herself have a pet, despite how she tears up over the love of an animal. And she chose me. At least she chose me to trust, and whether or not she realizes this bit yet, it hits me that I know I love her.

The feeling is nothing like the unfurling of a rose, nothing like the tentative, slow burn I recall.

It's like busting open a can of biscuits.

I know the feeling's there, I know what's going to happen every time I acknowledge it, but it shocks me nonetheless.

I should be scared about making myself vulnerable again. I really should. We live in different states, for fuck's sake. And even though I can see she belongs here, and I know that I do, I also know that she's in for a hairier turn in this journey, in finding herself again. I know it would be easier to let go.

I know she'll question this every step of the way, and the last thing I want to be is another hardship for her. How do I make her see, though? Am I man enough, or patient enough to give her the space to go through this on her own? To support her, reassure her, even when she inevitably tries to close me out? Will she even let me? I want to fix all of it for her, to imprint how I see her into her brain, to blow up that image so large that it leaves no room for doubt.

THIRTY-ONE

TAIT

Sex with Henry is . . . *more*. So much more than my dirty little imagination was capable of. There are more orgasms, sure . . . but there's also more laughter, more words—God, so many words of praise, more touching, more tasting.

The rain and our needs are relentless through the night, with sleep scattered in between tangled limbs. I woke up at some point in the night to get a glass of water from his bathroom—which, I can happily report is yet another lovely one. But when I saw him approach me from the reflection in the mirror, all thoughts of hydration fled.

He bent me over the cool counter, fucked me from behind while his eyes never left mine in the mirror. I remember the way he lifted my hips, the way his knees bent to the backs of mine as he lowered and as I went on my toes so we could align, the furrowed, determined expression on his face and his praise as I came apart around him.

"So fucking good, honey. God, look at you. So fucking beautiful when you come. I'll never get enough of you. Do you know that?"

I open my eyes to a still dark sky in the early hours of the morning when I feel him reach for me again, kissing slowly down the column of my spine. He gets to my lower back and groans.

"Do you know you have two dimples in your lower back here?" he asks against my skin, his voice husky in the morning, making my face smile into the pillow and my toes curl.

He kisses them with smiling, wet, open-mouthed kisses, and I discover a newly sensitive spot, the sensations bleeding from where he kisses down through my center.

"Mmmm, the only way this wakeup call could get better is if you let me sip coffee while you do this," I say.

He chuckles. "I'm offended that you think you'll have the focus for coffee sipping," he mumbles, kissing over to the other side. "Besides, we have all day to sleep. Can't set up for the party until this rain lets up, anyway." He kneads my backside as he runs his tongue back up to my shoulder blades and a little moan escapes me.

"And . . ." He suddenly whispers deeply in my ear, and I gasp. "Coffee is brewing."

I moan a breathy, pornstar-worthy, *"Yesssss!"*

At that he rumbles a low laugh, deftly flipping me over and beaming down at me. My breath hitches at the sight before me. Knees on either side of my hips, pinning me down, his massive body in all its glory in the gray morning light. There's nothing groomed about him; the whorls of hair on his massive chest trail down his hard abdomen (not exactly a six pack but defined and chiseled by work and use, with prominent obliques) to between his legs, and oh—I like that. I like that I can't imagine him taking the time to worry about grooming, or working out for aesthetics, just for what his body does for him. The dull ache between my thighs reminds me of all that body has done for me already. His cock nudges above my belly button as he leans over. "Eyes, up here, Tait." I watch in fascination as he begins to harden under my gaze, and because I can't help myself, I reach for him. He hisses, moving to kiss me, but I slap my palm over my mouth, dropping him to slap heavily against my belly. "Mrningbrth," I say beneath my hand.

"I don't care, Tait," he says, trying to pry my hand away.

"Nnnno!" I try to shout as he feigns a struggle.

"Has anyone ever told you that you are deceptively strong?" He laughs, but then easily flicks my hand away, pinning it to the bed. I clamp my mouth together.

"Let's have it, then."

I shake my head back and forth as he continues to bend closer and closer.

"Come on, honey, let's just get it over with. I'm dying to find out if this is your second flaw."

That gets me. "What's my first!?"

"Ha, gotcha. Oh, okay it's not great, maybe I have a spare toothbrush." I thrash underneath him, indignant, even as he laughs and kisses my re-sealed mouth.

"Asshole!" I spit out, and he bites my lip.

"Ooohh, feisty, are we?" He laughs all out as I try to breathe through my nose. Eventually I tire myself out—I'm running on fumes in terms of sleep here—and he kisses me.

I let him, but decide I just want to feel fresh anyway. I'm sticky from sweat and tongues and all manner of filthy, wonderful things, and I probably smell as such. "Really, though, I need my toothbrush, and a shower, Hen."

"But it's raining, Tait." He pouts adorably.

"Henry . . ." I try for my firmest, warning tone.

"Alright, alright. But no clothes. I'll drive you to your

place really quick and back . . . then, we'll put that bathroom you've been dreaming about to good use."

I feel my eyes and smile grow as we get up. I can't stop a squeal, kissing his cheeks before he stands all the way up. He turns, granting me the most perfect view of his ass as he heads to his dresser, firm and full above strong legs dusted in wiry hairs. And then I catch sight of him from behind—heavy, thick, and long, and my insides clutch around emptiness.

But then he pulls on some sweats and I busy myself fashioning the sheet into a toga of sorts. Before I move to do it, he bends to a knee and slips on my boots for me, one at a time, and I wonder how he's managing to make me blush with this simple gesture, despite seeing every inch of me already.

"Wait . . .," I hear myself say.

He looks up at me, all bedhead and strength, and I feel like an insane woman but I have to have him again, right now.

My face must read like an open book because without saying anything or breaking eye contact, he parts my sheet-toga and slides one long finger through my folds.

"One more, but then we need to eat and caffeinate before you turn into a real monster." He smiles up at me as he slides his finger in. I groan, letting my head fall back and eyes close again, tender and swollen and so sweetly sore.

He works me over slowly with that one finger, and I catch sight of him palming himself through his sweats, the outline of him impossibly hard again . . .

BANG.

BANG. BANG.

BANGBANGBANGBANG

"Tait! Are you in there?!" calls a familiar, faraway voice.

I feel the color drain from my face as Henry slips out of me. "What the fuck?" I say.

Fun fact: Hurrying down stairs sounds simple enough in theory, but it's actually hysterical and awkward, and painfully slower than you'd imagine. Especially when sharing those stairs with a giant, tightening a toga, and adjusting sweats accordingly. The slap, slap of our feet on the steps echoes as the seconds last hours.

"Stay here," I hiss-whisper.

"I think not," he says, clearly trying to protect me. "It's my house," he adds.

"Please," I plead.

He frowns down at me, standing on the bottom landing, but nods. I kiss his arm for reassurance . . . mine or his, I'm not sure.

BANGBANGBANG

"Goddamn it, Tait, it's pouring out here, let us in!"

Us?!

Finally, I make it to the door, and take a deep breath before I crack it open.

Lucy's face comes into view first, sporting a wince. Then Grady's, trying (and failing) to hide a smirk.

Lastly—"Ava? What the hell?"

THIRTY-TWO

TAIT

Ava shoves past me, followed closely by Grady and Lucy. All three of them freeze to stare up at Henry.

Ava's stormy expression immediately dissolves, replaced by a hysterical smile. "And who is *this?*" she exclaims with a delighted smirk.

Miffed by her initial indignation, my knee-jerk reply is, "Nobody. What the hell are you doing here?"

The expression returns. "I think the better question is what the hell are *you* doing here? You promised you would call me weeks ago, Tait. Enough is enough, let's have this out like grown-ups," she says, and I feel myself start to stiffen in rage.

"How *dare* you. You've got some nerve, Ava."

"I *do?!* What about *you?!*"

"*I'm* not the one who hid that I already had a relationship with all of them, Ave. You let me be the last to know. You want to talk about being a grown-up, well, *you first.* You know you hid that shit from me on purpose."

She sniffs, folding her arms and looking down. "I wanted that choice to be about me, not about how it would make you feel, Tait. I'm sorry if that hurt you, but there's always been so much that does not make sense about this, and I wanted to know the rest of my—*our*—family."

"I don't care that you wanted a relationship with them, Ava. I cared that you lied to me, that you hid things from me."

"As if you wouldn't have judged me for it. You're so self-righteous, Tait. You're so closed off to anyone and anything that might hurt you that I knew you would have resented me for it!"

"YOU DIDN'T EVEN GIVE ME THE CHANCE!"

At this, Lucy steps in. "Ladies, let's just . . . take a breath here. Tait . . . uhhh, do you want to change, perhaps?"

I'm tempted to say no, to stomp my feet and tell everyone to fuck right off, but then I remember that I'm wearing Henry's bedsheet.

"I'll take you home, Tait," Henry says. "The rest of you can help yourselves to coffee. There're some Danishes in the fridge and anything else you want." He grabs a T-shirt from his laundry room and swiftly guides me out the door.

The short truck ride over is silent, and I'm grateful.

It's when we get inside that I notice the solemn look on his face, and my brain plays back what I said. "Henry, I didn't mean that you were nobody. I just was . . . caught off guard."

"Tait, I'm a grown man. I don't care about that; I don't actually care what you tell your sister about us right now because I know what we are. I just . . . I've never been around sisters. I didn't know how, uh . . . I guess I'm a little taken back by how volatile you guys were back there." He half smiles apologetically, scratching the back of his neck, and I chuff out a laugh.

"You have no idea. That was nothing. She jumped out of my moving car once because I wouldn't let her borrow a sweater, but she had just lost my favorite pair of earrings! She called me a 'stuck-up, sour-faced bitch' and told me I smelled like cabbage. Then she bolted out of my car before I could take a swipe at her."

I really laugh, then, at his horrified expression. "I take it Grady never chased you around with a knife?"

"What?! No. Oh my god, you did that?!"

"Hey! I resent that assumption. She did that to me! And that's actually a very common sibling rite of passage."

"Aggravated assault with a weapon is *common* among siblings?"

"Not the actual assault part, just the threat of it."

"Ah, okay. Should I get back and hide the sharp objects?"

"No, just make sure *I* know where the best ones are."

He sighs. "Tait . . ."

"I know, I know. I'll just go shower."

I'M TEMPTED TO ASK HIM to shower with me, but I sense that I should use the time to sort out my thoughts. Instead of doing that, though, my brain starts doing this wonderful thing: oscillating back and forth between thoughts of him and last night, and violently pivoting back to Ava being here. By the time I get out of the shower, I feel a disturbing combination of annoyed and happy that my sister is here, and then horny over Henry again.

Yikes. The dam is broken and I'm feeling all my feelings rush at once.

I change into some leggings and a long-sleeve Lycra top, seeing through my window that the sun has broken the cloud cover. I catch my reflection on my way out and notice the smile I can't seem to suppress, despite my annoyance.

I know I need to get things sorted, to manage my own expectations, Henry's, and to keep my thoughts and feelings in check. To build a castle in the sky here would be a terrible, terrible mistake. But also, fuck it. I've got a few weeks to feel these good things again, and I want to just feel them, unapologetically.

Maybe that's why Ava's presence here feels so annoying. I am not happy that she lied, no, but I've enjoyed getting to know everyone too, so her lie of omission hasn't had any true negative consequences. Her presence is just a reminder that my reality exists outside of here, though, and maybe I don't want that . . .

"Henry?" I call out as I come around the corner of my room. "I just realized something—what's your middle name?"

But when I get to the stairs, it's Ava on the couch waiting for me, not him.

"Sorry to disappoint," she says with a knowing smirk. "But I bet it's something *über* manly, like Buck, or John-Wayne, or Major, or something."

I reply with an eyebrow lift.

"Sorry," she says.

"It's fine. I need to make some coffee really quick before we get into it, though."

"Henry already brought over his whole pot—or what was left of it, at least, after the rest of us got to it," she says, cocking her head curiously to judge my reaction. "He grumbled something about yours being garbage before he left."

"Oh. That was, uh . . . nice of him."

"Can't we just *start* with him, and then have out the rest after?" she whines, letting her arms fall to her sides.

"Ava, no. And not another word until I get some coffee,

please," I say, but I feel my lips pull up more as I head to the kitchen.

Properly armed with caffeine, I head back out to the couch and sit. After a deep breath, I ask her to go first.

"I'd been wanting to talk to you for a long time about it, but I kept chickening out whenever it came up in conversation and I just didn't know how to approach it. You always seemed to understand Mom a little more than I did, and while I've long since forgiven her, I just don't see why we weren't more encouraged to have a relationship with our father as kids, Tait. Since having Jack, that feeling has only intensified. I don't think there's anything Casey could do to me for me to not let him have a relationship with Jack. It'd be different if he did something to *him,* I guess, but Dad never did anything to me, Tait, to either of us. And we have a whole family here. I have my family and Casey's parents, but . . . Well, I guess that's why I didn't tell you. I felt greedy with wanting more. You'd lost your whole family when everything happened with Cole, and you just . . . caved in on yourself. So then when I started having a relationship with everyone, I didn't want you to feel like the one who was left out. I just started connecting to some of them through social media. It was really just Grady. Well, I guess LeighAnn also. And Lucy. And yeah, I wrote back to Dad's letters, but you knew that already, Tait." She finally looks up at me with watery eyes. "I'm so sorry I hurt you, though."

"It's okay. I think . . . I think you were right in wanting to get to know them. They're all pretty great. This place is pretty great." I sigh. "And I'm sorry I left you hanging for so long. I think I wanted to punish you, but I took it too far. I hope you didn't have to take time off of work, Ava."

"I did, but it's well worth it, and it's only a week. I'm here to celebrate your birthday, too."

"Oh, shit. I have to help Lucy set up. She's invited all the cast and crew from the show and they've got a huge tent and everything," I say, and move to get up in a panic.

"They hired people, Tait, it's fine. Please, sit with me. Tell me everything."

I hug her, then, because I have missed her. I let a few tears fall and so does she, but since we pride ourselves on not being overly mushy (we absolutely are) I sit back in a flourish, moving my coffee farther onto the table and away from the danger of my flying hands as I launch into it all . . .

"I'M JUST . . . I'M REALLY GLAD I came," I finish.

". . . Oh my god," Ava says, and she starts to cry.

"Ave, what the hell? What's wrong?" But then I see her laughing as she cries.

"You just . . . you sound, and look, like *you* again."

"Don't be so dramatic." I laugh back.

"No, Tait, really. I just have been so worried that the opposite would happen, you know? That all this would make you want to shut down and shut out more. But you're out here living life like a Tim McGraw song!"

I roll my eyes. "Stop."

"I mean, it literally sounded like that. You were all 'I went four-wheeling, I went Rocky Mountain hiking, I went—2.7 seconds—in a pond with Cowboy Thor,'" she sing-songs, badly.

"I'm truly impressed that you made that up actually. I can't even be mad."

"Tait, I'm really happy that you're scoring with hot Henry

over there, but I do have one piece of advice for you . . .," she says, ominously, and I nod for her to proceed.

"Always stay humble and kind." We explode, laughing so hard that tears are streaming down both our faces, until I hear the gravel crunching under tires outside.

"Oh my god," I say, "I have a good idea. Stay right there and follow my lead!"

I hop over to the kitchen and grab what I need, schooling my face into an appropriate expression. I hear boots hurry up the steps, and I can tell it's Henry by their heaviness alone. When I hear that he's close, I scream, "HOW DARE YOU!! GET THE FUCK OUT!!"

"NO, TAIT, NO!!! DON'T!!!!" Ava screams back.

Henry bursts through the door, pale and terrified when he sees me wielding the knife at Ava. He instantly hurls himself at me, but I drop it on the counter and snort out a laugh, followed by Ava. "We totally got you!" I laugh, pointing. But his expression remains. My laughter dies in the ether between us.

"IT'S YOUR GRANDMA. SHE'S IN the hospital."

THIRTY-THREE

"She fell," Charlie says when he sees me in the waiting area. "Knocked herself out on the way down, lost a lot of blood, but she's already spitting mad and trying to leave, so I'm sure she'll be just fine." I hug him, then, because he's as white as a ghost himself, and because despite his levity, he's clearly worried.

"I'm just glad she was at our house when it happened. You need to talk to her about moving in soon, Charlie," Grace says, and it's firmer and more irritated than I'd have guessed coming from her.

Emergencies bring out those differences in people, I suppose. Some thrive in chaos—their focus and calm sharpen; and some crumble—that panic ricochets out onto whoever's closest.

I don't expect, nor can I make sense of either reaction when they take notice of Ava behind me, though. Charlie grows impossibly paler, and Grace's brow crumples in confusion, devastated.

"Hi," Ava says, and it's clear by her timid tone she's noting the same reactions and interpreting them the same way—not happy.

"I called her," Henry says, and my head whips around to him. "She has a right to know what's going on with Em. They both do."

"What is he talking about, Dad?" I ask, my tone rising with the dread filling up my chest.

Charlie sucks in a deep breath, chokes on it, and looks up at Henry. "You should have talked to us, first."

To his credit, Henry doesn't back down, or even flinch. "She shouldn't have to miss out on time with her. They both should know. And clearly, I reached out just in time."

Grace speaks up, then. "You know I agree with you, Henry. But this wasn't for you to tell. It wasn't up to any of us, this was Em's choice."

Henry looks over at me, and I see the conflict there, something warring with the sadness in his expression. And then his words from the night before come back to me.

And I'm glad you're here, and that you're not wasting your time with anyone like I did. I hope . . . I hope you'll continue to.

His eyes stay intent on me as he grabs my hand, and I try to read what he's so clearly trying to convey. And then Duane and LeighAnn walk around the corner, arguing under their breath, and I pull away from that stare, pull my hand from his.

"Someone needs to clear shit up right this instant," I say to all of them. LeighAnn rushes Ava, though, covering the last of my statement with her excited cry.

Then Duane . . . Duane's face *shatters.*

He coughs, covering his mouth with a fist, failing to cover tears. Before he makes it to Ava, though, Charlie lunges at him and shoves him in the chest.

"Charlie! What the fuck?" LeighAnn cries, but both men immediately begin wailing on one another. Henry's arm wraps around my chest and he tucks me behind him as hospital security rushes in to break them up.

A little boy starts crying into his mother's lap, and in a blur of bloodied knuckles and noses, security badges, and admonishing glares, we are all ushered outside the hospital corridor, followed immediately by a deceptively small doctor with the deepest, scariest (and most British) voice I've ever heard.

"Oi!!! You lot! Get your shit together! Emmaline is being released momentarily, and I'll be damned if I'm to stitch up any uv the rest uv ya! Fuck's sake, this is why we don't encourage the entire family to join patients in the ER!" He shakes his head at all of us just as James, Grady, Lucy, and Caleb walk up.

"What'd we miss?!" Grady exclaims, which has the doctor turning around and growling more "fuck's sakes, bleedin' Yankee Doodle twats" under his breath as he leaves us and our special brand of bullshit outside.

"ALRIGHT," I say as loud as I can without shouting, since we remain in public, here. "Someone needs to start talking, *now*."

"I agree," LeighAnn says.

I look over at Ava, whose head is cocked, eyes moving back and forth like she's rapidly building a puzzle. I see when it clicks, her eyes flying up to look at . . . Duane?

"Tait, Ava . . . you didn't deserve to find this out like this. I'm sorry. Can we please go back home, and I promise to tell you everything, there?"

It occurs to me that in movies and shows, this is always what happens: The scene gets cut and they all leave for a more "appropriate" place to have their life-altering discussion. In this moment, though, I suddenly don't want to go anywhere with these people until I understand what the hell is going on.

"No. We need to know, now," I say, and Ava nods her agreement. I grab her hand.

"Ava . . ." Duane steps up, and Charlie begins to visibly shake.

"Don't you fucking, dare, Duane. You don't get to take this from me, too." Duane sighs, and Charlie continues. "Tait, Ava . . . I never told you this before, because it wasn't right. Your mom was a good mother, and she loved you both with such a fierceness that I would never have dreamed of getting between that. We just . . . didn't work anymore. I didn't want to lie to you, so I have tried not to . . .

"Tait . . . when I told you that your mom never knew how to fight, I meant that. She knew how to wound, though, and I'm sorry I didn't tell you before, but I just couldn't do it. It was my fault that she was so unhappy in the first place . . . plus, here I am now, with all my happiness. How could I risk taking away any of the respect you had for her when she's not even here to defend herself? I still can't. I need you to understand that this was still *my* fault.

"So, when I told you that I think, in a way, she wanted to force my hand . . . I meant that—that she had an affair with Duane. I don't know if she would have ever told me if he hadn't moved back at the time, though. At the time when we were already over in every other way.

"It happened when you were little, when I was taking on more after Dad's stroke. And Duane didn't even know that we'd had another baby until he moved back those few years later. He still acted so angry at *me* all the time for being with her . . . I never would have suspected.

"Viv said it was a mistake, that it was a one-time thing, but that she was scared that he would try to separate us if he found out . . . that we needed to move because of it. She wanted us to all go, to start over fresh."

"I never would have done that—separated you," Duane says. And this time it's me who stabs a shaking finger in his direction. "You shut the fuck up and let him finish." I feel Henry's hand come behind me, and I desperately want to lean into it and be held up, but I am holding up Ava.

Charlie runs a palm over his face, but proceeds. "She claimed she had told him that there was no way, but she admitted to me that she had no way of knowing for sure. So then, when Duane moved back, and he started asking questions . . . about how old Ava was . . . He made comments about her dark hair, and how she already loved math—at age three.

"And your mom suspected that he knew that Ava was . . . that Ava was his daughter. And I couldn't—I couldn't forgive her. I'm so sorry, girls. I'm sorry I wasn't man enough to forgive her, to take you both and move us all away, to be the father, the family you guys deserved. But we were already so bitter toward each other." He swipes angrily at his eyes. "We did some tests to confirm it."

"I remember that," Ava says. "I got to stay home from school one day and you guys called it our science day. You took me for ice cream after."

Charlie nods. "Your Mom didn't want you guys to be subjected to questions, to ridicule. And I didn't either."

"Obviously *she* didn't want the ridicule, either," Ava says, to no one in particular.

Charlie continues. "So she took you, and kept you as hidden away as she could. She knew that if Duane found out, that he'd push for a relationship with you, Ava. And yes, she didn't want that shame on her shoulders, but more than that, she didn't want you guys to suffer any unintended consequences from all of *our* actions. She didn't want to cause you any more confusion than the split already would. She moved you away. And I demanded that we all leave you girls alone. And, I want you to know, I wanted to call so much more than I did. I was angry at your mom, yes, angry at this whole situation, yes, but I didn't want to hurt your mother anymore. I'd already hurt her with a lack of love, so much so that she'd sought it out . . ." He sighs, deep and weary. "Up until Ava was eighteen, your mom, Grace, and I were the only ones who knew this. Although it's clear to me now that Duane had developed his suspicions, by the time that happened it was all too late."

"I knew," Duane says. "A lot longer than that."

"I had my suspicions," LeighAnn states.

"I, for one, had NO fucking clue," James says.

"But—wait, what about your letters?" Ava says to Charlie.

"Letters?" Charlie says in confusion.

"I wrote those letters," Duane says, barely more than a whisper.

"You . . ."

"It's why I didn't sign them for so many years. I knew you didn't know it was actually me, but I didn't care. I didn't want you to suffer either, nor your mom." He looks at Charlie when he says this, but Charlie doesn't meet his eyes. "I've only ever wanted to be in your guys' lives. I knew your mom didn't love me back. I knew what I was to her—a means to an end, a way of lashing out when her marriage was unhappy . . . I still did what I did, because I loved her. Even still, I wasn't about to go against her wishes later on. But I've been punishing myself for this since by not actively pursuing you. But then you guys grew up, past the years where it'd have been confusing and shameful—well, *more* shameful I guess . . . and I simply wanted to know you. That's why I started asking you to come visit. I wanted to tell you everything."

I look to my sister, then. I take in her dark hair, her tall frame, her blue eyes, and of course it's true. She turns to me, taking me in and mirroring all my thoughts.

Then, Caleb—quiet, reserved Caleb, who I think I've actually heard speak only three times in the weeks I've known him—says, "This is some *Jerry Springer* shit right here."

"*Maury,* dear. You're thinking of *Maury,*" Emmaline says from her wheelchair. Scary Dr. Who has brought her out without us noticing, a dumbfounded expression on his face.

". . . You know, *Maury? 'You're NOT the father!'*" Em elaborates. "*Jerry Springer* was the one where all the people threw chairs."

My mind decides to elbow its way through this revelation, back to the one at hand.

"Hold on. Henry, you said you called Ava because . . . because of something going on with Em. But you couldn't have known she would fall?"

"Henry Marcus Marcum," Emmaline says, shaking her head in disappointment.

Okay, I'm going to need to address that later.

That's a terrible teen heartthrob's name if I've ever heard one.

Henry seems to shake his head and come to, clearly as taken aback by this new information as the rest of us. "I'm sorry, Mrs. L. But they deserve to know."

She sighs in defeat, but shrugs. "Well, ladies, happy homecoming. I'm dying."

THIRTY-FOUR

HENRY

I can't stop wondering how a heart just fails. I have no medical background, so I guess when I think of the heart, I still think of it as its abstract identity. Not only as muscle, but as the thing that gives someone life; the very thing that drives their actions in turn.

It just seems like, maybe in a perfect world, they'd be related.

How can someone with a broken heart go on to climb mountains and run marathons, yet when there's so much life, vitality, and love in another person, their heart can just slowly fail?

I know that it's such a simpleton thing to mull over, but I can't bring myself to give it a Google search or ask anyone with a modicum of medical knowledge. It just seems unfair, and that's all there is to it for me.

Mrs. Logan asks the family to head home, and this time everyone listens. Ava and Tait get back into my truck, and I listen to Ava's quiet cries, and Tait's gentle words of comfort the whole way home. I feel like a right idiot for inadvertently throwing them into that revelation, but I can't bring myself to regret it. I know they'll get to soak up valuable time with their grandmother, now. I only regret that either of them feels hurt or confused.

Tait's eyes meet mine a few times in the rearview mirror before they dart away, though, and not knowing if she is angry at me is killing me.

I REMAIN QUIET WHILE EMMALINE tells all four of her grandkids what's going on back at the house. Congestive heart failure, she tells them. She was diagnosed over ten years ago, and it's been manageable since then, but she's started approaching the end stages of it. Her fall is evidence enough, and she agrees to move in with Charlie and Grace for her remaining months. She tells them how she's not in much pain, that she's already lived with it so much longer than most. She just forgets that she can't do as much as she used to, and she's grateful to get the opportunity to know that her end is coming, to "really suck the marrow out of my days," she says.

They all cry, gathered around her at the kitchen table, followed by some angry remarks from Lucy and Grady to their parents for not telling them. The anger fades quickly when Em chides them for it, and she laughs and exclaims how much she loves that she'll get to use this to her benefit.

As the conversation dies down, Lucy surges up from her chair and shouts, "Oh my god, I have to cancel the party!"

"You most certainly will not, Lucy. This is the first time we will have a celebration here with all of my grandkids, and it very well could be the last. We will dance, eat, drink, and celebrate yours and Tait's birthdays; I don't care if I drop dead between now and then, I want to know we all got one party together."

Lucy bursts into tears, but says, "Oh, thank God. Duke Wade is coming and I *have* to dance with him."

Em laughs, and says, "Oh, I'll play up my frailty and make that happen, don't you worry."

"Grandma!" Grady admonishes.

But Tait and Ava both laugh, too, and that makes the whole room brighten. They remain holding on to each other, and Ava eventually starts to fall asleep on Tait's shoulder.

"Hey, let's head back, I forgot you were on a plane early this morning too," Tait says to her.

"All my stuff is here, though. I met Grady and Lucy here this morning," Ava responds. She looks up self-consciously at Duane.

"That's okay. Let's both go stay in our old room tonight," Tait says, and they head upstairs. I never manage to catch Tait's eye before she disappears.

I HANG AROUND UNTIL EVERYONE leaves, with only Charlie, Grace, and Em remaining.

"I'm sorry that I disrespected your wishes, or if you feel I betrayed your trust. I should have, at the very least, given you all a heads up that I'd reached out to her," I say, and move to leave.

"It was the right thing to do. We know that. I hope . . ." Charlie seems to struggle with something. "I hope today gave you some explanation as to why I was the kind of father I was to them. It doesn't make any of it right, but I hope it makes a little more sense now."

"Charlie, I already knew the kind of father you were. That you are. Because I was the lucky one who got to live it."

Charlie nods tightly and leaves the room.

Emmaline says, overly loud, "Don't worry, dear, he just needed to leave the room to go cry again." She and Grace laugh.

"And you?" I ask Em. "Do you forgive me?"

"There's nothing to forgive, Henry. I love you. Forgive yourself, and don't give up on our girl."

She and Grace look at me knowingly, and I marvel at how I ever thought they might not be on to me.

I DON'T HEAR FROM TAIT that night, and I decide not to push her. The last thing she needs is anyone else to worry about right now, especially since she and Ava were hit with a double whammy.

I try to fall asleep without my top sheet, in a bed that I think already smells like her, and I wonder how I'll ever convince her to stay, if I even can. If there will be room in her broken heart for anyone after this, all while mine is breaking too. It feels like a cruel joke, this bad timing, and after tomorrow I know I'll need to give her space to process . . . everything. After tomorrow.

MY EYES ONLY *JUST* FINALLY feel heavy enough to remain closed when the knock comes, singular and quiet enough that if I wasn't fucking desperate for it, I may not have heard it. Belle barks excitedly, and before I know it the door is open and she's there, tearstained and beautiful.

"Ava was talking to Casey. She said she wanted to be alone, but I know she said she wanted that so I would come here," she says.

"So . . . you're trying to say you came here because your sister wanted you to?" I'm confused.

"Yes. No."

"Are you mad at me, Tait?" She searches my eyes, then, and the expression is so open and terrified that it scares me right back. "You're scaring me, honey. Talk to me."

"*I'm* scared. I always thought that sounded so cheesy before. That . . . *things,* this"—she gestures between us—"would just feel too good to worry. But *I'm* scared of how fast and how much I feel. I'm waiting for the other shoe to drop. For me to realize that I'm the one who cares more. Henry, all I wanted today was you. All I want right now is you."

I know this isn't actually good. I know that operating from a place of fear is a shaky foot to get started off from in a relationship. There's some part of my brain that also knows that using me to pass the time might not make any real progress either, and that she's never claimed she'd even consider staying here, that I could very well be setting myself up for complete destruction.

But I get hung up on the part where she says that she wants me, because all I want is her, too, and I decide to leave the rest for later, again.

THIRTY-FIVE

When Henry kisses me, I feel his eyes stay open and on me. He holds my face in his hands, swiping his thumbs across my cheeks as tears continue to fall.

"I'm right here with you Tait. I'm feeling all the same things. This isn't one-sided, and you're not imagining things on your end. I know I have to keep working for you, for that trust, and I'm going to."

I open my eyes then, but the tears keep falling because he's said exactly what I needed him to say, and it's both wonderful and terrible.

"I don't want to be neurotic anymore, though," I whine. "I don't *want* to make you work."

"You're worth it." He shrugs. "Plus, I think you and I have good reasons for not trusting ourselves when it comes to feelings. I'm going to be as straightforward with you as I can. Just hold my hand and I'll hold yours, and we'll both get to where we're headed together, okay?"

"Okay," I say, and pull his face back to mine.

Our kisses quickly become bruising, frantic, and my legs squeeze either side of him when he lifts me and carries me to the bathroom. He keeps holding and kissing me when he reaches in and turns on the shower, and we start undressing as much as we can in this position as steam begins to billow around us. When our top halves are bared, he sets me down and gently pushes me until I'm backed against the glass surrounding the shower.

He drops to his knees before me, kissing his way down my front as he lowers. He slides the tips of his fingers into the waistband of my leggings and slowly, painstakingly lowers them, lifting each of my feet with delicate care as he slides them out and brushes my bottoms aside.

When I'm naked before him, he looks up at me, planting slow, sweet, soft kisses across my lower belly, nipping lightly at my hips, working his way across and down until he makes his way right above my slit, until I feel my own slickness on the insides of my thighs.

He keeps his gaze locked with mine, continuing with slow movements, sliding his hands from my ankles, up to the insides of my thighs, around to below my backside. "Hold on to me" is the only warning I get before he's lifting my legs onto his shoulders, pressing my back into the glass, burying his face in my center. My hands fist in his hair and I gasp, my head falling back against the glass with a thud.

He laps, savors, humming sounds of ecstasy that rival my own. He circles his tongue relentlessly, the most perfect and consistent pace until I feel the build start at my core, until the steam around me feels almost as suffocating as holding it in any longer, and I overflow, the orgasm pouring out of me in rich, full, circular waves. My feet never touch the ground, and I'm floating, buoyed by Henry as he slides my legs around his sides and carries my boneless body into the shower.

"Hold on to me," he tells me again, and my hands grip the

hard muscles at his shoulders. I feel cool glass meet my back again, water sliding across my side. I feel him pause at my entrance, waiting. When I crack open my eyes, he rewards me by sliding in. It's slow, deliciously long thrusts and retreats that make my jaw ache in tension . . . until I feel his name ripped from my throat like a sob.

I've never thought the idea of saying someone's name was necessary, but with Henry it is. He's relentless in seeking and holding that connection, twining his fingers with mine and holding them against the glass when his shoulders grow too slick for me to hold on to. His face breaks when he finally does, his mouth falling open and his eyes falling closed, and we pant into each other's necks until we start laughing again.

I almost tell him, then. I almost tell him that I love him. But I get stuck in the vortex of my mind again, not wanting him to think I love him for what he's just done to me. He might not do *that* to everyone, but he does everything else for everyone, and I want him to know I love him for simply existing.

Later, in bed, with him curled against my chest and my fingers in his hair, I tell him that I'm sorry he's losing Em, too.

We both cry.

THIRTY-SIX

HENRY

In the span of little more than twenty-four hours, Tait's had approximately six rounds of sex, found out that her sister is actually her half-sister, found out that her grandmother is dying, and has now turned twenty-nine.

This is why I don't hesitate to let her sleep in on her birthday. And while I'm not judging the fact that it's almost noon and she's still splayed out like a starfish, softly snoring in my bed, I am anxious for her to get up.

I look down at the card that holds her birthday gift and grapple with myself for the hundredth time on whether or not to actually give it to her.

Now, after having five hours with nothing to do other than to obsess, the implications of the gift suddenly seem too great to pile onto her. Thus, when she finally gets up, and sleepily pads down the stairs, I shove the envelope into the pocket of my apron.

"Good—"

"Oh my god, what time is it?!" she says, clearly panicked.

"It's noon, but hey, calm down," I say, trying to wrap her up. She ducks beneath my arm and starts toward the door.

"Honestly, I really wonder if telling anyone to 'calm down' has ever, in the history of the world, ever, actually been successful," she spits.

What the—"Whoa, whoa. What the hell happened?"

"I gotta check on Ava. I need to go. I'm sorry. I'll see you at the party in a little while."

And with that, she bolts.

"HAPPY BIRTHDAY," I SAY TO the closed door. "You know what? Nope. Fuck that."

Pride be damned, my apron and I charge out the door after her.

"Hey!" I shout at her as she opens the truck door.

Back turned to me, I see her slowly duck her head between her shoulders, a turtle retreating into itself.

"Just what the hell do you think you're doing?" I say to the adorable patch of bed head before me. She turns, then, and juts her chin up defiantly.

"I need to check on Ava."

"And I understand that, but why are you being shitty to me?"

"I'm not being shitty!"

"You're being shitty."

"Henry, are you naked under that apron?"

"Stay on task, Tait."

"I'm sorry I was shitty. I woke up, and I panicked. Yesterday came rushing back to me, and"—she starts to cry—"and you're you, but I live in another state, Henry. I've done this before, this thing where it feels so wonderful so you just make it happen, where you forget yourself because you're ready to throw everything you have at being with another person."

"So you decided to pick a fight with me?"

"So I decided I needed to distance myself and stay away for a minute and breathe."

I sigh, and I feel it down to my bones. "I'm not trying to suffocate you, Tait. In this particular moment, I'm trying to feed you breakfast and wish you a happy birthday. Can we have this conversation over cinnamon rolls?"

"You made cinnamon rolls? Naked?" she squeaks, and I nod. "Well, alright . . . since no one else can eat them, since that's hardly sanitary."

SHE EATS SLOWLY, GAZE DARTING over to me self-consciously.

"Just spit it out, babe. I know you've got yourself backed deep into that head of yours again. It's been a pretty crazy twenty-four so I'll try not to hold it against you," I tease, but she doesn't return my smile.

She sets her cinnamon roll down with careful precision, and that's when it occurs to me that maybe I *should* be worried, seeing she's as worried as she is.

"When I got married, a big part of me chose Cole for the parts of him that I felt I were missing from me and my life. I fell in love with his family as much as him. I know that sounds childish, and maybe it was, but at the time it was what I was searching for. And I think—no, I *know*—that I internalized this feeling that I wasn't bringing that to the table. He had good relationships as good examples for him his whole life, so he was probably right in most things when it came to us, right? I chose a career path that would have worked with supporting his, I became friends with his friends and their wives. I found a version of what I felt I was missing and fit myself into it. Followed him to school, made myself feel like no work. And I convinced myself I was better for it.

"It was only when he wanted to start having a family that I came to, that I decided I wanted something for myself, for no other reason besides just wanting it—not because it would change the world, or because it would make me rich, or because it would be good or sensible or even stable.

"So, I started photography. And he was supportive on the surface and all that, but changing my job was only one part of the fundamental change that I went through." I take a deep breath.

"Now, I'm getting to know my family, getting to know myself again, and they're warm and wonderful, and also . . . clearly very fucked up. This is all so messy. And you . . . Henry, I owe you for making me want to be open to this, and I'll always be grateful. But don't you see that you yourself do everything *for* them? You don't owe them your entire life. Don't you want something for yourself, too?"

I feel myself rear back. "Tait, we've gone through this. Look at how much I have to be grateful for. It's obviously *you* that thinks that's not enough."

"I just . . . I think things can be great, that you can be grateful for your life, and you can still want something more for yourself. Not related to money, or even a job. But you guys are all plenty well off now—why haven't you traveled anywhere?"

"I haven't had time, Tait, I—"

"You could have made some time. And why didn't you finish your degree?"

"Christ. Maybe I decided I didn't need it."

"But that's *not* what you said. You said you were short because of family drama."

"Yeah, because my mother showed up out of the blue! And I had already spent years dicking around at school by that point anyways!"

"Why is it dicking around when it comes to something that's for *you*, though?"

I breathe in through my nose, out again . . . and play back all that she's saying to me. And that's when it clicks.

"Jesus, you think I want *you* because you're part of *them*, don't you?" I say, incredulous.

"I think maybe that's part of it. I think you are so loyal and devoted to this place and this family, and that I might just be a very convenient piece to that puzzle." She waves me off before I can interject. "But I also think that it took me years to find a sliver of myself, and I don't think that diving into a life here, fleeing even the small life I managed to build for myself, repeating history in a roundabout way, is what I should do without some serious time and consideration. I'm trying not to let go too easily."

I nod, not trusting myself to say or do much else.

"Henry . . .," she says in a watery voice.

"Can you see yourself building a life here? Someday, maybe?" I ask, still not able to look up.

"Can you see yourself building a life in California?" is her answer, and damnit, she's right. At this stage, I can't. *But I love you,* is on the tip of my tongue.

But it's not fair, to her or to me. If she doesn't want to set down roots here, for herself, I can't be the reason for her to. I'm not enough of a reason.

I think she very well could be enough of a reason for me, though. I think if she asked me to go with her, I couldn't deny her. And that realization terrifies me enough that I need to get out of the same room as her; I need to breathe.

Christ, this must've been what she was feeling this morning.

I get up—with as much dignity as a man can while naked and in an apron—kiss her on the cheek, and head upstairs.

AT SOME POINT I HEAR her leave, and I eventually work up the energy to get ready for the party.

I'm unsuccessful at keeping my thoughts on a leash, though, and let my mind wander to the future. There's no doubt that Tait is in my life, and will be in one form or another now, forever. We'll have to see each other at holidays, at minimum. I'll have to meet the guy she ends up bringing home one day. I'll have to swallow this love like glass, and I'll have to be her friend. While the thought of not loving her rakes its claws down my brain, the thought of not knowing her at all clogs my throat.

And shit, this is not how I remember heartbreak. I remember wanting it to be done, to be far away. To be the proverbial kid pushing away his peas at the dinner table because they're nasty—that's how silly that heartbreak felt compared to this.

I can't catch my breath for a second, for thirty seconds, for thirty minutes.

UNTIL I REMEMBER WHAT I do have, and that's now. Today. Until I remember that I need to be man enough to allow her what she needs, while she needs it. Until I know what I have to do.

THIRTY-SEVEN

TAIT

Lucy helps Ava and I get ready, cajoling us with 90s pop and lemon drops to pull us out of our funks. I ask Ava how she feels enough times that she eventually snaps, tossing her drink at me.

"I feel like the man I thought I was getting to know as my dad is still the man I was getting to know as my dad, damnit!! I feel like I'm fine! I feel like our mom was a spiteful, but sad woman, but that she tucked us away because she didn't want us to pay the consequences for her actions and have people call us sister-cousins our whole lives! I feel like I am still your fucking sister and I don't care that there's been a name change to the faceless man I've always thought of as Dad, anyway. I feel like I miss my son and my husband, and I feel like you're being fucking annoying. Now stop it and let's let ourselves enjoy a fun party for you and for Lucy, and for our grandmother!!!"

I stare at her, my face full of makeup running down in rivulets, and say, "Okay." And we all dissolve into laughter to the point that she pees herself and has to change her dress while I reapply.

* * *

THE PARTY IS BEAUTIFUL, AND way too over the top. It's the first real glimpse I get of Logan Range with its Hollywood glamour vignette. There are trailers everywhere behind the largest barn, the fanciest outdoor bathrooms (cannot be considered portable potties when they have stairs, mirrors, and actual flushing mechanisms), and lights strung up from the open barn across a blacktop dance floor, through the surrounding pines. There are great long banquet tables, small pub-style ones dotting the areas between, a bar with a full cocktail menu blocking the entry to the barn, and a DJ booth operating from a stage in the far corner. The night is cool but dry despite the other night's downpour, and Lucy even thought to set up multiple fire pit areas with Adirondack chairs, blankets slung over their backs.

"Lucy. This is incredible. You could do this for a living," I say in awe.

"No, thank you. Party planning usually involves planning for *other* people. I only like to plan for my own," she responds.

I meet the majority of the cast members, who all seem so much smaller in real life, but who also all seem surprisingly down to earth and kind. Duke Wade is handsome in a disarming kind of way. Big brown eyes the color of milk chocolate, tall and lean like you'd imagine an actor to be, with black hair that waves to his shoulders, and lips that would be feminine on anyone else, but that work with his sharp-boned face. Lucy may have feigned a brave interest in him before, but she loses her hold on the act the moment he greets us, and she sprints over to the bar.

Producer Jake is wheeling Emmaline dramatically in loops across the dance floor to "Purple Rain", still wearing his cowboy hat with a three-piece suit.

I'm delighted to find out that the journalist for the

entertainment article whom I'll be working with for the next few days is Jessa, a woman I've worked with before and adore.

James flirts shamelessly with Jessa, convincing her to dance when she starts bobbing her head to "Shut Up and Dance," shocking us all when he whips and swings her around with expertise. There are dips, there are swaying hips, swift spins in and out of his arms . . . Her face stays locked in permanent delight while Ava and I wear twin expressions of astonishment. "The Logans all *love* to dance. And are quite skilled," Emmaline says at my side, pride and laughter thick in her voice.

"Hey—are you supposed to be out of the chair?" I ask her, and she waves me off.

"I won't walk myself to death in ten yards, my girl." Then, to my stern expression, she adds, "I promise I won't go out on that floor unless I'm wheeled out there, though. Happy birthday, sweetheart." She kisses my and Ava's cheeks, exchanging compliments and exclamations when we spot Grady and Caleb dancing in the throng.

I see it in the distance when Duane intercepts Ava at the hors d'oeuvres, but she smiles brightly at him and they start talking, so I don't rush over to rescue her.

I spot Duke making an attempt at talking to Lucy again before she darts away. LeighAnn and Grace are breaking it down to Snoop Dogg's "Drop It Like It's Hot," each holding a wine glass high above their heads as they swing their hair back and forth.

Charlie and Jake are laughing at the bar, doing that man thing where they have an arm extended to the others' shoulder at the same time, beers gripped in their free hands.

There's chaos, bad dancing, the odd friendly argument, excellent dancing, delicious food, and copious amounts of booze. My senses are buzzing with the happiness around me, my heart feeling more hollow and somehow lonelier than ever.

"It's your party, and you'll cry if you want to, huh?" comes Henry's deep voice from behind me.

I shut my eyes at the flood of happiness, at the throat-thickening excitement.

"Hi," I manage to say, which is an impressive feat when I turn around and take him in fully. Henry dressed up is . . . a lot to take. Black button down that's pulled taut across his broad shoulders and chest, black tie, black slacks that mold to his powerful thighs.

"Hi," he says, not without warmth, and crooks a smile. "You look beautiful, again. Always." He sighs. And, when I don't come up with a response, only managing to stare some more, he continues, "So, what do you think of a Logan party?"

"I think that the music choices rival the randomness of my playlists, and they seem very off-brand for the place so far." Macklemore thumps out "Downtown," and synchronized dancing begins in a circle as Caleb lip synchs every word from the center.

"There's a broad demographic here. But don't you worry, they absolutely will be playing "Cotton Eye Joe" at one point or another, and they'll go apeshit for it."

"Thank you for coming."

"Of course."

The muscle in his jaw twitches again, and he slides the back of his hand down my arm before he asks, "Can we just enjoy the hell out of tonight? And worry about the rest tomorrow?" And when he says this, the feeling that fills me is equal parts love, gratitude, and mourning. Because Henry has always given me exactly what I've wanted, plus what I've needed. From that first night when he dropped the conversation and played card games, to each time he's said what I've needed to hear without expectation, to the space he's allowed for us to become friends—even after I drunkenly dry humped him in a pond. Here he is, even now, giving me this night, despite our earlier conversation, despite the fact that I can't tell him anything with certainty. I can't give up being me, again, just to hitch up my baggage to another person. And yet, here he remains, steady and strong, and insurmountably more mentally stable than I, offering me both a distraction and acceptance.

I feel the smile to my ears. "Hell, yes."

LADIES AND GENTLEMEN, HENRY MARCUS Marcum is a fun-dancing machine.

NO ONE MAKES ANY SURPRISED remarks or throws us any glances when, after barely a drink, he drags me onto the dance floor and tosses me around to Hot Chocolate's "You Sexy Thing." He finds ways to grind on me subtly, brushing his hands up my arms to wrap around the back of his neck when he presses quickly to my behind, before whipping me out of his embrace and letting me strut my way back in. We do a real-life country two-step and swing to "Boot Scootin' Boogie," his palm never leaving mine (even though he obviously knows real, proper, *actual* steps and I have no idea what my feet are doing to keep up with him). He yells into my ear to stay on my toes before he spins me around like a top to "Gimme! Gimme! Gimme!" (The *Mamma Mia!* version)—countless twirls before he tips me into a death-defying dip and plants a sweaty kiss on my face. We all laugh until we cry when he and Grady break down a pointedly on rhythm, overtly feminine, and dramatic rendition of BLACKPINK and Selena Gomez's' "Ice Cream." His tie takes turns being around his forehead or draped around my neck, and when "Cotton Eye Joe" inevitably comes on, everyone does indeed go completely, 100 percent apeshit. Even Duane clogs his way through the song, spilling his drink and smiling maniacally—like a deranged, country leprechaun.

Henry disappears for a moment when we fall over to the bar for our millionth cup of water. I think we both must want to remain as lucid as possible this night, drunk enough on fun.

When he returns, his face is flushed, but serious—forehead tie nowhere to be found. He holds his palm out to me ceremoniously as the slow song starts to play, the gesture asking *Will you dance with me?*

I catch Ava's eye from behind him, her sad smile that I return when she mouths "Twitterpated."

I look at this beautiful man and tell him yes, and then I'm in his arms, one hand around the back of his neck and one dwarfed in his palm, his other on the base of my spine. I'm afraid to look away, to blink and to have the night be over.

We don't say anything, but the more he stares into me, the more the panic in my chest climbs. I notice every twitch of his eyebrows, every time he swallows and I think he wants to speak. But neither of us does. The song's words cut into our bubble . . . the lyrics beg for someone to tell him what their heart wants, declaring it as if it's some simple thing.

When the song tapers to an end, he bends to whisper in my ear, "Come home with me?" And I know that I shouldn't. I know that tonight will just make tomorrow harder, but I say yes. We fit as many mini cakes in our fists as we can on our way out, giggling like idiots the whole way home.

WE TUMBLE THROUGH HIS DOOR, smearing frosting on each other's faces and licking it off. I catch his thumb in my teeth and his eyes flash with heat, and he picks me up and tackles me to the couch.

A memory flashes before me of the first night I laid here, when he fed me grilled cheese with apples and a whiskey ginger ale. He cages me in with a laugh, shoving an impossibly huge bite of a raspberry white chocolate cake in my mouth, and as I attempt to close my mouth around it, his eyes grow huge and his laugh disappears.

"I love you, Tait," he says, the words bursting from him like he couldn't stop them.

"RiiRuhRooRoo," I say around the cake, and then I laugh and cough cake into his face, but say with clarity, "I love you, too."

Then we are kissing again, wiping cake from eyelashes and eyebrows, and I'm untucking his shirt as he peels down my dress and then he's inside me and it feels like too much, like every time will feel like too much, too heartbreakingly good.

HE TELLS ME HE LOVES me, even as I claw at him later that night, crying out his name, keening out nonsense. He just says, "I love you," shaking his head occasionally, like he can't believe how much.

* * *

I WAKE UP TO A silent house, to the smell of coffee the following morning. The tears spring faster to my eyes than I'd have thought possible, because I know that it's over. Last night was our goodbye to us.

WHEN I MANAGE TO HAUL my weary body down the stairs and to the coffee pot, I see the envelope with my name on it. I open it, finding a simple green card that says "Happy Birthday" on the front. The inside would be empty if not for his handwriting. Two slips of paper fall out onto the counter, but my eyes pore over the note, first.

> Tait, you should know that if you choose to use this gift, I won't be able to go with you. They found it "exceedingly strange" that I would want to buy a gift card. Apparently, that's not something they typically sell there. They also didn't like that I wouldn't take any of the "merchandise" . . . I think you should nab, like, six of them, though. Don't be afraid to commit to something, give this kind of love a home. (Even if it's a little scary/aggressive/creepy when you refer to it as "not porn.") (See photo.)

I pick up the picture. It's the one he took of me with the llama. My smile is stretched to the limit, my eyes crinkled to the point of disappearance. I smile looking at the creature's furry, ridiculous face, even still.

The gift certificate is for an animal shelter, local to here, in Idaho. He's drawn an arrow indicating that I should look at the back, where he's written,

I called the animal shelter that I think is closest to you back home, too, but I couldn't get a physical gift certificate from them in time. Adopt as many animals as you want, wherever you want, Tait. In California, in Idaho, just grab any and every bit of happiness you deserve. Any living thing that has your love is the luckiest thing on the planet.

I want you to know that no matter where this goes with you and I, I am just happy to know you, and want you to do whatever it is that will make you as happy as you've made me, regardless of whether or not that includes us. I want you to know that you've made me want to be a better, happier man for ME. Thank you for having that kind of faith in me, for challenging me and pushing me as you have.

I meant what I said. I will be here, waiting, and ready whenever you are, however long you need. And here's the thing . . . As much as you make me want to be a better man for myself, you'd be the main character in my life, Tait, whether you like it or not. I don't think those things are mutually exclusive. I'd make sure you'd never forget how fascinating you are, always. If you'd let me, I'd cherish you. I love you.

-Henry

TEARS SPLATTER THE PAPER BEFORE I have the chance to move it.

IT TAKES JESSA AND I four days to get enough material for the article spread. With Henry gone on the hunting trip that

Emmaline insisted they still go on, I throw myself into work with something bordering violence. I retrieve my replacement camera, go back to filling my spare minutes with exercise and distraction, editing photos, and plotting the following shoots. I receive a checklist for the travel magazine's article and send those photos off almost immediately, having already covered each item in the time that I've been here.

I get the autograph of the actress who plays Sadie Dollar for Fletcher. She tries to corner me into talking about Henry, no doubt having heard about us at the party, but I don't even bother answering; I just smile and walk away.

I learn that Jake Lockhart might be a little cheesy on the surface, but it's easy to see that his vision for the show is anything but a sellout. He highlights difficult, uncomfortable, relevant social issues, finding a way to tie those in with the plotline surrounding the Dollar family.

Ava spends the nights this week in her old room, but she spends the days getting to know Duane.

Charlie sends photos and texts from different spots on their trip, so I know they have at least intermittent service, despite not hearing from Henry. I know it's for the best.

Emmaline remains stable, so when I finish up the majority of editing, I call Deacon and make arrangements to go home early. Dragging out another goodbye sounds like the last thing any of us need right now, and since Ava and I plan to come back in a few weeks for Thanksgiving, I decide to rip the Band-Aid off and head home.

Unlike traveling to Idaho, the flight home seems impossibly fast. Before I know it, I'm riding past Lake Tahoe, the blue somehow a little more dull, the terrain a little more tame. Then I'm walking through the door of my A-frame, greeted by my tastefully decorated, but pictureless walls, my too large, too cold bed, and the rootless life I built back here . . . a life that seems so unnervingly quiet and empty now.

I WAS BRAVE FOR A moment there, though.

I was brave enough to love, to reach out to a family that could have easily only hurt me more. I was brave enough to be vulnerable again, and it paid off, even if it did invite in so much more heartbreak . . . After all, I have grown to love more people that I will absolutely lose at one point or another—one in particular much sooner than the others, and her loss will be permanent.

ALL LOVE, AT SOME POINT, is going to be devastating, isn't it? We all just choose to be brave, to go after what we want, who we want . . . even if it means potentially losing a piece of ourselves. Even when it means being intensely vulnerable. I chose to let in my family, to let in friends again, to let in Henry.

INSTEAD OF LOSING A PIECE of myself, even with the pain . . . I found it there.

IT ONLY TAKES ME THAT hour, in that house that used to hold the smallest pieces of me, to realize what a complete, utter, total fucking idiot I am.

THIRTY-EIGHT

HENRY

The weather could not have been better this trip. Most years we end up with snow at some point, the painful, sleeting, knives-stabbing-your-face kind.

I had been looking forward to it. To hiking the brutal terrain, to being completely exhausted physically, to collapsing on my cot each night and sleeping like the dead—no matter how loud Charlie and James snore.

Instead, the days are crisp, clear, and colorful. God, they're so fucking colorful. Each morning feels like an insult. We get absolutely skunked on even seeing an animal, which, on any other year would be made up for with the beautiful weather. Not this one, of course.

The golds all remind me of Tait. I find ways to see her everywhere. When we play cards at night in the tent around the stove, I imagine I can hear her cackle at some of the arguments. The way Charlie and James pointedly say nothing about her only makes me think of her more. I imagine how her face would light up at the views, how she'd suck in a deep breath through her nose and smile before bringing her camera up to her face.

The more I think about her not asking me to follow, the more grateful I am to her. There's nothing else for me in California, no job opportunities, no family, no friends. There's her, and while that feels like enough for me, that pressure wouldn't be fair to her in the long run. There's foolish, and then there's *foolish*.

BY THE TIME WE GET home ten days later, I'm so desperate for my bed and a dark room—anywhere other than the colorful beauty around me—that I don't even go to the main house to get Belle first. I need to go say hi to Grace, to Em, and I will. I just need to lose it for a bit first.

And shower. And shave. We always come back smelling to high Heaven, but with the damned sun shining its smug face on us this whole trip, I know I'm ripe.

I DON'T KNOW HOW I know, but I know that she's gone back home. She was close to being done shooting before I left anyways, so it's not surprising. It still makes my lip curl in disgust when I pull up to the cabin, when I see how desolate the place looks.

The porch steps might as well be another mountainside for as long as they take me to climb.

When I open the door and move to hang up my jacket, I receive another swift kick to the gut. Tait's slug-parka is hanging there. She must've forgotten it. It's the ugliest damn thing I've ever seen, but my hands drop my own jacket and slide over hers of their own accord.

"Arf," the jacket says. Cool, now the thing isn't just ugly, it's haunted.

"Arf!"

My head whips down to my feet, and a creature of indeterminate origin is staring up at me, its curled, skinny tail wagging—a menacing smile on its face. The thing is probably ten pounds, six of which are made up by its ears—ears that flare up and out like the wings of a bat.

"Arf!" it says again, but that's gotta be a human just saying the word "arf" because that cannot be a bark.

"I named him Fennec. Doesn't he look like a fennec fox?" Tait says excitedly from the top of the stairs, and evil elfin woodland creature aside, my entire body lifts with unchecked joy. The feeling is nearly comical, like one of those inflatable men in front of a car lot.

She's there, smiling down beautifully, breathtaking in every way.

"What is it?" I ask when it starts to lick a spot on my boot frantically.

She frowns, put out. "It's a *dog*, Henry!"

"This"—I point down at the thing—"is not a dog. This is a creature from a 1980's movie. I hope you know not to feed it after midnight, or let it near water."

"He reminded me of you," she says, and she's at the bottom of the stairs now and I'm walking to her with the thing called "Fennec" at my feet, and then she's in my arms and my hands are in her hair and God, she smells like home.

Wait—"*That* thing reminds you of *me?!*"

She smiles a watery smile, shrugs. "Sure." And then the little bastard is humping her leg, and her lips finally slide up to mine. They're soft and full and warm. Home.

I manage to break away. "I'm sorry. I know I can't smell good."

"I could not give a fuck less, Henry Marcus Marcum."

LATER, AFTER THE LONGEST, MOST mind-blowing shower of my life, followed by a long, soapy, messy bath . . . Fennec and I have a heart-to-heart about his humping ways. I make it clear that she is mine, and that I don't share well, and I'm loath to admit it, but his ridiculous grin and ears are growing on me quickly.

I eventually work up the nerve to ask, later in bed, my head laid against her bare chest, listening to her heart, "How long are you here for?"

"You didn't hear?" she says, and I feel her smile. "I'm your new neighbor. You should know, I like to rage clean on Sundays. I blast my music as loud as humanly possible for hours on end, and I don't even make playlists when I do. I just hit shuffle on *all* my songs. Which means there will be Christmas songs that come up in the rotation, Henry, regardless of the month. You might hear a Doja Cat song, followed by Pentatonix or Celine Dion or something. I also expect to be able to borrow sugar whenever I want, in any amount I want. I want to be invited to any and all game nights. And you make really good coffee, so I'll probably be here every morning."

When I look at her smiling face, she's beaming, but I have to ask before I dare to hope, "Are you sure you're okay with that, Tait? Moving away from your sister?"

Her face turns more serious before she replies, "Yes, because you know what I realized, Henry?" She sits up and pulls the sheet up with her—a boon to my focus. "I realized that no matter what, this is going to end devastatingly."

Um. Okay. Did not expect that. My face falls.

She flails her hands around. "Let me explain," she says.

"What I mean is that this is a risk I've calculated, and I've decided that it's not even a risk. This place feels more like home because it's where I've been able to grow back into myself again. You helped me do that, and I'm *happy* about that, Henry. And a house or a state, a career, or even this ranch isn't *home*, just because of its location. My life is me, and you, and this chaotic family that I don't even have to worry about scaring you off with, since you already know how insane they are and love them anyway. My home, my life, is with the ones I love.

"What I also mean is," she continues, heaving a deep sigh. "Even if this ends up being forever, at some point something will happen and it will end—even if that end really is the whole 'till death do us part,' thing. It will end, somehow, someway, and it will be devastating. So, I'm not afraid of heartbreak again. What makes this worth it is that there *will* be heartbreak, because of how damn good it will be until that happens." Her eyes fill and when she smiles a tear spills. "Even if this fails in a less than spectacular fashion, Henry, I want to love you until then. I want to love you until it's devastating. Even in the best-case scenario, where I get to be with you until we are incredibly old, and then one of us gets tagged and bagged, baby. That's the *best*-case scenario, and it's still shit. I want all the stuff before then. I don't want to miss out on any of it—as much of it as I can get with you.

"I want to put down roots here: beside you, across a pond from you, somewhere new with you, I don't care. You've made me want to do that, to plant myself somewhere and flourish."

My forehead falls to her stomach until I can steady my breathing.

"I want to love you until I'm absolutely devastated too, Tait. I'm going to."

EPILOGUE

Emmaline Logan lived to be just shy of eighty-four. She lived to meet her second great grandson—my second, completely perfect, exceptional nephew, Arlo Logan Pruitt—and to share two Thanksgivings, two Christmases, and two New Years with all of us.

She even lived to see Henry go on to start a program at the Range for foster teens. During this highly regarded program, the kids spend a month over summer learning everything there is to learn about the ranching and farming factions here. In addition to that, those interested are able to learn about TV and film production. There's a little something for everyone this way.

Henry and Jake are currently working together to form an internship program under the umbrella of Jake's production company. Lucy is planning the first fundraising event, for which I've provided a few photography pieces for auction. There will be plenty of *Dollar Mountain*-related merchandise, and she's even convinced Duke to be auctioned off for a date.

GRANDMA PASSED AWAY IN HER sleep, on the night of Henry's and my engagement party, after a particularly raucous celebration. She defied the odds in almost every way in life, even in disease and death, having far outlived her doctors' expectations.

The entire cast and crew for *Dollar Mountain* attended her memorial, and even some from Deacon Publishing came in support.

We spread her ashes over the mountainside where she and her husband were married.

HENRY AND I MADE IT all of a month in our pseudo-neighbor situation before I gave up the ghost and moved in permanently. Belle tolerated Fen for the first few months, but he won her over like the rest of us, and they've been inseparable since.

What's been done in terms of wedding planning has been a breeze. Neither of us even wanted one, but when Lucy found out about our courthouse plan she staged a coup. Still, we want a day for and about ourselves, so we're in talks over destination spots. Henry is the most entertaining and thoughtful travel companion . . . in quite unexpected ways. Everything is a new wonder, and seeing the world through his eyes will never get old. He spends weeks learning key phrases in the appropriate languages before we go anywhere, then proceeds to charm cultures across the globe. I always notice how his smile relaxes and settles to its permanent, natural place each time we fly home, though.

TODAY IS THE BEGINNING OF our big move, and I can't help but feel suspicious over how smooth it's been. Our things are all boxed up, ready to go. We've admittedly been putting off clearing out Em's, however.

She's left her house to Henry and me, even going so far as to state in her will, "If I'm still alive, this part can be ignored, since they'll be getting my house as a wedding gift. Hopefully I'm dead so that they can't argue with me about taking it, though."

Henry and Charlie plan to add more cabins around the pond for the summer program's use. We'll have plenty of excuses to visit there, frequently.

We pull up to Emmaline's place, and I laugh because *of course* she's had the best views all to herself all of these years. It's been maintained since she moved in with Grace and Charlie, so even the landscaping looks quaint and tidy. Henry holds my hand up the porch steps, like he always does, and he pulls me to a stop, kissing me sweetly before we head inside.

It's simple and tasteful, a mostly open floorplan with a giant dining room and wet bar area. I don't worry about anything being old or outdated, anyway, because my guy loves a project.

The hallways are lined with shelves of pictures . . . so many pictures. A full and beautiful life reflected on every free surface.

I pause when I come to one of my mom and me, she with a heavily pregnant belly, smiling softly into the camera, crouched behind a dirty-faced, tiny me . . . I've got pigtails and am holding a giant toad, grinning from ear to ear.

"Tait?" Henry calls to me from somewhere in the house, and I set out to find him.

Toward the back of the house, through a pair of glass French doors, is what appears to be an office. The entire room is wrapped in windows, aside from one wall above a desk and a surprisingly high-end computer.

Henry wraps me up and says something about the view, but it's lost on me because I can't make sense of what I'm seeing on that wall . . .

My photograph, blown up to poster size, the one that got me my big break, the only copy this size in existence . . . the one I had sent to Gemma Nola when her book hit the NYT Bestseller's List. The handwritten poem, there, in my handwriting, that I wrote in the corner.

Why does a fire move with more speed uphill?
   Because it craves only light, only air.

Is my land, my soul, the parts of me only good when they feed your blaze?
   I can't fuel your flame nor build you a bridge to
      cross over my depths,
   so you move on to higher ground, destruction in
      your wake.

But, I will face the sun on my own, having traveled and climbed.
   There are parts of me that are safe.
   Untouched, wild, and free.

And it will be that much more beautiful.

MY MOUTH REMAINS SUSPENDED OPEN when Henry walks over to the picture, plucking down the envelope with "Tait" written across the front . . .

* * *

I OPEN IT WITH TREMBLING hands, bursting into a sob the moment
I open it and recognize my mother's handwriting. I ask Henry
to read it to me when it's clear that I won't be able to.

Tait,

I am sick, and the doctors now say I've only got a few
months, at most.

If you're reading this, then I can only assume I am
long since gone, and you've been back home (because
let's face it, that IS your home), and I'm guessing that
you've learned all that you needed to about me.

You, however, are so very full of life, baby. More so
than I have seen you in so many years.

A mother, even a very average one like myself, can
see it when their child is struggling. You've struggled
to settle, love.

For a while, I probably would have thought that
settling was a great thing to try to force yourself into,
honestly. After all, I couldn't seem to settle in my life,
couldn't manage to feel happy when I tried to.
Instead, I lashed out at those around me, expecting
them to fix it for me, to be my answer. And look
where that landed me. I still ended up brokenhearted,
and lonely.

Maybe I wanted to ruin that life so we could have
an excuse to start a new one. I truly don't know.
And instead of looking into myself and ever finding
that answer, I lived in perpetual distrust. I can't
trust myself, Tait, so why trust anything else? I
didn't have to be so lonely. I had you guys. Too often
I forgot that.

I've been selfish, though, and now it's almost too late. You, my beautiful girl, are bursting at the seams with excitement, for something new for yourself. And God, I am so in awe of you.

Did you know that your grandma was a writer? You must have inherited some of that artistic soul from her, because your passion is already contagious.

I want you to keep that zest for life, Tait. I want you to see things that I'd never even have dreamt of seeing. I pray you are still taking pictures of it all.

I have no way of knowing if this will all work, but there is one thing I can do to try.

I have written to your grandmother, and, sparing her the unnecessary details and trusting her to use her own artistic license for panache, have asked her to write something based on this poem you've written & this picture you've taken.

It reminded me so much of . . . well, me. Of the destruction I have caused.

I wrote to her about a story of a young woman who loved two young men, in very different ways and for different reasons, and the lives affected by her choices.

She has agreed to try, and to make sure you get the recognition you deserve. I pray she can help make your dreams come true.

I won't go on and on about how sad I am that I won't get to see you and your sister become mothers one day, because even though I'll be sad to miss it, I

know, without a shadow of a doubt, that both of you
will be wonderful. I will leave a separate letter for Ava.

I love you,
Mom

P.S. If Emma's there with you now, ask her to forgive
me for not telling you that your wedding gift came from
them. I was in the beginning stages of sickness then,
and already desperate to feel like I was giving you
something from me, in a way, and felt helpless in that
respect. You made an assumption and I couldn't bring
myself to correct you, for which I am sorry. I desperately
hope that this all somehow leads to something
beautiful for you, and that I make it up to you.

HENRY HOLDS ME AS I sob, for what surely must be hours,
until that sob turns to a hysterical laugh when I realize
something . . .

"Oh my god. Henry, her name . . . Gemma Nola."

"Oh." I see it in his face when he realizes it, too.

"It's fucking *Emma Logan* with the letters rearranged! She
goddamn Tom Riddled me!"

"She goddamn Tom Riddled you."

AND THAT, I THINK, IS how you make an exit.

ACKNOWLEDGMENTS

First and foremost, thank *you* for reading.

I'd be remiss not to jump right into it and start thanking everyone else, though. Because, for anyone not aware, the book community is so incredibly special. So many of you are the reason I felt confident enough to write this, and to want to continue. I know I'm supposed to say I'm doing it for me, and in a way that is the case. But you guys were the Meyer to my Fee; your support bolstered me until I found my voice and confidence. The fact that any of you takes even a moment out of your day to rate, review, or create something that cheers on my stories will never cease to amaze me.

Danielle, thank you for taking a chance on me sliding into your DMs in all my overly familiar and extremely casual glory. I'd love to claim professionalism, but self-deprecation and inappropriate content is more my speed, and you went for it. I'll never forget when you replied and told me you'd finished it and loved it. I'll never forget crying in my car in the Target parking lot when I saw that first aesthetic video.

Marisol, thanks for the therapy. What started as just fun back-and-forth became friendship. I'm incredibly thankful for your support, for how you always remember the links to things when I forget, and for how many times I teased you with mere portions of this story. I promise to never do it again (haha).

Krysten, I still think we were separated at birth. So grateful to you for your constant time and just letting me bounce things off of you occasionally—as in, all day, every day. It's crazy to think that sharing an ACOTAR conversation on the internet turned into friendship. I'm sure there are weirder starts to relationships.

M'Kenzee, Genesis, Hannah, Leah, Krysten, Stephanie, Kelly, Kelly, Allie, Liz, Katie—thank you for beta reading and editing and supporting me even in my disorganized state. Thank you for how much you've already shared this story, promoted it and pumped me up about it. I'll never take for granted how you gave me and my books your time. I know what a precious commodity it is.

Sam, my goodness. You're a magician. Thank you for giving me a cover that is so beautiful it will inevitably lead more people into reading my words. I am amazed by your talent and your ability to translate "vibes" into art.

Ty, Emery, and Aven: thank you for loving me through the crazy. When I cried over imaginary people that lived in my brain and when I lost sleep and chose writing over free time, so often. I love you.

Grandma: if you read this one, too, I love you, but I'm begging you to please lie to me and tell me you didn't. Thank you.

Don't miss out on the rest of Tarah DeWitt's steamy romances . . .

Available now from

Do you love contemporary romance?

Want the chance to hear news about your favourite
authors (and the chance to win free books)?

Kristen Ashley
Ashley Herring Blake
Meg Cabot
Olivia Dade
Rosie Danan
J. Daniels
Farah Heron
Talia Hibbert
Sarah Hogle
Helena Hunting
Abby Jimenez
Elle Kennedy
Christina Lauren
Alisha Rai
Sally Thorne
Lacie Waldon
Denise Williams
Meryl Wilsner
Samantha Young

Then visit the Piatkus website
www.yourswithlove.co.uk

And follow us on Facebook and Instagram
www.facebook.com/yourswithlovex | @yourswithlovex

PIATKUS